W9-CAY-682

REWIND

CAROLYN O'DOHERTY

AN IMPRINT OF HIGHLIGHTS
HONESDALE, PENNSYLVANIA

This is a work of fiction. Names, characters, places, and incidents are products of the author's imagination or are used fictitiously. Any resemblance to actual events, locales, or persons, living or dead, is entirely coincidental.

Boyds Mills Press
An Imprint of Highlights
815 Church Street
Honesdale, Pennsylvania 18431

Printed in the United States of America
ISBN: 978-1-62979-814-1 (hc)
ISBN: 978-1-68437-138-9 (eBook)

Library of Congress Control Number: 2017961199

First edition
The text of this book is set in Janson MT.
10 9 8 7 6 5 4 3 2 1

To the guys in my life:
Ryan, Connor, DanO

01

OUR CAR SKIDS TO A STOP AT THE POLICE BARRICADE. Ross rolls down the window.

"Agent Carson Ross." He holds his badge out to the square-faced cop standing guard. "I have a spinner with me."

The cop peers past Ross to stare at me with that familiar mix of curiosity and distrust. I pick at a ragged edge on my thumbnail. I hate dealing with people who haven't met a spinner before. They don't look at me and think: oh, there's a sixteen-year-old girl, they look at me and think: ooh, there's an escaped circus animal. The dangerous kind. That aren't necessarily fully trained.

The cop hands Ross's badge back.

"Chief's waiting for you."

Ross guns the motor and speeds to the open space in front of City Hall. I brace one hand against the glove box to steady myself. Today is the Friday before Labor Day weekend, and this street should be packed. There should be people juggling briefcases and cups of coffee, cell phones chirping, and exotic scents wafting from colorfully painted food carts. Instead, an unnatural emptiness screams *danger*, the warning underlined by the police cars barricading both ends of the block. Behind them, knots of uniformed men and women huddle, tension emanating from them like a bad smell. The sole person standing on the street is Portland's chief of police, Lamar Graham.

"Ross." Chief's lips part in a sigh of relief. "Thank God you're here." He bends lower, eyes skipping past me and into the back seat. "You only brought one?"

"Alex and I were close by when we got the call," Ross says. "If I'd gone back to the Center, it would have taken twenty minutes. Traffic is nuts out there."

Chief checks his watch. A nerve in his jaw twitches.

"How long do we have?" Ross asks.

"Fifteen minutes."

Ross climbs from the car. "You called someone from the bomb squad?"

Chief shouts a few words in the direction of the huddled officers. I step into the cool fall air, pretending the word *bomb* doesn't faze me. Up close, I can see sweat darkening the fabric under Chief's arms. My already clenching stomach tightens. Chief wants another spinner here because if two of us work together, we can combine our skills and hold the freeze longer. Now it's all going to be up to me.

"That's McDennon," Chief says, nodding toward a man striding up the sidewalk. "It's his first freeze."

McDennon marches up to Chief and salutes. He's got a brutal crew cut and is wearing this spotless uniform that makes him look like a character from those Vice War video games the other Center kids play, except for the bag he carries—black, lumpy, and with BOMB SQUAD etched across it in white letters. My mouth fills with spit and I swallow, hard.

"Let's get to it," Ross says.

I stretch out my arm, exposing the three-inch-wide metal bracelet clasped tight against my left wrist. It looks like those bands Wonder Woman wears in the old cartoons, except mine is called a leash, it's stamped with the Center's logo, and I'm required to wear it whenever I leave the building. Ross pulls a key from his pocket and twists it in the band's lock. The knot in my stomach loosens. Leashes emit a low-level electromagnetic current that, when pressed against a pulse point, blocks my ability to link with time. The instant it falls away, I relax a little. It's like inhaling a mouthful of fresh air after being cooped up in a stuffy room.

"You'd better hurry," Chief says, taking the leash from Ross. He glances at his watch again. It's a sporty thing, and even from four feet away, I can read the time: 1:47.

"According to the guy who called it in," Chief says, "we're down to thirteen minutes before the bomb blows."

My stomach twists back into a pretzel. If I can't hold the freeze long enough for McDennon to find the bomb *and* figure out how to dismantle it, then City Hall is toast. There isn't time for another spinner to get here and try again.

"Don't worry," Ross says. "Alex has never failed a mission yet."

Chief doesn't look comforted, but Ross's faith helps restore some of my confidence. I roll the tension from my shoulders and hold out my hands. Ross grasps my right one, and McDennon slides a damp palm around my left. I breathe slowly, the way Ross told me to do when I feel anxious.

"You ready?" Ross asks me.

I look into his eyes. They're blue with flecks of darker color in them, like waves in a picture I once saw of the ocean. I take another breath. Release it.

And then I freeze time.

Everything stops. Sound disappears. The bright September air grows perfectly still. People turn to statues. A clutch of fall leaves, caught in a passing gust of wind, hovers a few inches above the pavement. In the sky over City Hall, a flag hangs in a half-furled wave. Nothing—not a person, insect, machine, or object—moves anywhere in the world.

Nothing, that is, except me and the two people whose skin I'm touching.

McDennon's hand twitches in mine. He's gawking at all the strangeness: a squirrel suspended mid-jump between two trees, tail bristled by a breeze that no longer exists; the fact that our shadows won't follow us since we can't block an unmoving ray of light; the impossible, absolute silence.

My breathing steadies; it's calm, no longer forced. The frozen quiet laps me like a warm bath. It's not just lack of noise. It's the absence of sound. Pure. Undisturbed. For the first time since I got out of the car, my body relaxes. This is my element. A freeze is the one place where I am in control. I release the two men's hands.

"Let's head in," I say.

McDennon doesn't move. Instead, he bends to pick up one of the floating leaves and rips it into pieces. When he opens his hand, the shreds flutter to the ground like confetti.

"We need to get going," Ross says. "Alex can only hold time for about half an hour when she's dragging along two other people."

McDennon makes an obvious effort to regain his focus. He straightens, dusting the leaf scraps off his palms.

"The briefing notes said the security cameras caught a suspect leaving the building at the west entrance. We'll start there."

Inside, City Hall radiates abandonment. The building is designed with an open lobby that soars all the way to a skylight three stories above. To the left and right, stairs lead to the upper levels. There are no people. We cross the open space and head down a hall to the right.

Everyone must have left the building quickly. Doors hang ajar on either side of the hall. I catch a glimpse of jackets drooping on the backs of chairs, coffee cups forsaken on window ledges, pens dropped on top of half-finished notes. Every desk we pass holds a lit computer screen, and for a second I wish we weren't walking quite so quickly. I am always curious to see how Norms spend their days.

The west entrance lies at the bend of a stairway leading down into the basement. It's a solid door with glass on the upper half and a sign saying *Exit Only*. A security camera hangs over the top molding, its green light shining dully through the still air. I stop on the landing, facing the door.

Ross waves a hand in my direction. "It's your show."

I nod. McDennon switches his attention from the door to me. I smooth a stray strand of hair into my ponytail.

"How long ago did the suspect leave?" I ask Ross.

He glances at his watch. The hands, of course, haven't moved since the freeze. He flicks its metal casing.

"The camera caught him at 12:25. It was almost 1:50 when you froze, so you'll need to rewind a bit less than an hour and a half."

I close my eyes. In my mind, I picture time as strands woven in the air. Usually the strands slide by freely. During a freeze, they hang still, like fiber stretched across a loom. Mentally, I tighten my grip and pull the strands toward me. Time shifts backward, a gently rocking current that flows through my body. I pull harder, gathering momentum so the minutes rush by fast enough that the hour and a half will pass quickly, but not so fast that we can't see what's happening. The rewind settles into a smooth rhythm and I open my eyes.

Shadows flicker along the stairwell, light fading and brightening to match the rapidly altering pattern of sun and clouds outside the window. The air is filled with a whispering hum, a combination of all the background noises so easily ignored in real time: distant voices, the drone of a heater, the faint buzz of electricity. To me it sounds like white noise. Ross describes the sound as an overlarge mosquito lodged in his brain. He says it's doubly irritating since everyday noises like a sneeze or a clap get unrecognizably distorted when heard speeded up and backward.

McDennon pulls on his ear. Ross watches the closed door, tapping the handrail with one finger. I sit down and write my name in the dust on the edge of the step. *Alexandra Manning.* It's my own little ritual, a temporary signature on the scene I've created.

A maintenance guy zooms up from the basement and flits past us. He's lugging a bucket and mop, his image as insubstantial as the sounds are hushed. McDennon lurches out of the way.

"Don't worry." Ross slaps the wall next to him. "All you can touch is what was here at the moment of the freeze. That guy's like a memory. We can't affect the past at all. All we can do is rewind it and see what happened."

McDennon rubs a hand through his crew cut. I let more time slip past. The strands move through me more sluggishly than usual. A time headache has already woken up in my temple and I'm extra aware of the draining sensation from dragging along two Norms. Probably stress from the bomb. Despite the comfort of the freeze, there's a tightness in my stomach that hasn't completely gone away.

"How are things at the Sick this week?" Ross asks.

McDennon tugs his ear again. "I beg your pardon?"

"He's talking to me," I say. I point to my shirt. It's part of the uniform I always wear when I go out on a mission: khaki pants and a collared maroon shirt embroidered with the words *Crime Investigation Center, Northwest Division.*

"The C-I-C," I tell him. "Pronounced phonetically it's *Sick.*"

"I see." McDennon doesn't sound like he does. "And are things good there?"

I consider telling him that when the highlight of your week is rewinding violent crimes, it's generally not considered a sign of a happy home. I refrain. My life isn't this man's business.

"Stop!" Ross calls.

I pull on the mental strands to halt the flow of the rewind. Superimposed over the closed west door, a shadow door stands open, revealing the dim figure of a man backing into the building.

"Is that him?" Ross asks.

McDennon studies the man carefully. He's young—I'd guess early twenties. A white guy, average height, wearing jeans and a dark windbreaker zipped up to his chin.

"Can you rewind it a little farther?" McDennon asks. "Real slow."

I do as he asks. The young guy backs all the way in, then pauses with one hand on the door. Tipping his face up toward the security camera, he lifts his other arm and waves a defiant one-finger salute at the glowing green light.

"That's our suspect." McDennon shakes his head. "Must be a real whack job. Can we follow him?"

"Absolutely." Ross pats my shoulder. "Good job, Alex. That was fast."

The compliment sends a flush across my cheeks. I raise my chin and start unreeling events again, this time at a steady pace. The suspect lowers his arm and continues his backward walk into the building. When he heads up the stairs, we follow him.

Rewound images of people fill the hallway. Voices well up, the sounds subdued, and the images ghostly. McDennon stares in fascination as Ross walks right through a group of school children on a tour. We pass a man in a suit yakking unintelligibly on his cell phone, and a woman waving manicured hands as she babbles instructions to a younger man jogging backward at her side. Our suspect shuffles among the shadow people, hands stuffed in his pockets, actively avoiding eye contact. No one pays him any attention. I speed the pace of the rewind, the beat of our footsteps keeping pace with my growing excitement. This is the part of investigations I like best: my own carefully controlled rewind, the emerging certainty we are on the right track.

We trail the suspect up another flight of stairs and down an empty hall. Recessed lights illuminate beige walls, their blankness broken up by framed black-and-white photographs of city landmarks: children playing in the Salmon Street fountain, cherry trees blooming beside the river, the Portlandia statue holding her trident. The doors here are all closed.

The suspect stops at a large, blue recycling bin. The bin's lid pops up into his hand and he reaches out over the yawning interior. A backpack, black and limp, rises up to him. He slides it onto one shoulder, lowers the lid, and then glances around before scuttling to a door marked *Conference Room 3.* Once there, he reverses into the room, pausing at the threshold to check if anyone is in the hall, then pulling the door shut very slowly. Ross waits until the memory of the door closes before opening the real door. I nearly step on his heel in my eagerness to follow him inside.

The room is dark. It's a windowless interior room, the only light bleeding through an opaque glass panel beside the door. Any glow from the hall stops where the door blocked it when I froze time. I squint, and the shadows resolve themselves into a long table surrounded by chairs.

"There he is." Ross lunges to the right of the conference table and drops to his knees. McDennon and I hurry to join him. My vision has adjusted to the murkiness, and I can make out the suspect sprawled on his back with his head under one of the chairs. Frowning with concentration, he pulls a strip of duct tape off the bottom of the chair and returns it to the roll in his other hand. McDennon's indrawn breath hisses near my ear.

"Bingo," Ross whispers.

I wedge my head under the chair beside Ross to get a better view. A brick-shaped object is stuck to the underside of the seat, mummified with a crisscross of tape. Ross reaches out a hand and fingers the bomb. I shiver. Even in this inert form, the thing oozes threat.

"I wouldn't touch that," McDennon says. I can't see his face from my position under the chair, but his voice trills with alarm.

"No?" Ross winks at me. "What about this?"

With a quick tug, he pulls the tape away, letting the bomb drop to the floor with a loud clunk. McDennon leaps to his feet, tripping over my legs in his rush to get away.

"Mr. Ross!" I say, smothering a laugh.

Ross shoots me a grin, and then says to McDennon, in a perfectly serious voice: "I'm sorry. I didn't mean to startle you."

Ross stands to help McDennon back to his feet. I remain on the floor until I can control the giggles tickling my throat. Our suspect's wraithlike shape hovers next to me, methodically taping the shadow bomb in reverse. When I manage to rub the smile off my face, I stop the rewind.

Frozen silence settles around us as I crawl out from under the chair. Ross picks up the bomb and holds it out to McDennon. The explosives expert approaches it warily. Released from the tape, the bomb is a mess of wires around a square of something that reminds me of modeling clay.

"It's perfectly safe," Ross says. "The bomb's got an electrical trigger, so there's no way it can go off. Electrical impulses freeze just like everything else. None of it works." Ross sticks a finger under one of the wires and wiggles it. "Even if it did explode, it wouldn't hurt us. If Alex lost control, time would melt, and we'd go back to where we started, standing next to Chief, and all in one piece."

McDennon lifts the bomb from Ross's hand with admirable resolution. He probably heard all this in training; it's just the reality of it that rattled him.

"Let's take this somewhere there's better light," he says. "I need to figure out how to dismantle it."

The three of us trek out into the hall. Even the muted brightness of frozen light seems glaring after the dark conference room. Ross opens a door across the hallway to reveal a small office, furnished with a desk, a couple of file cabinets, and a visitor's chair. A bald man sits behind the desk, fingers raised in the act of typing. The sun streaming through the window makes him appear particularly insubstantial. Dust motes hang like glitter inside his chest.

McDennon places his bomb squad bag on an empty space on the desk.

"How much time do I have?" he asks me.

I focus my attention inward. The current of time is pulling harder now. It's still manageable, but I know from experience the pressure will grow.

"Fifteen minutes?" I say. "I can hold it for twenty if you need it."

"McDennon, you have ten minutes."

Ross's voice is firm. The bomb expert turns to his work without comment. He must be used to working under deadlines.

"I can hold it longer than that," I say to Ross, softly, so I don't distract McDennon. "If Mr. McDennon doesn't figure this out now, they'll only have thirteen minutes in real time."

"You worry about your job," Ross says, "and let McDennon worry about his. Come on, we'll talk in the hall."

A smile twitches the corners of my lips as I follow him out of the room. Ross is hands-down the best agent on the squad. Don't get me wrong—he can be as abrupt, demanding, and critical as all the other cops, but Ross, unlike any agent I've ever heard of, always shares the details of a case. And not only that, he even asks my opinion.

As soon as we're out in the hall he starts talking.

"Chief said the person who called it in claimed to be the bomber himself. From what Chief told me about the call, McDennon is right. The guy's a total whack job."

"Why would the bomber report his own crime?"

Ross shakes his head. "Why would he give the video camera the finger? Clearly, he doesn't care about getting caught. Either that or he thinks we won't catch him. In the call he ranted about the ineptitude of the police department. He thinks all cops are crooked and that our reliance on spinners is a perversion of nature." He glances at me. "Sorry."

I shrug. "That's nothing new. What else did he say?"

"That the reason Sikes has never been caught is because Chief Graham is accepting bribes to cover up his crimes."

I lean against the wall. If that part of the call leaks out, it's not going to go over very well. Sikes is the name the press has given to the city's most notorious criminal and the police department's Achilles heel. Ten years in and no one has a clue who the man is or how he manages his operation. Or if he's even a man. Sikes is blamed for the theft of at least fifty million dollars. He steals from banks, high-end jewelry stores, elegant homes, and flourishing businesses. He leaves no clues and always manages to time the thefts so no one discovers them for at least three days—too late for a spinner to rewind the crime. Although there are a few outliers who call Sikes Robin Hood—even spreading rumors that he gives all his riches to charity—most of the city is furious about the police's failure to catch him.

"Do you think it's true? That Chief is helping Sikes?" I ask.

"You know my opinion," Ross says. "I don't know if it goes all the way to the Chief, but there is no way Sikes could have avoided capture all these years without some inside help."

The headache building in my skull throbs. Ross is fanatical about unmasking Sikes. Before he was an agent, Ross was a regular police detective. He and his partner, Salvador Rodriguez, were the main investigators on the Sikes case. One day, when Ross was out with a nasty flu, Sal called him up to say there had been a breakthrough in the case. He'd gotten some new information and now had three likely suspects he wanted to interview. Ross asked him to wait, but Sal was too impatient, so he followed up on the leads by himself. The next day, a Friday, Sal disappeared. On Tuesday, his body was found floating in the Willamette River. Ross swore he'd catch Sikes and make him pay. Instead, Chief sent him on leave for a few months. When he came back, Chief said the case had become too personal for Ross and that it would be better for someone else to handle it. Ross was transferred to the Time Department. He's supposed to have let the case go, but he still works it on his own. He and I have spent many hours in the car talking through evidence.

"What would the suspect gain by bombing city hall?" I ask Ross.

Ross frowns at the floor as if there might be answers in the linoleum's abstract swirls.

"Given that he called it in, I don't think he planned to actually hurt anyone. Probably just wanted to show how powerful he is. Did you notice the schedule outside the room where he put the bomb? The meeting this afternoon was about the precinct's budget. Chief would have been there, along with the mayor and lots of upper level staff."

I rub my temple, trying to think like a psycho bomber.

"Maybe he really does have information about which cops are working with Sikes. He could have known about the meeting and set the bomb as a warning to them."

"If he did have information about Sikes, this kind of attention would not make our master thief very happy."

"There must be a pretty clear image of the guy on videotape. Surely the cops will be able to identify him."

Ross's frown deepens. "I wonder . . ."

I know what he's thinking. If he could get a chance to question the bomber, find out who on the force was working with Sikes, it might give him a lead to crack the case. The pounding in my head bounces up to match the spike in my pulse. All the spinners at the Center tease me about my dedication to time work, but none of them would laugh if I helped solve a case this big.

"Agent Ross," McDennon calls. Ross's head jerks up, and we hurry back into the room. The bomb expert is standing in the middle of the small office, his face split with a Cheshire cat grin. Wires and bits of plastic are strewn all over the desk.

"I got it," he says. He wipes his brow against the shoulder of his shirt. I rub my head, too. Time is pulling at me hard now, a current with definite intentions of dragging me downstream. McDennon starts packing things back into his bomb squad bag. A tiny screwdriver. A magnifying glass.

"There's no need for that," Ross says. "Let it go, Alex."

I release my hold on time with relief. The scene around us blurs. Ross told me once that the melt made him momentarily dizzy, like missing a step off a curb. For me, the sensation is more violent. Scenes from the freeze swing crazily in my head: the suspect placing tape, manicured nails waving in a crowded hall, the janitor's bouncing mop. I try to relax the way we're trained, to let time wash over me, but it still feels like the seconds are being forcibly ripped through my chest.

The world steadies. I am standing on the steps in front of City Hall, staring into Ross's ocean-blue eyes. He blinks and lets go of my hand.

Chief starts. "You're back?"

McDennon's neatly packed bomb bag slips from his fingers and hits the ground with a thud. The leaf he'd shredded during the freeze, once again intact, floats past his feet on its draft of wind. The squirrel completes its journey to the neighboring tree. The flag on the rooftop flutters.

Chief looks up at the building. "Did you find it?"

"Yes, sir," McDennon answers, scrambling to recover his bag, "and I know how to dismantle it."

"Quick," Chief says. "Go."

McDennon races back up the stairs. Chief turns to Ross and hands over my leash.

"How long were you inside?" Chief asks him.

"I'd guess twenty, twenty-five minutes."

Ross refastens the leash around my arm. I wish he'd been less prompt. My head is still swimming from releasing the freeze, and adding the leash's hum makes me queasy.

Ross walks over to stand next to Chief. Neither man speaks. Chief keeps glancing at his watch, then back up at City Hall. The cops waiting down the street mutter together, the sound echoing the buzz in my head. I want to go over and stand with them, just in case, but the effort is beyond me. Instead, I sit on the steps and lay my head on my knees. Time headaches usually fade after a few minutes.

"All clear, Chief!" McDennon yells.

He bursts through the front door, arms raised as if he's just won a championship race. When he waves pieces of the bomb, cheers break out from the waiting police. Chief rushes to shake his hand. He's smiling so widely I catch glimpses of silver on his back teeth.

I stand up and instantly regret it. This is the worst time headache ever. It feels like someone is squeezing the back of my eyeballs.

"Agent Ross." Chief is back, one arm draped over McDennon's shoulders. "You did all right today, you and . . ." He nods over at me, my name clearly gone from his memory.

The other cops flood around them. They're laughing and shoving each other, all eager to congratulate the new heroes. I slump back down onto the step, grateful for once to be ignored. If this was the time someone actually came over to thank me, I'd probably puke all over their shoes.

The steps grow crowded. Nervous sweat taints the air with bitter perfume. People yell, cell phones jangle. The noises bounce around my head like a mistuned orchestra. And it isn't just the noise, it's the light, too. Everything around me seems too bright, the edges so sharp they hurt. I put a hand up to shade my eyes and touch clammy skin.

Nausea, fever . . . Realization thrusts me back to my feet. It's normal for me to get a headache from freezing. This is different.

"Mr. Ross!"

I must have shouted. Heads turn, confusion interrupting their celebration. I don't care. Panic is drowning me in a way time never does.

Ross hurries over.

"What is it?

I clutch his proffered hand. "I'm sick."

"A headache?"

"No! I'm sick, Mr. Ross. Time sick."

Ross's face crumples.

"Come on," he murmurs, wrapping an arm around my shoulders. "Let's get you out of here."

"Where are you going?" Chief calls. "I need you for the press conference. It's set up for four o'clock."

"I'll be there," Ross says over his shoulder.

"Don't worry," he tells me as he shepherds me to his car. "It's going to be OK."

I stumble along beside him. I know Ross is lying. Things are not going to be OK. Time, that invisible essence I control with a twist of my mind, always takes its revenge. Once a spinner gets sick, the end is inevitable. A few months, a year at most, and then ... Sixteen is young, but not unheard of.

No spinner lives past twenty.

02

I WENT ON MY FIRST MISSION WITH CARSON ROSS SIX months ago. I'd been certified to work missions as a fully qualified spinner since I was thirteen, and had been through three different agents already, enough to learn that since rewinds make most people uncomfortable, the cops assigned as agents aren't always the city's finest. My first agent, Amanda Spruce, worked vice, so we unwound a lot of prostitution cases. In between, she'd tell me stories about her teenage daughters—their clothes, soccer clubs, boyfriends, and parties. She'd laugh about the time her eldest got caught skinny-dipping with her boyfriend in a city reservoir, or when the youngest was found with a joint. Later, we'd round up another drug-addicted hooker and rewind her day before arresting her pimp and any of the johns we managed to ID. Ms. Spruce called the girls whores when she questioned them and once shoved one so hard against the side of the police car she broke the girl's tooth.

Tito Marquez was a beat cop in a neighborhood known for gang violence. He drank gallons of coffee and spent a lot of time intimidating witnesses before we got around to the rewinds. I'd sit in his car wishing I could speed time up instead of slow it down. The only upside was that we did work some interesting cases. It was with him that I first tasted the grim pleasure of uncovering a murderer.

The last guy was the worst. Jonas Saul was about fifty, with graying hair and a gut he had to wedge under the steering wheel in order to drive. He called me honey and tried to put his arm around me during rewinds. *Frozen time doesn't count*, he'd tell me, then laugh his disgusting smoker's hack as if this phrase might be considered original. Or funny.

That first mission with Ross involved a dead baby. The probable verdict was that the death was natural. SIDS, they called it—Sudden Infant Death Syndrome—but the cops thought something might be off, so they brought in Ross to check it out. I was not supposed to be there. Calvin had been Ross's first spinner, but he'd gotten sick a couple months before, and Ross had been reassigned to the oldest—and theoretically most experienced—spinner at the Center, nineteen-year-old Jack. In his typically loud fashion, Jack had been annoying everyone all week, crowing about how he'd won the agent lottery. That morning, though, Jack got caught making out with another spinner in the second-floor bathroom—a cardinal, if frequent, Center transgression. They were both given extra chores, and I got pulled for Jack's mission.

Ross and I drove out through an unseasonably hot spring afternoon that even the air conditioning in his car couldn't tame. Ross asked me lots of questions, which at the time I found disconcerting: What did I like about the Center? What jobs did I do there? Did I think Dr. Barnard, the Center's director, treated us fairly? None of my other agents wanted to know anything about me except my name. I answered him in monosyllables while surreptitiously studying his profile. I pegged him at late thirties, still fit, with gray peppering his dark blond hair. He gestured with his hands a lot and had laugh lines around his eyes that crinkled when he squinted into the sun.

As we moved east and the city's hustle shrank down to streets of tired houses, Ross's conversation slowed. By the time we reached our goal, Ross was frowning with a focused concentration I admired. The house we stopped at had a falling-down fence around a lawn whose only green spots were dandelions. When we got out of the car, the heat descended like a flaming hand pressing the back of my neck.

Ross rang the doorbell. Twice. No one answered. He had just raised his hand to knock, when the door cracked open to the width allowed by a chain lock.

In the shaft of darkness, the woman looked insubstantial, as if she'd already been rewound. She wore a thin bathrobe without a belt and her feet were bare. Misery wafted from her, mingling with the stench of spoiled milk and unwashed skin.

"Mrs. Montgomery?" Ross asked.

The woman's face remained so blank she might have been the one who died.

"I'm Agent Carson Ross." He showed her his badge. "And this is spinner Alexandra Manning. We're here to look into the death of Rosalind Montgomery. We have a time search warrant."

The woman stared vaguely at the paper in Ross's hand. No spark showed even the faintest hint of comprehension. Ross stuffed the papers back into his pocket. When he spoke again his voice was gentle.

"May we come in?"

The door closed. I thought Mrs. Montgomery had dismissed us, but a moment later I heard the slide of the lock, and the door swung open. I had to force myself to follow Ross inside. Mrs. Montgomery was already shuffling over to a forlorn sofa. She must have been there a while. An open pizza box displayed congealed pieces of barely eaten pie while a television flashed images through a muted screen. Somewhere nearby, a diaper pail needed emptying.

Ross cleared his throat. "Can you show me where Rosalind died?"

Mrs. Montgomery pointed vaguely toward a closed door. Ross thanked her. I tripped over a stroller in my eagerness to get away from the unresponsive woman.

The bedroom was worse. For one thing, it turned out to be the home of the overflowing diaper pail. The cloud of ammonia that hit us when we entered the room made me gag. Ross put a hand up to his nose.

"Give me your arm," he said.

"What?"

"Freeze time, quick, so we can lessen the smell."

I held out my arm and he unlocked my leash. As soon as the metal left my skin I touched two fingers to Ross's bare wrist and stopped time. Ross grabbed the door, waving the wood back and forth to make enough breeze to disperse the stench-laden molecules. It didn't erase the smell, but at least my eyes quit watering. I blinked, taking in a blanket-strewn mattress on the floor, a sagging dresser, and window blinds that didn't close all the way. Only the far corner showed signs of care. Here, the wall was painted a soft yellow. On the floor, a makeshift changing station made of a stack of towels rested next to a pile of neatly folded baby clothes. Above that, someone had taped up three photographs. The first showed a dozing infant in a stretchy pink-and-blue hat. The second was a studio portrait of a startled-looking child with a flowered band around her bald head. The last was a snapshot of a laughing woman holding the baby tight against her chest. The girl's fat cheeks were split by a gummy smile, one little hand wrapped around a strand of her mother's hair. The mother was a barely recognizable version of Mrs. Montgomery.

"Let's get this over with," Ross said.

I nodded, grabbing time so hard the rewind spun backward with a force that made me sway.

"How far back do I need to go?" I asked.

"A neighbor called it in this morning. I gather the child died sometime the day before. We'll have to go back at least twenty-four hours—will that be a problem for you?"

"No, sir," I said.

The phantom police backed in first, quickly followed by a guy from the morgue, who replaced a tiny body into a coil of blankets in the center of the bed. Rosalind's rosebud mouth hung open, relaxed far beyond the temporary release of sleep. I kept the rewind moving at a fast clip. Police wandered in and out, poking in drawers and un-taking pictures. Their rewound voices kept up an incomprehensible hum, punctuated by ugly squawks from their radios. Mrs. Montgomery never appeared. Presumably she'd already taken up residence on her sofa. Light leached away from the afternoon until last night's darkness settled an overlay of gloom, though the fetid air around us kept its real-time heat. Sweat tickled the edges of my hairline. Rosalind lay alone in her blankets, unmoving and definitely dead. I spun the rewind harder. Light returned. I pulled faster still, racing a growing tiredness as we moved farther back. The sun brightened, receded.

In the rosy light of dawn, Mrs. Montgomery staggered backward into the room. She moved like a barely animate china doll, as if any fast movement might shatter her. My grip on time slipped. The image stuttered to a halt.

"Is this as far as you can rewind?" Ross asked. "I understand. This is much farther than I expected."

"No." I pressed my lips together, barely giving my words enough room to slip out. "I can go further. It's just . . ."

Mrs. Montgomery's body strained with a barely suppressed scream. The idea of seeing her turn around and face the dead baby terrified me.

Ross put an arm around my shoulder.

"Hey, it's OK."

I stiffened beneath his touch. He let me go.

"You don't have to watch," Ross said. "Close your eyes. I'll tell you what to do."

I escaped into the darkness of my closed lids and concentrated on the strands flowing through me. I eased them out, fast or slow, depending on what Ross asked. Only when I heard his soft *oh* of comprehension did I peek. The shadowy form of Mrs. Montgomery slept, her body rising and falling in rhythmic exhaustion. A thin bedspread covered most of her body. It must have been a cool night because her exposed arm was dotted with goosebumps. Next to her, baby Rosalind lay packed into a carefully constructed nest of pillows and blankets. Mrs. Montgomery's outstretched arm curved around the soft pile, the unconscious gesture of a mother protecting her young. Except the arm was not protecting. Its weight had pushed the heap of blankets forward, so that the edges of the nest caved over, pressing down onto the form beneath and covering Rosalind's head with smothering comfort. As I watched, one chubby hand waved, the tiny fingers unable to coordinate an assault on the warm excess.

I slammed my eyes shut again, wishing I hadn't ignored Ross's directions. Time scraped through my mind like fingernails.

Ross let out a long sigh. "You can let it go now."

I released my hold, suffering the swirling dizziness before opening my eyes. The horrible urine smell exploded in my nostrils. A time headache pounded inside my skull.

"Come on," Ross said.

Mrs. Montgomery still perched on her sofa, staring at the soundless TV. The flashing images cast strange lights on her skin, now red, now green. I imagined Ross telling her the baby's death was her fault, saw the words falling on her like hammers. I wondered if it were possible for someone to dissolve. Mrs. Montgomery already seemed so frail. This news would surely crush her into multicolored dust.

"We're done, ma'am," Ross said. I held my breath. Despite the heat, my body shivered.

"The initial assessment was right," he said. "Your baby died of SIDS. It was nobody's fault. I'm so sorry."

An earthquake could have rocked the building and not stunned me as much as Ross's words. Not because I'd never heard a cop shade the truth before, but because I'd never seen one do it to protect someone like this: a poor, unimportant woman with nothing to offer in return.

Mrs. Montgomery raised her head. Her mouth worked, as if she barely remembered how to speak.

"Are you sure?" she asked.

"I'm positive." Ross gestured toward me. "We both saw the rewind."

Her eyes went wide. Whole worlds could be lost in the blackness of those pupils. I wondered what she knew. Or suspected. What she was willing to forget.

"Thank you," she said.

Ross ushered me out to the car and drove to a fast food restaurant. He ordered three hamburgers, fries, and two chocolate milkshakes. I hoped he'd eat quickly. I wanted to put as much distance between me and that rewind as possible. We parked under a tree. Ross adjusted a vent on the dash so cold air blasted over me.

"I'm always famished after a rewind," he said, handing me a burger. "Aren't you?"

The unexpected reward filled my hand. I'd never heard of an agent buying a spinner lunch before. Ross slid his seat backward and settled in to eat.

"Won't the Center wonder where we are?" I asked, worried Ross's generosity would get us into trouble.

Ross shrugged. "They don't know how long the mission lasted." He noticed my untasted food. "Unless you want to go back?"

"No, sir." I unwrapped the burger and took a bite. Ketchup squirted onto my tongue, the tangy flavor a perfect counterpoint to the chewy meat. I realized I was starving.

"You were good back there," Ross said. "Your rewind was really clear, even after almost thirty-six hours. How long can you go?"

"I rewound two and a half days once," I said, my words muffled by the food stuffed in my cheek. Ross whistled appreciatively. Spurred by the praise, I added, "And I've held time for over two hours."

"Impressive," Ross said. "I might have to keep you around. Think you can handle homicide?"

I swallowed the entire lump of burger in one painful gulp. He wanted me as his permanent spinner? I wiped the ketchup from my lips.

"I've seen worse, sir," I said, though I wasn't sure it was true.

"Don't call me sir," Ross said. "If we're going to be partners, there's no need to be so formal."

Partners. The word sounded like a promise. The idea that this decent man wanted to work with me was the best present I'd ever gotten. Happiness made me brave.

"Why did you do it?" I asked. "Why did you lie to Mrs. Montgomery?"

Ross handed me one of the milkshakes and unwrapped his second burger. "Let me ask you a question. Why do you do rewinds?"

"Because I have to."

"Fair enough. Does the job ever make you feel good?"

"Sometimes." I considered the question. "I rewound a case for Agent Marquez once that proved the guy the police had arrested was innocent. The real culprit had framed him. That felt pretty good."

"It felt good because the truth led to justice. Truth isn't always that straightforward, though. In Mrs. Montgomery's case, the truth would have destroyed an already devastated woman, and for what? The truth wouldn't bring back baby Rosalind. The truth would only have made things worse."

I swirled some chocolate shake around in my mouth. It tasted sweet and deliciously cool.

"What will you write in your report?"

"That the baby died of SIDS." Ross turned toward me. "What do you think about letting what happened in that rewind be our secret, known to nobody in the world but us two."

I smiled at him so widely I probably looked like a demented jack-o-lantern.

"I'd like that," I said, and took another bite of burger to staunch the ridiculous grin.

Thoughts sprouted in my brain like shoots after a spring shower, fragile and teeming with possibility. For as long as I could remember, people had told me that my abilities made me different. Ross was the first person to say they made me special.

03

"I SHOULDN'T HAVE LET YOU HOLD THE FREEZE SO LONG," Ross says as we pull away from City Hall. "Not with you bringing two people with you."

"Freezing doesn't cause the sickness. When it's your time, it just happens."

I lower the visor on the windshield to block out the sun's glare. I'm trying really hard not to cry. After spinners get sick, staff pull us off time work until our chronotin levels stabilize. Some spinners' time skills are so weakened by the sickness they never go back. My hand closes around the door handle. The idea of not going on another mission with Ross, of spending the rest of my life doing mindless chores inside the Sick, makes me want to throw myself from the moving car and just end it all now.

Ross and I drive through the city without speaking. The Crime Investigation Center is in Portland's Old Town, languishing among single room occupancy hotels, soup kitchens, and a cluster of the city's grittier businesses, which makes the drive from the glossy City

Hall area feel like a lesson in urban decline. I massage my churning stomach. Ross turns the police radio's chatter down low and chooses a roundabout route so I'll have time to calm down. Sometimes, after a mission, Ross will park somewhere so we can hash over the case or speculate on Sikes's identity. Sometimes we talk about time work, and he tells me how vital rewinds are to successful police investigations. He says no one likes to acknowledge how much our work helps because most people are uncomfortable having their public safety depend on a bunch of institutionalized orphans. *Guilt*, he says, *is a great silencer.*

With the press conference a little less than two hours away, the only stop Ross makes is at a mini-mart to buy me a soda. Caffeine helps relieve time headaches. I watch him paying the clerk through the store window and consider all the ways my life is basically over. It's not just the missions. Kids who get sick, they're not pariahs, exactly, but other spinners tend to start avoiding them. I know. I've done it. It's like, if you've already cut someone off, then you won't miss them when they die.

The scene in front of me blurs. Of course I've always known this day would come, but I didn't think I had to worry about it for at least another year. My best friend, KJ, is eighteen and he's never gotten sick.

KJ.

My stomach flips, and I have to clench my teeth to keep from throwing up all over Ross's squad car. KJ has been down ever since Calvin, his former roommate, got sick. KJ's such a good friend he doesn't ignore Calvin. Instead he hovers over him, carrying his lunch tray and bringing him books. Whenever KJ talks about him, his spine wilts a little, like the world is too heavy for him to bear. How will he stand it if I tell him I'm dying, too?

"Are you sure this is time sickness?" Ross asks a minute later, as we ease back into traffic. "Maybe it's just nerves. The bomb, all those people."

I take a long swallow of soda, forcing the carbonated bubbles to push down the acid rising to meet them.

"I don't think so," I say.

We stop at a light. In the car next to us, a little boy sits in a booster seat, sucking his thumb with an enthusiasm usually saved for lollipops. The boy stares at me. He's a normal boy, with a mom in the front seat, and a sister beside him. A normal boy with a normal life. I doubt he'll ever appreciate how lucky he is.

"You kids are so special." Ross slams a hand against the steering wheel. "Letting you die is a complete waste."

I shrug. I've never had a real home. The ability to freeze time comes from a rare gene mutation that makes the body produce an enzyme called chronotin. All babies have their blood tested for it at birth. I assume my parents cried when the nurses took away their newborn, but I sometimes wonder if they were also relieved to rid themselves of a mutant. Not that they had a choice. By law all spinners are raised in a Children's Home. Once we can start to control our time skills, usually around ten, we get assigned to a Center for training. Lots of us die in infancy and even the healthiest of us are unstable without medication. Violent. Paranoid. Who would want to raise a child like that?

Ross is still talking. "The hardest part about being an agent is seeing how tough it is on you kids. It's been especially hard since I started working with you."

The light changes. Ross pulls away from the little family.

"You're a really great kid, Alex. Not just a good spinner—which you are. The best. Most spinners don't really care about the work. But a good person. And right when we're *this* close to catching Sikes." He slams the steering wheel again. "You've been such a help on this case. You deserve to see it through."

"Thanks," I mumble.

Any other day, Ross's speech would have lit me up like a torch. Ross, though generally kind, has never said he cares about me so explicitly. Today, his words just sink into the pain wrapping my body. They are a gift I can never open. Not when I can count the weeks I have left. Not when I might never see him again.

"Look, Alex." Ross clears his throat. "What if there was a way I could help you? Keep you from getting another attack of the sickness?"

"You can't." I look out the window. "Everyone gets sick."

"I've been emailing with a scientist," Ross says, "a researcher in Germany named Dr. Kroger. He's been developing a new medicine for treating time sickness. In his trials he's been able to postpone a second bout for a year—sometimes even longer."

A year. The words hover in the air between us, a spark of hope in a world gone dark. I keep staring out the window. I know about fires. People can get burned.

"Will Dr. Barnard prescribe it?" I ask.

"Probably not."

We turn a corner. The Center rises up at the end of the block, a hulking stone building on a small hill that raises it a full ten feet above street level. It's not a friendly looking place: A low wall and a narrow strip of thorny shrubs discourages passersby from getting too close. Arched windows set at even intervals along the ground floor offer the blank stare of opaque glass. Small cameras tucked in the eaves warn of the constant surveillance around the building. All the windows are barred.

Ross slows the car.

"This new treatment hasn't been approved yet by the FDA, but I could ask Dr. Kroger if he'll let you be part of his clinical trial. The problem is, if he agrees, you'll have to take it without Dr. Barnard's knowledge. In fact, you can't even tell him you got sick today, or he'll start monitoring you so closely he'll figure out you changed your meds."

I drink the last of my soda.

"If I don't tell Dr. Barnard," I say, "he won't increase my Aclisote dosage and my chronotin levels will really go nuts."

"If there's too much Aclisote in your system the new medicine won't work."

I roll the soda can between my hands, hope and caution battling it out inside my head. Dr. Barnard is an international expert on Aclisote. He has decades of experience keeping chronotin levels in check. What if these untested meds just bring on a second attack sooner? Or have some horrible side effect?

"Won't Dr. Barnard notice anyway?" I ask. "Amy checks our blood every month whether we're sick or not."

"True." Ross pulls the car into one of the reserved parking spots in front of the Center and cuts the engine. "When is your next blood test scheduled for?"

"Two weeks. Dr. Barnard just raised my Aclisote dosage, too."

"He did?" Ross frowns. "What was your last chronotin reading?"

I shake my head, afraid if I talk my voice will crack. I have no idea what my chronotin reading was but I do know that if I got sick so close to an increase, my chronotin must have totally spiked.

"Don't worry about your next test," Ross says. "I'll deal with it. The question is whether you're willing to try the new medicine."

"I don't know, Mr. Ross." I squeeze the empty soda can so hard the sides crush together. "It sounds risky."

Ross runs a finger along the steering wheel.

"Dr. Kroger is a well-respected guy, and the early results he's getting have been amazing. I'm sure FDA approval is only a matter of time. The problem is you don't have time." He twists in his seat so he's facing me. "I know there's some risk, but sometimes a chance is all you ever get. After that, life is what you make of it."

I study the crumpled metal in my hand, the edges sharp against my palm.

"It's not your risk, though, is it?"

Ross's face softens.

"It's absolutely my risk," he says. "I don't want my partner to die."

I can't stop the tears anymore. The salty wetness blurs everything: Ross, the car, the street outside. Ross rummages in the console for a tissue. I hear something banging and it takes me a second to realize that Charlie, one of the Center's front-desk guards, is knocking on the window of Ross's car. I keep my head down as Ross unrolls the window.

"You guys get locked out?" Charlie asks. "Sorry. Dr. Barnard said I could run out for some coffee. Slow day."

Ross climbs from the car, distracting Charlie with chatter about last night's football game while I mop my face with a tissue. The caffeine from the soda has finally kicked in and bright things don't hurt my eyes anymore. I barely notice. All I can think about is Ross's offer.

Charlie waves his key card across the sensor that lets us into the cramped Center lobby. I inhale the familiar scents of burnt coffee and bleach, letting my vision adjust to the dim light. A framed black-and-white photograph hanging near the entrance shows what the Center looked like a hundred years ago when it was a newly built hotel. Back then, the lobby was an elegant space, open and airy, with sofas scattered among potted palms. Now the lobby is chopped up into offices. Brick has replaced the glass windows, choking out any source of natural light, and the front door bristles with electronic locks and security cameras. Only a pair of curving staircases leading to the second floor hints at the space's former glory, and even these potentially graceful lines are ruined by the guard station plunked down at their base.

Ross walks me over to the glassed-in station. Charlie goes inside and slides open the window partition, letting loose a waft of air tinged with the smell of unwashed socks. Charlie spreads out a page of the logbook. Ross signs me in while I hold out my arm for Charlie to unlock the leash. Its release lightens my lingering headache.

"I'll see you soon?" Ross asks, turning over the leash key to Charlie. I know he's really asking what I've decided, but he can't say anything more explicit in front of an audience.

"Mr. Ross, I . . ."

My stomach gives another lurch. Four months ago, when Calvin got sick for the second time, KJ and I visited him in the clinic. He looked awful. Sweat dotted his forehead, making slick diamonds that nestled in the roots of his kinky hair. KJ and I were sitting together, watching him sleep, when suddenly, Calvin's eyes popped open. *Did they get you, too?* KJ leaned forward and Calvin grabbed his shirt front. *Don't let them hurt me*, he begged. *They want to send me to the Central Office. I won't go with them. I won't!* Amy came running, and Yolly, the Center's manager and resident den mother, bustled us out of the room. *Don't worry*, Yolly soothed us, *it's just the chronotin talking. The real Calvin will be back once he stabilizes.* He isn't, though. Calvin's body is healthy, but his mind dwells on wild conspiracy theories and a deep conviction that someone is trying to hurt him. He isn't the first spinner to go crazy at the end, just the first one I knew well.

Did the studies Ross read track quality of life or just quantity? What if I live longer but I also lose my mind?

The main office door swings open, and Dr. Jeffrey Barnard steps out into the lobby. Everything about the Center's director is crisp, from his neatly pressed lab coat to the knife-edged crease running down his pant leg. Even his hair is perfectly contained, the gray strands clipped into a tidy circle around his receding hairline.

I tilt my head down, aware of my red-rimmed eyes and puffy nose. A lock of hair has gotten loose from my ponytail and I let it dangle over my face.

"Agent Ross, Alexandra." Barnard nods his head in our direction. "How did your mission go?"

"Very successfully," Ross says. "We found the bomb and the expert was able to deactivate it before it could go off. We got a pretty good look at the perp, too. Shouldn't be too hard to track him down."

I pretend to be interested in the rotating pictures from the security feeds inside Charlie's station: a grainy image of the Center's front steps, a group of Youngers reciting lessons in a classroom, Yuki mopping an empty hallway. The common room looks busy and I make a mental note to avoid it.

"Good." Barnard sounds no more impressed by Ross's answer than if he'd said we'd prevented a fender bender. Instead, he asks Ross when he'll be receiving a copy of his last report. Ross isn't known for stellar paperwork. I touch the spot on my forehead where my headache still throbs. Dr. Barnard turns abruptly in my direction.

"How are you feeling, Alexandra?"

Ross stops talking. Barnard peers at me over his wire-rimmed glasses. The lobby suddenly seems very crowded. Three pairs of eyes fix on me: Charlie's gaze mildly curious, Barnard's clinical, Ross's anxious. A warm flush creeps along the side of my neck. Who do I trust? Barnard the efficient scientist? Or Ross and the possibility of a longer life? My heart rate jumps, no doubt sending heightened levels of chronotin gushing through my veins. I take a breath.

"I'm fine," I say.

Ross rewards me with a massive grin. The pain in my head fades to a dull pulse.

Dr. Barnard frowns. "No worse headaches than usual? Any nausea?"

I scuff the worn tiles under my feet.

"No," I lie.

"It was a rough day," Ross says. "We ended up cutting it a little close. Things were pretty tense in there for a while."

"I see." Barnard sounds thoughtful, perhaps wondering why the gruesome murder I'd rewound a few months ago hadn't fazed me when a plastic box had. I keep my attention glued to the floor. One of Ross's shoelaces has come untied. Barnard's leather oxfords gleam.

"If you need to rest," Barnard says, "you can spend the afternoon in your room."

"That's OK," I mutter. If my days *are* numbered, the last place I want to spend them is shut up alone in my room. "I signed up to work with KJ in the garden."

"If that's what you prefer." He turns to Ross. "We have a free office, why don't you write up your report here."

"I won't be able to do that." Ross backs away. "I'm supposed to meet Chief Graham for a press conference."

"Make sure you get us a copy of both reports when they're complete," Barnard calls after him.

Ross says something vague. Behind Barnard's back, he winks at me.

Charlie buzzes the door open and Ross strolls outside. Sunshine picks up lighter threads in his hair, making them glint like strands of gold. At the threshold, he turns and waves to me. I watch him leave, holding our secret inside my chest, a tendril of hope to protect me from the shadows that descend as the front door's locks click back into place.

04

THE CENTER'S COURTYARD ISN'T A GREAT PLACE FOR a garden. Shade covers most of it, so there's only a small area that gets enough sun to grow anything besides rhododendrons. All of us have to take shifts working in it—part of the do-gooder Society for Spinner Rights's theory that we'll be happier spending time outside and eating locally sourced organic food. A theory that will be hard to prove since we've never harvested more than two meals' worth of greens in a season.

Cool air touches my face as I step outside, bringing with it the scent of freshly turned earth. KJ is pulling up some weeds that invaded the space between the beds. The steady work must have warmed him, because he's ditched his sweatshirt, leaving his long brown arms bare. I watch him for a minute. Everything about him—the focused concentration, muscled shoulders, dark brows, and the proud arc of his nose—already seems tinged with the nostalgia of loss.

"Hey," I call.

KJ settles on his heels, smiling. "You're back early."

KJ's full name is Kaleel Jabar, which means his birth parents must have been of Arab descent. One of the Society's first initiatives back in the 1960s was a campaign to replace randomly generated first names for spinners with ethnically appropriate first and last names. Like all the Society's efforts, this one is kind of a joke, since none of us are raised with any kind of cultural identity. KJ dropped Kaleel when he was still a Younger after another kid started calling him Kaleel the Heel. KJ is over six feet tall now, out of reach of most teasing, but his chosen nickname stuck.

I cross toward him. KJ shoves his overlong bangs away from his eyes with his wrist, the only part of his hands that isn't muddy.

"How'd it go?" he asks.

I grimace. "Not great."

"What? No fun huddle with Ross to speculate on the latest Sikes theory?"

"No."

The abruptness of my answer wipes the cheer from his face.

"What happened?" he asks. I move closer and my expression must give something away because he adds, "Are you OK?"

"It's just . . ." *that I'm dying.*

I can't do it. And I certainly can't tell him about Ross's offer of a new, unlicensed drug. KJ is a worrier, and I don't think I can handle his fears on top of my own. I plunk myself down on a patch of grass near the beds. At this point in the afternoon, the sun has abandoned all but a small corner of the courtyard. In the spot where I sit, the air carries a definite chill.

"I'm just tired," I say. "We ended up getting called in on a bomb scare at City Hall. There were, like, thirty cops there, and all of them were freaking out."

"A bomb? You're kidding. How come you always get the glory jobs?"

Coming from anyone else, the words would have made me defensive. KJ is the only spinner in the Center who doesn't give me grief about how much I like time work. Not that he particularly enjoys the job. KJ's agent is in the traffic division so mostly he unwinds car accidents. He says the missions are usually dull and occasionally gruesome, and he sees no reason to spend more energy on them than he has to.

I pluck half-heartedly at a patch of dandelions making inroads on some nearby lettuce. "What'd you do today?"

"Barnard's computer froze up, so I spent all morning cleaning off a virus. It was actually really cool."

A dreamy expression creeps over KJ's face. Despite my own worries, I can't help smiling. KJ is fascinated by computers, the same way I'm drawn to solving crimes. He sees viruses as puzzles—untangle the code and the whole thing comes apart. I only follow about half of his explanations, but I love that he's passionate about something. Most of the kids here waste all their time on video games and TV.

I throw my handful of dandelions at him.

"You're such a dork."

KJ laughs and picks up a rake.

"Hey, come on, dork is the new cool."

I flop onto my back and stare upwards. The walls surrounding the courtyard hide most of the sky, leaving only a rectangle of blue overhead. The more I stare up at it, the more the walls seem to be leaning, as if they're closing in around me.

"If you weren't a spinner," I ask, "what would you want to be?"

"Lots of things." KJ rakes the scattered weeds into a pile. "Computer programmer, obviously. Or maybe a scientist."

"You could run the experiments they do on the sick spinners at the Central Office. Find out why no one ever comes back from there."

"Not medical science. I'd want to be a marine biologist. I've always wanted to see the ocean." He leans against the rake. "I would freeze time and get really close to great white sharks. Or see what it looks like underwater when a wave crashes into a reef."

"I said imagine if you *weren't* a spinner."

"I'd rather stay a spinner *and* be able to do whatever I wanted."

Dampness from the ground seeps through my CIC shirt. I shiver.

"If you were still a spinner, Norms would think you were too much of a freak to let you join their expedition. Plus, you'd die before you learned enough to be useful."

"Aren't you Miss Cheerful today." KJ bends to scoop up the pile of weeds. "What would *you* want to be?"

A cloud drifts over the edge of the Center's walls. I study it, trying to force the bit of fluff into some kind of shape, but all I can see is a blob. I turn KJ's question around in my mind to the one I really want to ask: what would you do with your life if you knew you had only a few months left to live? An ache fills me, the longing as unshaped as the blobby cloud.

"I'd want to be someone important," I say. "Someone who makes a difference."

"That's funny." KJ carries the weeds over to the composter. "Shannon and I were just talking about that last night. About how we all need to feel useful. She says that's why she likes working with the Youngers."

Something about the way he says her name, just a shade too casually, catches my attention. I lift my head.

"Shannon?"

"Yeah." KJ is still messing with the compost so I can't see his face.

"You know she's not as much of an airhead as you always claim."

I wriggle my shoulders. The grass itches my back, each blade an individual irritant. Shannon is my roommate. If she weren't a spinner, she'd be a cheerleader, all pep and bounce, with a deep desire to indulge in volunteer work. I sit up.

"You and Shannon, huh?" I'm trying really hard to make my voice sound light. "Anything I should know about?"

"I don't know." KJ finally turns around. "Would it bother you if I went out with someone?"

The walls of the courtyard shrink a bit closer. I force myself to picture it: KJ and Shannon, together. My best friend distracted by someone else in what might be the last few months of my life. The acid remnants of nausea rise up to scrape the back of my throat. When I swallow, my mouth tastes bitter.

"Why would it bother me?" I stand and pick up KJ's abandoned rake, scraping it across a mound of dirt. "It's not like I'm your girlfriend or anything."

KJ's mouth pinches shut and the quiet from his unsaid words is loud enough to muffle the rasp of my unproductive raking. I focus my attention on my task, bending the thin tines under the strength of my stroke. KJ and I arrived at the Center the same summer. At ten, I was the youngest kid there and so shy I barely made eye contact with anyone. He was twelve, super scrawny, and suffering from a bad case of acne. The teacher at the time, Mr. Thomas, paired us up for a class project, and we started sitting together at meals. By fall we were inseparable. Two years later, things changed. I overheard another girl sighing about how cute he was, and after that I couldn't stop noticing the adorable way his hair curled over his ears. Then KJ started getting tongue-tied in the middle of the simplest conversations, and it no longer seemed casual if our shoulders touched. When we finally kissed I felt like I'd entered a three-dimensional world after living in two dimensions all my life. The Center looked brighter. Food tasted sweeter. Every song on the radio was about us. We both rearranged our schedules so we could spend every possible minute together.

And then . . . I don't know. It got weird. People teased us. The staff started assigning us to separate jobs to "keep a healthy perspective." KJ saw me laughing with Simon and got mad. We argued. I was only twelve and it all just seemed like too much. So I told him I wanted to break up. The six months that followed were the worst of my life. I slunk around the Center trying to avoid him, yet unable to talk to anyone else without thinking how dull they were in comparison. Shannon did her best to make me feel better, but she had recently broken up with Aidan, and listening to her inane theories about healing chakras was worse than being alone. The only way I could sleep was to practice freezing during the day for so long that I'd be exhausted by the time it was lights out. It took ages before KJ and I worked through all that awkwardness and regained our friendship, so now I'm always very careful not to do anything that might screw things up again. Acting like I'm jealous is definitely in the screw-up category.

"I'm sorry," I say to KJ, "that sounded bitchy. You should do whatever makes you happy."

"Yeah." KJ wipes some of the dirt off his hands. "Well, there is something nice about being around someone who thinks you're special."

I pull harder on the rake. He's clearly annoyed, so I must not have done a convincing job of acting supportive. Should I offer to say something to Shannon? A splinter flakes off the wooden handle, shooting beneath my skin with a sharp stab. I yelp. KJ is beside me in seconds. He takes my hand and opens it inside his own. The jagged tip of the splinter sticks out from my skin and KJ rubs at it, trying to ease it out with his thumb.

I breathe in the smell of him—dirt and sweat and crushed dandelions—and the formless ache inside me stretches even wider. All the secrets I'm keeping from him rush so close to the tip of my tongue I have to bite it to stop myself from screaming them. I know if I tell him about getting sick, he won't hook up with Shannon, and I also know that keeping him away from her is a selfish reason for fessing up. A sigh works its way from deep in my gut, a long rasp of air that only expands the ache inside me. KJ looks up.

"Are you really OK? You seem, I don't know, distracted."

"I'm fine," I say, automatically. KJ frowns.

"I just have a lot to think about." I search my brain for an excuse that doesn't involve new girlfriends or death or untested drugs. "Ross thinks the City Hall bomber might know something about Sikes. If he's right, we might be able to uncover Sikes's identity."

KJ pokes my palm, trying to grasp the end of the splinter.

"Aren't you worried that if you and Ross get close to Sikes, he'll come after you like he did to Sal?"

"Ross is careful. Whenever he makes inquiries he always pretends they're about some other case. Besides, I live locked up in the Sick. What safer place could there be?"

KJ makes an irritated sound in the back of his throat. "I think you're getting kind of obsessed with this Sikes thing."

"I told you, I want to make a difference. This is how."

"I get that, but what about, I don't know, hanging out with your friends?"

He looks at me, his eyes dark and unreadable. I shift my feet.

"We do hang out," I say.

"We could hang out more. It's not like we have endless time."

His hand tightens around mine. When we were an item, all those years ago, KJ used to hold my hand like this, as if it was the most precious gift in the world. I rub my temple, trying to erase the memory. Getting sentimental about the past is just going to make things awkward between us, which is not something I can afford. There is no way I'll survive the stress of a drug trial without KJ's friendship to lean on.

"You're right," I tell him, making a huge effort to sound casual, "we don't have a lot of time, which means we really need to focus on the things we want to accomplish."

KJ makes another unsuccessful swipe at my splinter. He looks like he wants to keep arguing, so I slip my hand free. He'll never get the splinter out, anyway. He's too afraid to hurt me to really dig in and yank.

"I'm going to go find Yolly," I say. "See if she has some tweezers."

"Are you coming back?"

"I'm really tired. Dr. Barnard said I could go up to my room. I might do that."

I walk back into the Center with KJ's disappointment burning a hole between my shoulder blades. Ten minutes ago, the idea of being alone sounded awful, right now it feels like a reprieve. At least then I won't have to lie.

05

YOLLY POUNCES ON ME BEFORE I'VE TAKEN THREE steps down the hallway.

"There you are!" she cries. "I've been looking for you everywhere. The press conference about the bombing is about to start. Barnard gave permission for us all to watch it together on TV!"

My stomach sinks all the way to my toes. Sitting in a room with the other spinners, pretending nothing is wrong, sounds about as appealing as spending a month scouring toilets.

"That's OK," I say. "I already know what happened."

"Don't be silly. It will be fun to see Mr. Ross on TV."

We're supposed to call Yolly Ms. Yolanda, but only Dr. Barnard uses her full name. She's a large, comfortable-looking woman with short black hair curled into an immobile cap around her face. She constantly reminds us how lucky we are to be living in a Center run by the famous Dr. Barnard. *You're getting the best care in the world here*, she says. Jack calls her Jolly Yolly behind her back because she always talks in an aren't-we-having-fun voice.

I try a new angle.

"I'm such a mess." I wiggle my grass-stained fingers in her direction. "I need to wash up."

"Be quick, then, so you don't miss any of it." Yolly beams at me. "It's going to be on in less than ten minutes!"

I try to dig up another reason to refuse her invitation. Nothing comes to me. Besides, I am a little curious to hear what Chief Graham will say about the tip-off call, so I nod and trudge off to the nearest bathroom.

The common room is much less cozy than the name implies. It's a big, shabby space on the ground floor with blinds covering the windows so outsiders can't see in. Fluorescent lights hum over linoleum floors and an assortment of mismatched furniture. A bookcase stretches across one wall, mostly well-thumbed paperbacks—romance and thrillers are popular—mingling with pristine good-for-you classics, courtesy of ever-hopeful Yolly. A shelf on the opposite wall holds a haphazard stack of puzzles, board games, and some neglected art supplies. Besides the TV, there's also a table holding a CD player and three computers with lots of games but no internet access. Jack claims they don't want us in contact with people outside the Center. Yolly says it's not in the budget.

Despite Yolly's enthusiasm, only five of the nine other qualified spinners are in the room. Jack is sorting through a pile of CDs, avoiding everyone under a pair of headphones. Aidan and Raul are playing the card game War. Yuki is lying on a sofa, flipping through a dog-eared copy of *Glamour* magazine while simultaneously tracking the dubious hilarity of a TV sitcom. She must have been on a mission today, too, because she's sipping from a giant mug of Center coffee.

Shannon sits on the second sofa surrounded by four of the Youngers.

She's got them all playing one of those writing games where each person adds a line to a story and then passes it on, an exercise that seems to involve more giggling than concentration. When Shannon isn't on a mission or doing her main Center job as Amy's nursing assistant, she tutors groups of Youngers in reading and math. I suspect half the kids fail their tests on purpose in order to spend time with her. My Center job is training the Youngers on time skills. None of them shows particular interest in spending extra time with me.

Yuki sees me come in and waves her magazine in my direction. Yuki adores clothes or, as she would call it, *fashion*, and can't quite comprehend that other people don't share her fascination. I shake my head at her and slink across the room to curl into one of the armchairs facing the TV.

"Look who's here," Aidan calls when I pass him. "Our very own celebrity. Think I could get your autograph later?"

Raul chuckles, which he does every time Aidan says anything even vaguely resembling a joke. I scrunch lower in the chair and pretend not to hear them.

The common room door opens and KJ walks in with Calvin. The sight of Calvin's anxious face floods my brain with second thoughts about not telling Barnard I was sick. KJ and Calvin are almost the same height, but where KJ's limbs are lean, Calvin has always had bulk. Lately, though, that bulk has shifted—it's like he aged from eighteen to forty in half a year. His shoulders lost their athletic swagger and his belly ballooned into a swaying bump. When he enters the room, pushing his glasses up on his nose, he takes quick glances left and right, as if checking for attackers behind the sofas. KJ guides him over to a chair in the corner, murmuring presumably reassuring things. When Calvin opens the thick book he brought with him, KJ turns it over so it's right side up. I bite down on one of my thumbnails. Is this what I have to look forward to?

Yolly bustles in and starts counting heads. "Everyone here? Who are we missing?"

"Angel says she's got cramps," Yuki says, throwing in an eye roll to underline her skepticism, "and Simon's on dinner prep."

"Too bad they'll miss out," Yolly says, picking up the remote. "We've got a special show today."

The music on the sitcom grows to a crescendo. The on-screen couple kiss, prompting the studio audience into a canned *awww.* The credits start rolling as Yolly switches the channel.

"Coming up next," a smooth voice announces, "a shocking bomb scare evacuates downtown Portland." The camera pans over images of harried people being ushered out of City Hall. "Was this a random act of violence? Or something more sinister? Stay tuned for a special press conference, coming up live right here on News Six."

The channel's logo fills the screen and the scene cuts to a commercial.

Yuki sighs. "Do we really have to watch the news?"

"It wasn't a real bomb," Calvin announces. "It was all faked to raise the profile of the agents. They're in the middle of salary negotiations, you know."

Nobody pays him any attention. KJ, I realize, has moved away from Calvin to sit by Shannon, who slid over to make room between her and one of the Youngers. I hunch down in my seat and pick at my splinter. I forgot to ask Yolly for tweezers.

"Jack," Yolly calls over a jingle advertising low-cost car insurance, "turn that thing off and come join us."

I expect Jack to ignore her, or mouth off and tell her how he doesn't care whether City Hall blows up. Instead, he snaps his headphones off with atypical obedience.

"Wouldn't want to miss the city celebrating its amazing spinners."

He bounds over and drags an armchair so close to mine I am doused in the cedary scent of his body wash—a grooming item he must have purchased himself, as it is not supplied by the Center's minimal hygiene budget. Shortly after Ross dropped Jack for me, Jack suffered his first bout of time sickness. It was really mild, and he hasn't had a second one, but he's also only been on one mission since it happened. Jack's current Center job is working in Barnard's office. I guess Barnard likes him, because Jack gets more day passes than anyone else and, I suspect, more allowance. He's always bragging about this hoodlum Norm friend of his, Javier, who supposedly taught him to drive a car and showed him how to sneak into movie theatres without paying. Given Jack's loose relationship with the truth, I have my doubts.

"So tell me, Alex." Jack holds his fist under my chin, imitating an overeager reporter. "Think the mayor will mention you? Give credit where credit is due?"

"Now, Jack." Yolly pushes Yuki's feet off the sofa so she can sit next to her. Two of the Youngers, their group story complete, wander over to curl up against Yolly's wide hips. I notice neither Shannon nor KJ make any effort to reclaim the extra space.

"You know Dr. Barnard thinks spinners should keep a low profile," Yolly says. "The rest of Portland is still getting used to you."

"Yeah." Jack's voice drips sarcasm. "Forty years unwinding crimes in this city and people still think we're dangerous monsters. Good strategy."

"Steve got publicity after his rewind nailed that nightclub owner for selling drugs," Shannon says, referring to her last boyfriend. "Remember what happened to him? Piles of hate mail and then those protesters . . ."

She doesn't need to say more. We all remember. After the club owner got arrested, protestors chanted angry slogans on our steps day and night for a week. They blasted loud music, screamed at passing cars, and waved signs that said things like: *Lock Up the Deviants*, *Time Spinners = Tax Suckers*, *No More CIC for the Sick.* The cops only dragged them away when they started breaking things. Meanwhile, we all stumbled around so sleep deprived it was like living in a home for the undead. Steve got sick for the first time in the middle of the protest week. He died last spring.

"Half the city still thinks Steve faked the evidence." Shannon's voice falters. KJ puts a consoling hand on her shoulder.

"The mayor faked the evidence," Calvin says. "The mob wanted the club owner shut down because he was working their turf."

Jack interrupts. "A spinner puts away one popular scumbag two years ago and that makes it OK to get no credit when we stop a bomber from blowing up City Hall?"

Without thinking, I glance across the room. Jack always rants about how spinners don't get enough respect, which KJ thinks is funny given how little Jack has ever cared about time work. Whenever Jack starts up, KJ always winks at me behind his back. Today, though, KJ isn't paying attention. He's still consoling Shannon, head bent to catch something she's telling him. I look away.

"I know it's hard for you to understand," Yolly says. "Freezing time feels normal to you, but it's unnerving for other people. It makes them uncomfortable to think there are things happening they don't know about."

"Like this, you mean?"

Jack leans forward and smiles directly at Yolly, a wolfish grin that shows too many teeth. There's a short pause and then the freeze monitor starts beeping. Everyone looks up at the narrow screen bolted to the wall over the TV. The words *Jack Whiting* scroll across it in red letters.

Yolly starts. All spinners have tracker chips implanted in the back of our necks. They link to the monitors, setting off an alarm within a few seconds of the freeze. The links run through cell towers so staff can also track our location. For our own security, Yolly always reminds us.

"Jack," Yolly says, "you know it's against the rules to freeze time outside of training."

"Why? Does it make *you* uncomfortable, Yolly? Wonder what I've been doing?"

Yolly's cell phone rings—always a disconcerting event, since she set it to meow like a cat. She pulls it from her pocket.

"Hello? Yes, I'll check." She puts her hand over the mouthpiece. "Did he take any of you with him?" She looks at me, since I'm the one sitting closest to Jack. I shake my head.

"He froze alone," Yolly says into the phone. "OK, I'll tell him." She hangs up. The freeze monitor stops beeping.

"Dr. Barnard let you off with a warning," Yolly says. "I hope you appreciate the leniency."

Yuki looks up from her magazine.

"Seriously?" she says. "He only gets a warning?"

Jack smirks. It's so unfair. Ever since he started working in Barnard's office Jack has become untouchable. The last time he got in trouble for anything was a couple months ago when he punched

Raul because he insulted some band Jack loves. Even then he was just assigned to an extra dishwashing shift. Anyone else would have been scrubbing out the inside of the dumpster with a toothbrush.

I lower my voice so only Jack can hear me. "Why'd you mess with Yolly? She's OK."

"Yeah, if you're five," Jack says. "Why do you care? She's just a Norm. And besides," he lifts one hand and places it on my thigh, "how do you know it was Yolly I was messing with?"

I slap his hand away.

"Give it up, Jack."

Most of the girls at the Center have had some kind of fling with Jack. Shannon says he's cute enough to be a movie star. I don't see the attraction. For me, cuteness is totally erased by acting like a jerk.

"Your loss." Jack smirks. "Saving yourself for someone special?"

I turn away and pointedly face the TV.

"Hush," Yolly calls. "The mayor's on."

Mayor Tully stands at a podium surrounded by microphones, her image flickering under multiple camera flashes. Behind her, Ross, McDennon, and Chief Graham stand shoulder to shoulder. The mayor adjusts her glasses and starts reading from a prepared statement, laying out the basics of the mission to the members of the press. The common room starts buzzing with sounds of inattention. Yolly might have trapped everyone in front of the TV, but she can't make them listen.

". . . crisis was averted thanks to these brave men," the mayor sums up. "They all risked their lives today and I, for one, can't thank them enough." More lights flash as the mayor turns and shakes hands, first with Chief, then Ross, and finally McDennon. When she's done, she invites Chief to the microphone and opens the floor to questions.

“Do you have a suspect?” someone asks.

“We do,” Chief says. I perk up. I hadn’t expected the police to ID our guy so soon.

“The suspect has been identified as Jason Torino, age twenty-four.” A blurry photograph of the man I saw in the rewind flashes up on the screen. His body is turned away from the camera, face creased in an expression of fierce concentration. The photo must have been taken from one of the security cameras at City Hall because he’s wearing the same dark windbreaker I saw him in earlier.

“Mr. Torino has a history of civil disobedience,” Chief says, “and has had previous encounters with police. Anyone who has information about his whereabouts is asked to call 9-1-1. Do not approach him. Please remember, he may be dangerous.”

“So young,” Yolly sighs. “What can happen to someone to make them want to do something like that?”

“I can think of a few reasons,” Jack says.

Yolly waves dismissively. “You don’t mean that.”

Calvin clears his throat. “Statistically, most terrorists are under the age of twenty-five. They tend to come from troubled homes, often suffering some form of abuse in childhood—”

“Give it a rest, Calvin,” Aidan says. Raul gives him a fist bump.

Across the room, Shannon whispers something to KJ that makes him laugh, a rich, happy sound that floats across the overcrowded room. I pick at some dirt under my fingernail and try to remember the last time KJ laughed like that at something I said. I can’t. In the courtyard KJ complained I was distracted. Am I really so caught up in catching Sikes that I’m not that fun to hang out with anymore?

A chubby reporter, holding an oversized spiral notebook, raises his hand.

"The room where the bomb was found was scheduled for a meeting to discuss the annual police budget, and the first agenda item was the Crime Investigation Center. Are the police investigating this as a possible anti-spinner hate crime?"

A lull empties the common room of sound as everyone in it turns to hear Chief's answer. My stomach, still not completely recovered, clenches. Ross and I didn't think of this possibility. Maybe this Torino guy doesn't care about Sikes at all. Maybe his real target was us.

Chief puts on the blank expression that must be a requirement for any public service job.

"It's too early to tell what the bomber's motivations were," he says.

"That's a lame political answer," Jack sneers.

"Jack," Yolly says, "we need to show respect towards our city officers."

"It doesn't matter if he answers or not," Raul says. "Now that the reporter asked the question, everyone will assume it's true and then somehow the bombing will be our fault."

On screen, the reporter is pushing his point.

"A recent survey showed that seventy-nine percent of the population believes spinners are mentally unstable. We've all heard the reports of spinners behaving erratically, even violently, especially at the end of their lives. Given the overwhelming unpopularity of spinners among most Americans, doesn't the location of the bomb imply someone is making a political statement?"

"Instances of spinners suffering from mental illnesses are vastly overreported," Chief says. "Spinners can do some unusual things, but at the end of the day they're just kids."

The chubby reporter looks unconvinced. He raises his hand to ask another question. Chief ignores him, pointing instead to the reporter sitting next to him, a young woman dressed in a tight-fitting red suit.

"I have a question for Agent Ross," the woman says, with a smile so eager she could be posing for a toothpaste commercial. Chief grimaces, but he steps aside so Ross can join him at the microphone. The camera zooms in on Ross's face.

"How stressful was the rewind when you found the bomb?" the reporter asks.

Ross leans against the podium, the essence of relaxed nonchalance. He's told me that his goal is to one day be chief of police. Watching the way he projects reassurance on screen makes me believe he'd be way better at the job than Chief Graham.

"The rewind wasn't very stressful," he says. "I trusted my team. I had a good spinner with me and Chief assigned Mike McDennon from the bomb squad. Mike has an excellent reputation, and he certainly proved his worth today."

"There you go, Alex," Jack says. "You're a *good spinner.* Doesn't that make you proud?"

"She should be proud," Yolly says. "We all know how hard the work is."

"Yeah, right." Jack snickers. "Calling her a good spinner makes it sound like she's his dog."

Yuki gives a disgusted snort, but Aidan and Raul erupt in laughter. I glare at them. If I *were* a dog I'd go over and bite them. Across the room, Shannon is holding KJ's hand, whispering as she traces his palm with one finger. She and Yuki took up tarot card readings a few months ago. I suppose now Shannon's moved on to palms.

The reporter asks Ross what the rewind was like and Ross launches into a long description. I curl back into my chair, wishing I'd chosen a seat closer to the door so I could more easily escape. It's not like anyone will miss me. I peek over at KJ again. His dark head is bent close to Shannon's blond one, face lit with something I doubt has anything to do with a newfound belief in the occult.

Jack leans over and whispers in my ear. "Looks like endless love isn't so endless after all."

I snap back upright. "KJ's not my boyfriend."

"I wasn't talking about you." Jack twists his fingers together, making the knuckles crack in a quick line of pops. "Didn't Shannon swear she'd miss Steve forever? Or was that the guy before him?"

"Shannon enjoys being in love," I say, not quite managing to keep the snideness out of my voice.

"Unlike you. All you care about is solving crimes with your—" Jack raises both hands to make air quotes "—wonderful agent."

"Ross *is* a wonderful agent. He actually values my time skills."

"Ross only values you because you hero-worship him."

My cheeks burn. I wish I had the guts to slug him, but I'm pretty sure Barnard wouldn't offer me the same slack he just gave Jack.

"What's the matter?" I taunt, instead. "Still pissed Ross dropped you for me?"

"I'm not pissed about that." Jack sniffs. "I work with people much more important than Ross."

My anger fades. Jack doesn't work with important people. All he does is file and run errands for Barnard. Jack leans toward me.

"You're so big on investigating that robber guy. Maybe you should be looking a little closer to home. Ever wonder what the great Dr. B. is really up to?"

I stare at him. He sounds as delusional as Calvin. Is Jack losing it? It happens sometimes. Jack is nineteen and it's been over five months since he first got sick. He's surely due for a second attack any day.

Lots of people fall apart toward the end. The sickness is an ax falling in slow motion and I'm just beginning to understand exactly how terrifying it is to be standing under it.

"Jack," I start, unsure what I want to say, when a voice on the TV grabs my attention.

"Can you address the rumor that the bomber has contacted the police?"

My head swivels back to the screen. Chief has returned to the microphone stand, making Ross again a mere background figure. Cameras are flashing like strobes. Chief squints against the media's glare.

"I beg your pardon?"

The reporter who asked the question straightens his shoulders. He's short, with hair that sticks up around his head as if he's only just gotten out of bed.

"There's a report that Jason Torino has information about Sikes and he's willing to talk if he gets immunity."

Chief clears his throat. "I have no knowledge of the suspect contacting the police."

"I got this tip from a reliable source," the reporter says.

Chief's lips settle into a tight line.

The reporter presses on. "Assuming the rumor is true, can you share the city's stance on negotiating with terrorists?"

"No comment," Chief says.

Questions explode from the press gallery. Hands wave, cameras click. Chief leans into the bank of microphones and thanks everyone for coming, promising to let them know as soon as they have more information. His expression holds thunder.

Jack leaves the seat next to mine and asks Aidan to deal him in for a new card game. Calvin starts rambling about some theory involving leaks and hit men. Yuki grabs the remote and switches the TV to a reality makeover show. I sit alone, staring at the flickering screen. For all his efforts to project professional calm, Chief's surprise at the reporter's revelation was obvious. Ross, however, looked pleased, even calculating, like a cat trying to figure out which way a cornered mouse might run. Does that mean the rumor is true? My heart does a little flip. If Jason Torino has information, Ross will find a way to get it. Which means that, with Ross's medical help, I can potentially live long enough to solve this case.

06

BY THE NEXT MORNING, MY EUPHORIA HAS FADED. The 6:30 alarm jolts me awake, and before I even open my eyes yesterday's grim realities crash over me like a massive sandbag dropped onto my chest. I was sick. Time sick.

"You up?" Shannon asks. My roommate is standing in front of the window twisting her long hair into a tidy braid. She's already dressed in her mission uniform, though it's topped with the pink smock she wears when she's assisting Amy. Under her breath, she's humming an old pop tune. I can't remember the title, but I know the chorus includes a line about a girl being amazing the way she is.

I mutter something incoherent without getting out of bed.

"It's a gorgeous day out there," she says. "Look at all those people heading out to enjoy it."

She cranks open our window the three inches the security bars allow. Traffic noises drift up from the street along with the smell of car exhaust.

"It's Labor Day weekend," I tell her. "All those happy people are setting off for the accidents KJ will be rewinding this afternoon."

Shannon shoots me a sharp look. "That's pretty morbid."

I shrug. "I just don't see why you're so chipper about the weather, it's not like *you'll* get to go outside and enjoy it."

"Is something bothering you?"

"No."

The word comes out particularly harshly. Shannon bends to smooth a minute wrinkle from her bedspread, carefully not making eye contact. The weight on my chest shifts uncomfortably. I feel like I just stepped on a kitten.

Shannon vanishes into our miniscule half bath. I turn on my side. Our dorm rooms are compact squares with one window, two beds, and a couple of dressers. Shannon's side is spotless, mine littered with copies of Ross's old case files and a criminology textbook I found a while back in the donated book bin. I stare at the wall across from me. The photo of Steve that Shannon used to have pinned over her bed is gone, replaced with a line of drawings from the Youngers. Three of them are bunches of flowers with the words *I love you* scrawled in sloppy letters.

Julio, one of the night guards, starts the secondary wake-up call, banging his nightstick against each dorm door as he unlocks it. Out in the street, a siren blares past the building, a high-pitched scream of recent disaster. I burrow deeper in my blankets, stopping time with a mental flick before Julio reaches our door. Spinners sometimes freeze time as an instinctual response to nightmares, so staff turn the monitors off at night, not turning them back on until our dorm rooms are unlocked.

Stillness settles around me, slipping through the cracks of my closed lids. I make an effort to relax. Besides high chronotin levels, the only other trigger I know of for an attack is stress. Which is a pretty useless warning since stress is inevitable once the clock starts ticking. I practice steady breathing. I can't actually fall back to sleep without losing control of the freeze, but maybe a few minutes of peace will settle my nerves.

The heavy mass crushing my chest refuses to be soothed. Tiny things, like the faint bleach smell from my sheets and the headache lurking in the back of my skull, grow larger in the vacuum. I imagine I can feel my chronotin levels rising, the cells duplicating, unchecked by my insufficient dosage of Aclisote.

I have only a few months left to live.

The words clang through my head, knocking away any lingering wisps of sleep. I sit up. The vastness of the unmoving world stretches out endlessly. I am completely alone, and today the thought is chilling rather than freeing. Will death be like this? A solitary soul moving through a world that neither knows nor cares about its existence?

I let time go, shifting instantly back to my earlier prone position. Julio's stick smacks the door with a sharp crack just as Shannon emerges from the bathroom wiping her face with a towel. I grab my robe and head down the hall to the showers. How much of a risk am I taking by not reporting my illness? I ponder the question, standing under the spray so long the timer clicks the water off before I remember to wash my hair.

A cacophony of clattering spoons and raised voices envelopes me as I make my way down to the basement for breakfast. I scan the cafeteria, stopping when I find KJ. He's sitting at a table with Calvin, who is talking vehemently about something, his hands pounding the table as he makes his point. KJ nods as if whatever nonsense Calvin is spouting makes perfect sense. When KJ sees me watching them, his mouth lifts in a smile and a tiny bit of the tension wracking my body eases. KJ has forgiven me. The urge to race across the room and pour out my fears is almost unbearable, but I force myself to hold back. KJ's already got Calvin to worry about. Adding the pain of another sick friend would be cruel.

"There you are, sleepyhead," Shannon chirps at me from her spot at the meds table set up just inside the door. "Feeling better? I was thinking I'd have to go back up and drag you downstairs."

For a split second I consider confessing that I'd felt sick yesterday and asking her to run a surreptitious blood test. I squash the impulse. Shannon follows the rules. If the results came back high she'd be sure to report me to Barnard.

Shannon selects a pre-measured dose of Aclisote from the meds basket. I watch her initial the logbook next to my name and try to decide the merits of faking a cold so that I'll get sent up to the clinic. If I get a high chronotin result from a routine test would they pull me from time work? Or just raise my dosage?

"Here you go," Shannon says, peeling the plastic seal off the vial with a practiced hand.

"That's not mine," I say. "I don't take that much."

Shannon checks the label. "Yes, it is."

I read the tiny writing on the tube she holds out. *Alexandra Manning, 5 cc, twice daily.* Five cc's? Yesterday, I'd been taking four and a half. My cheeks warm, relief at getting a higher dosage mingling with guilt, as if somehow Barnard had caught me lying.

"Why did Dr. Barnard change it?" I ask. "He just raised my dose after my blood test two weeks ago."

"I don't know," Shannon says. "But between us two, I bet Amy copied the dosage wrong and no one noticed until now." She leans over the table and lowers her voice. "She's totally distracted these days. I think she has a new boyfriend."

My first smile of the day spreads across my face. This must be why I got sick yesterday. Amy, our cute, scatterbrained nurse, messed up Barnard's prescription. I toss the medicine down like a cowboy shooting whiskey. The chemical-sweet flavor tastes reassuringly familiar. I remember the pointed questions Barnard asked me in the lobby yesterday. That must have been why he'd been so curious: he'd noticed the error and been worried about the possible repercussions.

I turn my smile on Shannon, determined to make up for my earlier surliness.

"I'm thinking Amy isn't the only one who might have a new boyfriend."

Shannon's face turns bright pink and she seems suddenly intensely interested in straightening the logbook.

"I don't know. Maybe." She glances up at me. "Would it bug you?"

I wish people would stop asking me that.

"Of course not," I lie. If I'm KJ's friend, it's my job to do what I can to make him happy. Plus, as Shannon would say, it's good karma, and I could definitely use some help in the luck department.

I chuck the empty vial into the trash and head over to the breakfast counter. There's a big pot of oatmeal on the hot pad, and I serve myself a healthy dollop. All that worry, when the only problem was . . . The oatmeal slops into my bowl. The problem was I'd gotten sick. Whatever the reason, I'd suffered a bout of time sickness. Sure, it was mild, but the first ones usually are. And then first bouts are inevitably followed by second ones, then third. Most people don't get four.

The oatmeal quivers. I spoon on brown sugar. Ross said if my Aclisote dosage was too high, the new medicine wouldn't work. Is five cc's high? How much is someone like Calvin getting?

"You gonna leave any of that for me?"

Jack is standing beside me, pointing at the mound of sugar I've heaped into my bowl.

"Sorry." I put the spoon down. Jack snatches it up and piles twice the amount of sugar I just used onto his own oatmeal.

"Hey, Jack?" I ask. "How much Aclisote do you take?"

"I don't know." He adds a generous scoop of raisins. "Six cc's, I think, why?"

"Just curious."

I pour a cup of coffee and follow Jack over to the table where KJ and Calvin are sitting. It's dawning on me how little I know about Aclisote and chronotin, a knowledge gap that suddenly seems glaring. All I really know is that chronotin rises as you age and that high levels are bad. Nothing about exact numbers.

"Yuck," KJ says, as I set my tray down across from him. "Are you eating that?"

I look down at the mountain of sugar in my bowl, gray oatmeal barely visible along the edges.

"I guess I wasn't paying attention," I say.

"I'll take the extra," Jack says, scraping off a generous spoonful of sugar and dumping it in his coffee. "The one upside of a short life: there's absolutely no reason to eat healthy."

"The Center purposely feeds us low quality food to limit our life spans," Calvin says. "It saves them money. I should write to the Society for Spinner Rights and ask them to push for a macrobiotic diet."

"Please don't," Jack says, digging into his mound of barely diluted sugar.

Calvin launches into a theory about how the Center profits from buying inferior food—something to do with farm subsidies and using up the nation's excess corn. I pick up my spoon. If Ross is going to change my meds, he's going to need to know what my chronotin levels are. Maybe next time I see him we could stop at a drugstore and he could get someone to take a blood sample? I swirl the spoon through the thick oats. No, that's not going to work. Even if he gets my blood, how would he test it? The only chronotin analyzers are here in the Center.

"Hey, Alex." KJ nudges my foot under the table. "You still signed up for laundry this afternoon?"

"What?" I blink at him. "I think so, why?"

"Jack and Aidan and I all have the afternoon off, so I reserved the gym. You can join us between loads."

"OK." I take a bite of oatmeal. Even with the scoop Jack syphoned off, my breakfast tastes so sweet it hurts my teeth. I put the spoon down.

"Do you think there's a chart somewhere," I ask the table at large, "that shows what your Aclisote should be based on your chronotin levels?"

"That's a random question," Jack says.

KJ shifts his gaze to something past my shoulder, and his face opens into a smile. "Here's someone I bet can answer it, though."

"Answer what?" Shannon sweeps around the table to claim the empty chair beside KJ. He scoots over to make room, and I repeat my question.

Shannon shakes her head. "Not that I've ever seen."

"What's a normal chronotin reading?" I ask her.

"There isn't really a normal." She nibbles on the dry toast she chose for breakfast. "Everyone has their own range."

"Why are you suddenly so interested in chronotin?" KJ asks.

"Barnard just raised my Aclisote dosage to five cc's. I was wondering if that related to a specific chronotin reading. I mean, if there were a way to predict when you're likely to be sick, wouldn't you want to know?"

"I wouldn't," Jack says. "Sounds totally depressing."

Shannon picks up her tea. "There's no magic number," she says. "Dr. Barnard just watches for changes in our levels and adjusts our meds to keep the increases gradual. I don't think even he knows the trigger for sickness."

"Well, what's a high reading?" I push. "Like, what's Calvin's?"

"I can't tell you that." Shannon wipes her lips with a napkin. "It's confidential."

I glance over at Calvin, but he's focused on his toast, which he is carefully cutting into perfect triangles. I don't bother asking. Even if he did tell me a number, there's a very good chance it wouldn't be accurate.

"I don't know why you're all hyped up about your chronotin readings," Jack says. "We all know who the likely candidates are to get sick next, don't we?" He raises his coffee cup to toast KJ and Calvin, who, along with Jack himself, are the oldest kids at the Center.

A leaden silence falls over the table. Jack slurps his coffee. KJ stares down at his tray. Shannon reaches over to pat his hand. I stir my oatmeal. All that sugar has turned it a particularly muddy shade of brown.

Shannon checks her watch and gives a little gasp.

"I've got to run," she says, jumping from the table. "My agent is picking me up at eight."

"Anything fun?" I ask, in an effort to lighten the mood. Shannon rolls her eyes.

"When are missions ever fun? They just mean I'm stuck spending hours with Agent Sourface. She flinches whenever I get near her. You'd think I smell or something."

The cafeteria is starting to empty out as kids move on to their various assignments. Jack wanders off to snag some toast before the cafeteria closes, leaving KJ, Calvin, and me alone at the table.

"You're not really worried about getting sick, are you?" KJ asks me. "You're only sixteen. You should be fine for ages."

"I know," I say, too quickly. KJ frowns.

"It's just . . ." The oatmeal has now congealed to a point where my spoon stands up all by itself. I push the bowl away. "Getting sick doesn't seem as far away as it used to, you know? Don't you think about it sometimes?"

"Of course I do, but it's not like there's anything we can do to stop it. When it's time, it's time."

I open my mouth, Ross's offer perched on my tongue.

"KJ?" Calvin's voice is tight. "Why did everyone leave? Did something happen?"

KJ turns instantly. "No, buddy. Everything is fine. It's just that breakfast is over. Come on, I'll walk you up to the library." He looks at me. "See you this afternoon?"

"Sure," I say. The two boys collect their trays and head out of the room. I pick up my coffee. If I want to keep from getting sick again I'll have to find out my chronotin readings. I wrap my hands around the warm mug, picturing my last test—the narrow exam room, its gleaming surfaces and lingering smell of disinfectant. Amy had been complaining about being hauled in for an extra shift. She'd taken my blood, added something to the sample, and then shooed me out before she put it through the chronotin analyzer. I sip my drink, only realizing after I swallow that I forgot to add milk. I put it down. What I need is to get hold of my medical chart.

Living at the Center doesn't leave a lot of free time to brood. Spinners not being particularly popular with taxpayers, the Center keeps the cost of running the place low by making the twenty-five kids who live here do most of the work. Just like a real home, Yolly always says. We take turns tidying the common room, helping in the cafeteria, emptying trash, and cleaning bathrooms. Once we're fully qualified spinners, we get assigned bigger jobs, too, like Shannon working with Amy in the clinic, or KJ's job as general handyman and computer wiz.

I got assigned to help train the Youngers because I can hold freezes really well. Mostly I help with Class A, the beginners group, all between ages ten and twelve. It's an OK job, made better by the fact that I love the room itself. Tall windows let in light dappled by the trees outside. The windowpanes are so thick they muffle most of the traffic noise, and the Center is built high enough off the ground that passersby can't see in. When the trees are in bloom the room reminds me of a giant tree house. This time of year, with the leaves blazing into fall colors, it feels like sitting in a nest surrounded by flames.

The teacher, Julie, taps her watch when I walk in. Class is already in session. Julie is a young woman, with curly brown hair and so many freckles her face appears tan all year long. She always dresses as if she's about to head out on one of the treks she takes on her days off—jeans, sturdy shoes, and bright bandanas. The kids like her because it's easy to get her off topic. She'll give up multiplication tables in a heartbeat if they ask about her latest fishing trip.

Today looks ripe for a distraction. The eight students are spread out across four tables, and all of them are yawning with boredom.

"How many spinners are there in the US?" Julie asks the class.

"Two hundred and eighty," the kids chorus in a monotone.

I pick up the list Julie left me on a clipboard by the door. As usual, I'll be taking kids aside so they can practice freezing and rewinding time. My day grows a little bit drearier when I see Kimmi Yoshida's name at the top of the list. Kimmi hates time work.

"That's right," Julie says, "or approximately .0017% of the nation's population under age twenty. How many spinner babies are born each year?"

Jenny raises her hand. "Miss Julie, is it true spinners used to be called witches?"

A ripple of interest passes over the slouching students. Even Julie perks up. Who doesn't think witches sound more fun than birth rates?

"Well . . ." Julie only hesitates for a second. "Back in the 1700s, before Aclisote was developed, spinners were pretty unstable. They tended toward severe paranoia, and some even became violent."

"Did they send them to the Central Office?" Emilio asks.

Julie smiles. "There was no Central Office back then. Freezing time was considered black magic, not a genetic condition. There are lots of old stories about spinners spying on people or even making things disappear."

Emilio leans forward. "How'd they do that?"

"They didn't really," Julie says. "Changing things during frozen time isn't possible. They're just stories, like the ones about really old people being spinners. The real thing people fear about spinners is that they can sneak around and find out secrets."

Julie talks more about the old days when spinners were chained up, or killed as soon as their powers were uncovered. The Youngers listen with rapt attention. Jenny's bottom lip trembles a little when Julie tells them about spinners getting burned at the stake, which Julie must notice, because she switches over to talk about Aclisote and how its development has made spinner life so much better. I grip my clipboard. Aclisote has been working for three hundred years. What if the new medicine makes me go crazy like Calvin, or worse, turns me into some kind of rabid monster?

The edges of the clipboard bite into my palm. I loosen my hold and beckon to Kimmi, who pretends not to see me.

Emilio's hand shoots up again. "Have spinners always worked with police agents?"

"Not always," Julie says. "At first Aclisote made spinners kind of, um, slow. They couldn't really function very well. It's only been since the 1950s that the dosages were refined enough that spinners could control their skills and still live relatively normal lives."

Kimmi finally acknowledges my waving and drags herself up from her table. Julie launches into a description of the first case ever solved by a rewind. I usher Kimmi into the time room, a glassed-in space at the back of the class, empty except for a couple chairs and a small cabinet. Tariq, the student sitting closest to the door, slides the lock once we enter. The Center is really strict about controlling where we can freeze time. Yolly says the staff don't want the kids to dig through Julie's desk and find answers for tests. Jack says they do it because they don't trust us to run around unsupervised, which, frankly, in Jack's case, makes sense. I might not feel it if he hit me while I was frozen, but that doesn't mean I want him to have the opportunity.

"Hey, Kimmi." I rub my ear, trying to clear the images created by Julie's now muffled voice: hatred, insanity, death. "Want to try a freeze?"

"No." Kimmi is a round-cheeked eleven-year-old with the attitude of a teenage thug. "Let's just *say* we did and you let me out of here. It's not like anyone would know."

"Come on," I say, doing my best to dredge up some patience, "the longer you can hold a freeze, the better assignments you'll get as a qualified spinner. Besides, freezes can be fun."

"Not locked in the practice room they're not."

I bring out my final piece of leverage. "I'll let you eat the chocolate bar."

Kimmi gives a huge sigh and takes my hand as if she's doing me a favor. A slight stutter tells me she's stopped time, an internal blip like an extra heartbeat. On the other side of the glass, Julie stands with one arm raised, in the act of pointing at one of the seven remaining students frozen in their chairs.

"Good job," I say. "That was really smooth."

Time hums through our linked hands like a very low electric current. As long as we're touching, our powers mingle, a minimal drain on me, but a real support for the spinner holding the freeze. I slide my hand away from hers. There's a momentary blur, and then time springs forward. I retake Kimmi's hand.

"Try again. Close your eyes and picture time in your head. Can you feel it? Focus on the currents flowing around you. Now imagine pulling them taut." The world freezes again. "That's it. Now you hold it alone."

I let go. Time wavers for an instant, before Kimmi catches it and pulls it tight.

"There," I say, "you did it."

Despite herself, Kimmi looks pleased. I mentally push against her hold. It's her freeze, so I can't break it, but I can gauge the strength. The flow of time hangs around us like a sheet of gauze, fragile but unmoving.

I open the cabinet and take out the chocolate bar the kids have been eating in frozen time all week.

"Here."

Kimmi rips open the wrapper and takes a bite. I watch her eating. In the frozen silence her chewing sounds loud. I touch my ear again. If I plug it, I can hear the thump of my pulse. I think about chronotin, a slow poison taking a second of my life with every beat of my heart. I drop my hand.

"Do you want to try a rewind? It's more exciting than just standing here."

"How about we go out there?" Kimmi gestures at the frozen world outside the glass. "That's more exciting than just standing here too."

"We can't," I say, "the door is . . ."

The words drift into the quiet air. A flash of brilliance has just hit me, and I suddenly know a way to get the information I want about my chronotin levels. I rock on my heels. I'll be breaking every rule in the book, but if it works, I don't see how I can get caught. I give Kimmi a huge smile.

"Let time go," I say. "We're done."

Kimmi is so taken aback by my sudden capitulation she forgets to finish the chocolate bar. She releases time immediately, whirling us back to our prefreeze, chocolateless positions. Vaulting to the door, she starts banging on the glass so Tariq will let her out, presumably worried I might change my mind. The classroom noises surge when the door opens: voices, shuffling feet, and the scratch of a pencil. The freeze monitor, however, remains quiet. Monitors are blocked in the practice room since it's one of the few places we're *supposed* to use our power. I wrap my arms around my body, hugging myself to keep from jumping up and down with impatience. Emilio shuffles from his seat to take Kimmi's place. The instant the door closes again I freeze time.

Peace settles around me and I relax into it. Ten-year-old Emilio's body is easy to pick up and move out of my way. Tariq falls over when I shove the door open. He hasn't had time to lock it. I pause to settle him more comfortably on the floor. Even if he won't remember it later, it seems rude to leave him collapsed over a chair.

Walking through the Center is eerie. I've never wandered around here in a freeze before. The rooms have a dreamlike quality, familiar and also strange. My footsteps send out a lonely echo as I walk up the stairs.

The clinic takes up half of the second floor. Beige wallpaper stamped with pale sailboats covers the walls. There's a waiting area with a couple of padded chairs, separated by a half wall from Amy's office. Closed doors mark two sickrooms, a half bath, and an exam room. The air smells like disinfectant. Amy must not have come on duty yet because the whole place is empty.

The filing cabinet I've come to search stands behind Amy's desk. It's beige with four neatly labeled drawers. I skip the administrative one on top and reach for the one labeled *Records.* It's locked.

The headache lurking in my skull since yesterday pulses. I massage the taut muscles in the back of my neck, sending them calming thoughts. They don't listen. I find the key in the second place I look, casually tossed in the top right drawer of Amy's desk between a tin of mints and a crumpled tissue. I unlock the cabinet with sweaty hands. The folder labeled *Manning, Alexandra* is stuffed near the middle.

My file isn't particularly thick. I plop on the ground so I can spread the pages across my lap. The information I want jumps out immediately, scribbled on a stack of papers clipped to the left side of the file. One column shows the date, the next, my chronotin reading, then the tester's initials (primarily Amy's), followed by another notation showing my Aclisote dosage, this time initialed by Dr. Barnard. I focus on the last few entries:

6/23	172	AS	4 CC	JB
7/21	171	AS	4 CC	JB
8/18	172	AS	4.5 CC	JB
9/2			5 CC	JB

I frown. My chronotin levels have *not* spiked. In fact, with all the Aclisote I'm taking now, my levels are probably even lower than they were when they tested me two weeks ago. So why did Dr. Barnard raise my Aclisote not once, but twice? I rub my neck again. Is 172 some kind of warning threshold? Or are there other signs of imminent time sickness besides chronotin readings? I wipe my palms against the front of my sweatshirt and dig into the file. The pages on the right side hold records of my physicals since I moved to the Center, notations of height, weight, blood pressure, a time I'd taken antibiotics for strep throat. There is no mention at all of time sickness.

I flip the chronotin chart back a few pages. Amy's initials are replaced by her predecessor, Jessica's, and then someone called TR whose face I can't remember. When I first came to the Center, my chronotin level was 126. Over the years, my readings have crept steadily upwards, interspersed with occasional crashes when Dr. Barnard raised my Aclisote prescription. Not surprising. Not helpful.

The cabinet drawer creaks as I reach in and yank out more files. KJ's readings for the last year range from 163 to 165, Shannon's from 152 to 155, Aidan's from 158 to 160. Their Aclisote levels seem to line up more closely to their age and weight than their readings, which backs up Shannon's statement that everyone has their own version of normal. I open Jack's file. Before he got sick, his levels climbed to 162. Barnard raised his Aclisote to six cc's and his chronotin dropped down to 155. It's been slowly climbing ever since. His last test put him back up at 159. Is 162 his critical number? The point where he'll get sick again? I look for a file from someone who died but they've all been cleared out.

The last file I pull is Calvin's. He's getting eight cc's of Aclisote. His last chronotin reading was 150. I flip back to a year ago, then move through the sheets so I can read his report chronologically. Before he got sick, Calvin's levels hovered between 169 and 171. I turn the pages. I know he got his first attack in January because it was only a few days after KJ's eighteenth birthday.

11/8	171	AS	5 CC	JB
12/7	171	AS	5 CC	JB
1/5	170	AS	5 CC	JB
1/10	171	JB	7 CC	JB (SUBJECT ADMITTED)
1/12	140	JB	6 CC	JB (SUBJECT RELEASED)

My finger hovers over the words *subject admitted.* Calvin's chronotin readings hadn't changed, so what triggered the attack? Stress? I dig through the sheets on the right-hand side of the file. Calvin's admittance paperwork is a jumble of acronyms and numbers. The only part I can decipher indicates that he had a fever of 103. Was the high temperature a symptom of the sickness, or did he get the sickness because he was weakened by a fever? I flip the pages forward and back, searching for any kind of additional notations, but I don't find anything. If Barnard keeps more detailed case notes, he doesn't store them here.

I turn back to the sheets tracking Calvin's chronotin levels. In February, they started to rise again but his dosage remained the same until May, the month of his second attack, when his chronotin was back up near 165 and his Aclisote dosage increased to eight cc's. Why did Barnard wait so long to raise it? Why did he reduce it in the first place? If there were side effects to high doses of Aclisote, I'd never felt them.

I lean back against the metal cabinet. Files litter the floor around me, reams of information adding very little to my knowledge. I pitch

Calvin's file in among the others with so much force the pages spring loose from the clasp. Paper scatters everywhere, numbers and sheets hopelessly tangled. I pick up a random piece of paper and crumple it. More than anything, I wish KJ was with me so we could think through everything together. Things always seem clearer when I talk to KJ.

Pain twinges inside my temple. I need to let time go. I fish out my file one more time and read the numbers out loud, committing them to memory. At least that information will be helpful. If I can get it to Ross. The sheet in my hand rips as the chart slides off my lap. How long will it be before Ross needs me for another mission? Our missions are based on crimes, events completely out of both of our control.

Time squirms in my grasp, seemingly as impatient for release as I am. I let it go. One swirling instant of dizziness, and I am back in the freeze room listening to an untoppled Tariq click the lock on the door. Emilio is watching me expectantly. I rub my temple with one hand and hold out the other to the little boy.

"Want to eat some chocolate?" I ask.

I'm taking a break after my fifth Younger when Dr. Barnard pokes his head into the classroom.

"Excuse me, Julie," he says. "I need to claim Alexandra."

I flinch, immediately convinced Barnard somehow knows about my illicit trip to the clinic. I trail him from the classroom as slowly as I dare. Except for his soft spot for Jack, the Center's director is never lenient about infractions.

Barnard speaks without preamble.

"Mr. Ross just called to ask for you to come on a mission. It seems the police found a body."

I lift my head.

"Great," I say.

Barnard raises one eyebrow. A blush burns my face.

"I mean, a body, that's awful."

I wipe my flushed cheeks, pausing to rub the spot on my temple where a time headache still flickers. Barnard catches the gesture.

"You're not worn out from yesterday's mission, are you?"

"Of course not." I drop my hand. The opportunity to spend the day with Ross is worth a pounding headache.

"Good. Mr. Ross was very insistent that you be assigned to this case."

I straighten my shoulders, doing my best to look like the qualified professional I am.

"Who died?"

"A woman found the body this morning." Barnard adjusts the faultless edge of his cuff, a gesture that somehow implies disapproval. "It's Jason Torino, the bomber you saw yesterday. It seems he was murdered."

07

MY EAGERNESS TO GO ON A MISSION OVERCOMES even the dull buzz of the leash. Ross seems equally hyped up, tapping his foot while Charlie goes through the process of signing me out: logging the mission number and who I left with, clearing me to freeze time without setting off the monitor, and handing Ross the key to my leash. When the Center doors lock behind us, Ross jumps the stairs three at a time in his rush to reach the waiting car. I scramble after him, barely getting my seat belt clicked before he guns the engine.

"I think this is it, partner," he says, zooming around a truck with enough acceleration to pin me against my seat. "The case that will change everything."

Adrenaline shoots through me, though whether it's from Ross's driving or the upcoming case, it's hard to say.

"Did Sikes kill Jason Torino?" I ask. "To keep him from talking to the police?"

"That's what we're going to find out. It makes sense, though, doesn't it? If he thought Jason was going to spill, Sikes would want to shut him up."

We drive around a corner so fast, Ross's tires squeal.

"Did anyone get a chance to talk to Jason before he died?" I ask.

Ross shakes his head. "Jason never contacted the police."

"But that means . . ." The speed at which we're driving is making it kind of hard to breathe evenly. I wrap one hand around my seat belt. "That means that by asking the question, that reporter basically caused his death."

"The reporter was just doing his job," Ross says. "It's Sikes who acted. He's the one who bears the blame."

"I guess." I shift in my seat. "Maybe Jason didn't even know anything about Sikes or dirty cops. He might have died for nothing."

Ross barely slows the car before running a red light.

"You feeling better today?" he asks.

"Yeah," I say, though this isn't strictly true. The headache from my earlier freeze still hasn't faded.

"Actually, Dr. Barnard raised my Aclisote." I tell Ross everything I discovered since we last talked, including my illicit trip to the clinic.

"All of which makes the sickness even more confusing," I conclude. "It seems like it's not just triggered by high chronotin. Jack got sick and his level never rose above 162. Calvin's level dropped to 150 after his first attack and he still suffered a second."

"Those are questions only Dr. Barnard could answer." Ross points to a notepad tucked in the well between the seats. "You should write down your readings before you forget them. And I have to say, I'm impressed with your initiative. Freezing in the practice room was a clever trick."

I smile into the pad as I scribble down the numbers I've memorized. It's a struggle to write them legibly in the moving car.

"Have you heard anything from Dr. Kroger?" I ask.

"He overnighted the medicine to me last night," Ross says. "I'm just finalizing my plan to get it into the Center."

The pen slips from my fingers. Everything is moving so fast. The worries that plagued me this morning about side effects and quality of life crawl back up to nibble on the edges of my excitement. Before I can frame my concerns, Ross cuts the wheel, skidding to a stop in the parking lot of a brick-red one-story building.

The lot is empty except for three cop cars. Ross springs out onto the pavement. I wobble after him, my legs welcoming the solid ground. A big red-and-white sign announces the place as Franz Meats. Blinds cover the store windows, and a note saying *Closed for Labor Day Weekend* is taped to the glass. Ross ducks under a strip of yellow police tape and opens the door.

Jason Torino's body lies on the floor ten feet from the entrance, face down in a pool of congealed blood. Nausea rises in the back of my throat. As much as we'd talked about Jason's death, I'd managed to avoid thinking about his actual corpse. He seems even younger than he did in the rewind, his body slight and vulnerable splayed out on the cold floor. One arm is flung up over his head, the other lies twisted awkwardly beneath him. At the side of his neck, a deep gash shows the source of all the blood. The edges of the slash curl back like a pair of obscenely pursed lips.

"Agent Ross."

An officer separates himself from the cluster of uniforms on the other side of the room. Ross moves toward them. I follow, stepping as far around the fallen body as the space allows. The police start a round of greetings. I tune them out, scanning the store so I don't have to look at Jason Torino. Closed freezer doors line one wall, their metal fronts gleaming in the overhead lights. On the opposite side, racks offer various meat-related products: barbecue sauce, seasonings, and grill tongs. In between, a line of glass display cases divides the public and vendor sections of the store. Even though the cases are empty and wiped clean, the room still carries a lingering aroma of raw meat mixed with the peppery scent of salami. The smell makes my stomach heave.

"How long since he died?" Ross asks.

"The woman who runs the shop found the body about two hours ago," says one of the cops. He's a beefy man with red hair and a nose that's been broken at least once. He leans back on his heels while he talks, arms crossed, chewing loudly on a piece of gum. "It was totally by chance she came in today. She and her husband were planning to go away for the long weekend. They locked up the store around eight o'clock last night. It would have been a perfect crime. No one should have been here for three days, way too long for a rewind, except the woman came back this morning. Said she left some sandwich meat they planned to bring in the freezer."

Ross catches my eye over the cop's shoulder, confirming what I already know: the planned set-up is textbook Sikes.

"So," Ross says aloud, "time of death was somewhere between eight last night and nine this morning."

"Your rewind will pin it down," the cop says, "but I'm guessing it was last night." He nods toward Jason, his squashed nose wrinkling with distaste. "That guy's not real fresh."

I dare another peek at Jason. The cop's right. Rigor mortis stiffens the corpse's limbs. The blood that didn't escape through his throat has settled, turning his hands an unnatural shade of blue. Near his head, a couple of flies hover like tiny helicopters. I turn my attention back to Ross.

"Is the shop owner a suspect?" he asks.

The cop shrugs. "She sounded pretty shook up when she called. We've got a guy checking her out, though."

"OK. We'll get to work then."

Within seconds, I am unleashed and resting two fingers on Ross's bare arm. Movement stops. Sound ceases. The flies hang motionless over the blood.

Ross rubs his hands together.

"Let's start the rewind."

The unnatural quiet hangs around me like a smothering blanket. Even through the freeze, the stomach-turning raw meat smell saturates the air particles. I must be more tired than I realized. Time always fights against me when I freeze it, but the feeling today is more pronounced. Even my thoughts move slowly, as if they have to push themselves through a barrier to reach my consciousness.

I pull on the time strands. They shift sluggishly. I pull harder. Undecipherable buzzing noises float through the air. Shadowy doubles of the cops around us move with quick little jerks. I watch an echo of myself get released, hover for a split second, then hurry backward out the door with Ross. The cops pace the room for a bit, mouths moving in muted gibberish as they probe the crime scene. Pretty soon they start leaving in small clumps. A short-haired female cop, her partner, and a civilian woman reverse their way inside. The cop undrapes a police blanket from the woman's shoulders, talks to her a while, then backs away with her partner and leaves the woman alone. The woman crouches, letting out a weird, high-pitched sobbing before lurching upright to stumble back-first to the phone. She gestures frantically as she speaks into it. After a few seconds of this, she replaces the receiver, runs backward away from the phone, and then opens her mouth in a long scream. Finally she, too, toddles out the door.

Shadows flee along the checkered tile floor as darkness descends on the unmoving shop. Faint car noises pass outside. The large refrigerators hum. The sense of heaviness seeps deeper into my bones. I speed up the rewind, impatient to get to the murder. The shadow hands of the clock over the counter spin backward. 6:00 a.m., 2:30, midnight. I wish there were a place for me to sit down. The slipping minutes seem to be leaking from my brain, the seconds taunting me, struggling to free themselves from my control.

A headache bursts into my skull with the force of an explosion. Panic dries my mouth. I brace myself against the edge of the display case, the truth too obvious to ignore. I've done rewinds two days in a row before. I've done them after a worse night of sleep than I got last night. This headache is different. This tiredness is different. Something is going wrong.

"Mr. Ross . . . ," I say. I must have missed something important when I was looking at those charts. A critical bit of information that shows when an attack is imminent.

The blood around Jason Torino starts to move.

"Alex! Slow it down." Ross leans forward. Blood seeps up toward Jason's body, scarlet rivers returning to their source.

I struggle to control the time strands even as they pull away. Jason starts twitching. I concentrate. Hard. If I can just hold on a little bit longer, Sikes will show up. I clench the strands with all my strength. Even if we can't follow the killer, at least we'll see who he is. If I can just hold on.

Blood flows out, then back in as the rewind wavers from my control. Jason's shadowy double writhes. Something inside me rips. The shadow image of Jason disappears. Ross gasps. Time pours from me in a rushing torrent. The scene around me breaks up. Images pour into a tangled soup: the crying woman, the cops, the wings of the fly.

"No!" I try desperately to pull the rewind back. I can't fail now.

We *have* to see the killer. Sikes is so close. Pain floods the emptiness left behind by the rush of time. I moan, bent double by the blast. Ross turns toward me. His mouth moves, but I am way too far gone to understand. My fingers scrabble for purchase on the glass case. Air moves against my cheek. The beefy cop moves toward me, blinking anxiously.

Time is moving again. The rewind is over.

"I couldn't hold it." I feel like a husk of a person, a shell empty of any spark of life. "I messed up."

Ross catches me when I fall. "Alex?"

I've been an idiot. I should have told Dr. Barnard I'd gotten sick as soon as I went back. He would have done something, prevented this from happening again so soon.

"What's wrong?" the cop asks.

"I'm sorry," I manage, just before the world goes black.

08

THE LIGHT SEEMS UNNECESSARILY BRIGHT. WHITE SHEETS, white walls, a shining metal tray. I close my eyes. Thirst swells my tongue. *Water,* I try to say, except the word comes out as a groan. Faces fade in and out of my vision: Amy, Ross, Chief. I'm not sure which are real. Someone calls my name. KJ? It sounds like he's crying. My head pounds. When the darkness returns it feels like mercy.

The next time I wake, it's night. Stiff sheets wrap my body. The air is cool and smells like rubbing alcohol. An IV pulls against my arm. Moonlight leaking through a slatted window outlines the furniture filling the room: bed, sink, cabinet, and an empty chair. On the wall hangs a poster of a painting with melting clocks. It's all very familiar.

I am in the clinic.

A familiar weight settles on my chest, sinking slowly down until it fills my stomach. I've never heard of anyone suffering two bouts of time sickness in two days. Usually kids have months between episodes. At this rate, the third one might hit me tomorrow. Or tonight. Self-pity closes my throat. Only the lucky few survive to face a fourth. *You knew it was coming,* I tell myself. *You always knew.* The reminder doesn't help. Tears drip past my temples into my hair.

Footsteps pad outside the room. I close my eyes, not wanting anyone to see me crying. The door opens with a soft whoosh, and someone moves close to my bed. Amy? Yolly? I hold still, keeping my breath slow and even. I'm not ready to face the world yet.

A gentle tug on my arm tells me my visitor is changing the bag on my IV. I wait while she fumbles with it, wondering why she doesn't turn on the light. The few other times I've been here I don't remember the staff being so considerate. Maybe the standards go up when the patient is terminal.

The fiddling stops. I turn my head infinitesimally and slide one eye open a fraction. Through the haze of my lashes I see a bulky figure shuffling through the bottles of medicine in the cabinet next to my bed.

Another head pokes around the door.

"Is she still asleep?" Even in the half light I recognize Amy's outline. The figure beside me starts.

"Like a baby."

Surprise pops my eyes all the way open. I know that voice, and it isn't Yolly's. It's Ross. Ross slides his hand from the cabinet, neatly pocketing something before turning toward Amy in the doorway.

"I thought you were keeping watch out front?"

"Julio just passed the door a few minutes ago. He won't be back for at least half an hour." She comes to stand close to Ross, her face lifted toward his. She's paying no attention at all to me.

"Besides," she says, "why do you care if the night guards see you here? Agents are allowed in the Sick anytime."

Ross shrugs. "Barnard already gave me a report on Alex's condition. I wouldn't want him to think I don't trust him. And it's not that I don't, it's just . . . I want to be sure the kid's going to be OK."

Ross's concern warms me like a burst of sunshine. I am just about to tell him I'm awake, when he adds, "Besides, we wouldn't want Julio to see this."

There's a rustling sound and the squeak of a soft-soled shoe sliding across the linoleum floor. Amy giggles. I slam my eyes shut. To my infinite horror, I recognize the wet slurping sound of people kissing.

Shock keeps my eyes sealed. When Shannon said Amy had a boyfriend, it never crossed my mind that it could be Ross. I'd always pictured him with an elegant lawyer or a brilliant professor. Not someone like Amy. I mean, sure, she's cute, but all she ever talks about are the clubs she and her friends hang out in after work. Half the time I show up at the clinic she's texting instead of working. I wonder if I am sicker than I think. Maybe this whole scene is a hallucination.

"Carson!"

The admonition breaks on another giggle. More rustling. I crack open one eye. The writhing shape reminds me of an oversized hunchback, the chest too large and head deformed. I close my eyes again and wait, hating myself for witnessing this scene.

"I'm so glad it's you here taking care of Alex," Ross says. More kissing, some indistinguishable murmurs. "She's a good spinner, you know. She can hold time much longer than the others." Smooch, rustle. "I have a case coming up I could really use her on, too. A Sikes case."

"Can't you take someone else?" Amy asks. "Any spinner would be proud to work with *you*."

"Alex is special."

I'm too mortified to take any pleasure in the compliment. I concentrate on breathing, making each intake of air deep and even.

"I wish *I* could help," Amy sighs.

More kisses.

"Actually . . ." An idea dawns in Ross's voice. "You *could* help me."

"I could?"

"You know how Dr. Barnard never releases patients after a bout of time sickness unless their chronotin levels drop below 160? Well, Alex's chronotin levels are naturally high. Dropping them that low might take weeks. And Alex really likes the work, making her sit around thinking about dying is only going to make her worse."

"So how can I help?" Amy sounds eager.

"Fake the test results for me." Silence greets this suggestion. Dense, kissless silence. I second Amy's astonishment. Monitoring chronotin is a cornerstone of Center routine, the essential foundation for a spinner's life and health.

"It won't be hard," Ross says. "When you draw Alex's blood tomorrow, pretend to run the sample, but instead just write in that she dropped to, say, 167, and then the next day write in 148."

Ross sounds disturbingly cavalier about my health. In the car, he told me Barnard couldn't test my blood anymore once Ross changed my meds. Is that what he was doing when he ransacked the cabinet? I take a mental survey of my insides without detecting anything different. If Ross did change my meds, isn't it even more critical to track my chronotin than it was before?

I open my eyes again. Amy stands stiffly in Ross's embrace, her head craned back so she can see his face.

"What if I get caught?" Amy asks.

This is her first question? I clench my fists beneath the sheets. Shouldn't she be worrying more about me getting sick?

"How could you get caught?" Ross bends his head to nuzzle Amy's neck. His words grow muffled. "You toss the samples after you test them, right? So if for some reason anyone else retests her blood they'll just think the first result was faulty."

My thoughts must have winged their way through the room

telepathically, because Amy asks, "Isn't it dangerous for her?"

"Of course not!" Ross's indignation relaxes my gripped hands a little. "Remember all those books you lent me? The ones from Dr. Barnard's library? I've studied this really carefully. The doctor is just being overly cautious."

"What if I run the test and her levels are rising?"

"Don't run the test at all. Give the blood samples to me, and I'll check them at home. If there's a problem, I promise I'll tell Barnard."

"You're so clever." She strokes Ross's cheek. "I bet you know as much about chronotin as Dr. Barnard."

My hands loosen a little more, though I'm still not as reassured as Amy seems to be. At least someone will be checking my chronotin, but I still wish it was Barnard. For all the books Ross may have read, he's not a famous spinner scientist.

Amy leans her head against Ross's chest.

"I'm only on shift a half day tomorrow," she says, and even to me the protest sounds halfhearted. Ross kisses her. I close my eyes.

"A smart girl like you will figure something out."

There's more rustling. Ross whispers something, and his words turn into the suck and slurp of kisses. Amy gives a little moan.

"If it will really help you . . . ," she says.

"You'll be my heroine. My invisible partner in crime." Ross gives a throaty chuckle. "In *solving* crime, I mean. When I catch Sikes, you'll know it was partly because of you."

Amy moans again. I lie still, pretending to be asleep and trying not to listen. Finally, Ross says, "I better go. Wouldn't want to get you in trouble when Julio comes back for a check."

"You'll stop by later?"

He answers her with a final kiss.

A few minutes later I open my eyes to an empty room. Shadowy shapes lurk in the dark, the outlines of furniture turned vague by the night. I stare up at the ceiling and listen to the clinic's night sounds. Something mechanical beeps at steady intervals, a radio plays classical music in the distance, a car sputters outside the window like an old man coughing. Memories from my last rewind play against the gloom: the seeping and receding blood, Jason's disappearing body, and the door that never opened to reveal the killer. I twist onto one side, then the other, my positions limited by the dangling IV line. I feel tired and dirty, soiled by my unintended voyeurism, my failed rewind, and—though I hate to admit it—flickering doubts about Ross's principles. Ross. The man who just made a midnight visit to secure my ability to work again, even after the disaster of my last attempt. The professional agent who is risking his career to extend my life. The guy who will stoop to seducing Amy to get what he wants.

When I wake up the sun is shining. Yolly stands near my bed, twisting the little rod that opens up the blinds. When she sees I'm awake, she smiles.

"Back among the living, I see."

It's not the most tasteful comment, given my current condition. I prop myself up against the pillows. Someone has dressed me in pajamas. I'm guessing Shannon picked them out, since they're royal blue, a color she claims is flattering on me. My IV is gone, too, which I take as a sign of recovery. I am also starving.

"What time is it?" I ask.

"You really ought to ask what day it is."

Yolly whips a plastic thermometer from her pocket and pops it in my mouth. The multicolored kittens decorating her smock smile encouragingly.

"You've been in here for two days," she tells me. "We've all been terribly worried."

"Two . . ."

The thermometer clatters against my teeth, and Yolly makes a zipping motion across her lips with one hand. I wait impatiently until the probe beeps and she takes it out.

"Two days? What's today?"

"Monday." Yolly squints at the thermometer. This close I can smell the sweet vanilla scent of her hand cream. The familiar everyday perfume raises a lump in my throat.

"Looks good," Yolly says. "Amazing really. When you came in you were as sick as I've seen anyone." She picks up my chart from a rolling supply table and makes a note. "And to answer your original question, it's almost noon."

Noon. I've been out for over forty-eight hours. Except for last night. I cringe as images crowd into my head. Ross and Amy. All that heavy breathing. As if my uncomfortable recollections conjured her, Amy sticks her head in the door. She wears street clothes, jeans and a green cardigan with big square pockets.

"Hi," she says, giving Yolly the kind of smile little kids offer when you take their picture, lips stretched with no emotion behind them.

Yolly's eyebrows rise. "Didn't you just get off shift?"

"Yes." Amy blushes. "I . . . uh . . . just wanted to check on Alex. Car—Mr. Ross said he was worried and . . ."

"Alex is doing really well."

"That's great," Amy says without enthusiasm. She hovers in the doorway, one foot in the door and one outside. "Well, since I'm here, I guess I'll run her blood test. Mr. Ross said he'd be by later to find out her results."

Yolly looks at her sharply, and my memories from last night snap into focus. Ross asked Amy to fake the results of my chronotin test. I twist a strand of hair around my finger. It feels greasy. If Ross *has* changed my meds then one unexpected result will expose the truth. Is that what I want? I brush my hair back. Ross has gone to such lengths to help me. I owe it to both of us to at least try.

"That's a great idea." I dredge up a reasonable sounding lie. "When Shannon does the blood draw it always pinches."

Amy looks relieved. She moves into the room and rummages around the cabinet for a sealed needle pack.

"You hungry?" Yolly asks me. Adding, when I nod, "I'll see what I can dig up from the cafeteria."

Amy takes my arm and pats the vein in the inner curve of my elbow with a damp swab. The sharp smell of alcohol invades my nostrils.

"There are quite a few people who will be happy to hear you're on the mend." Amy slides the needle under my skin with a familiar prick. "Your friend KJ has been here every day. I practically had to shove him out the door yesterday to get him to leave."

KJ. The thought of seeing him and not having to hide being sick makes me almost dizzy with relief. So much for my altruistic wish to spare him pain. I promise myself I'll tell him everything. There's no more time for secrets.

Amy pulls the needle free and caps the blood vial with a quick twist. "That should do it."

She heads off, presumably to steal my blood and fake the results, just as Yolly returns with a tray bearing soup, toast, a carton of orange juice, and, my favorite, a bowl of chocolate pudding. There's a small metal tabletop attached to an arm beside the bed, and she swings it around until it rests in front of me. The scent of chicken soup and chocolate makes my stomach grumble. Yolly watches as I slurp up my soup.

"How do you feel?" she asks, with genuine concern.

"Great." As I say it, I realize it's true. My headache is gone. The food is restoring my energy, and I actually feel more clear-headed than I have in ages. I guess it's true that keeping secrets takes a physical toll.

"I'm still kind of weak," I say, "but other than that I'm pretty normal."

Yolly smiles and says she has some work to do in the clinic office and to call her when I'm done with my lunch. I inhale the soup and toast and pick up my pudding. A sweet cloud of chocolate slides over my tongue. I lick the spoon, thinking about Ross and what our next mission might bring. Maybe he used another spinner to rewind the scene at the butcher shop again, or found some other lead that we can follow together when I get out. A whisper of worry interrupts my dreamy visions. What if the sickness has interfered with my time skills? Lots of spinners go back to work after their first illness, but not so many do after their second.

The chocolate coating my mouth turns slimy. If I can't hold freezes anymore, then I won't be able to keep working the Sikes case. Sweat dampens my palms. What if I freeze right now? Just to see if it still works? When the monitor goes off, I can claim I fell asleep.

I set down the half-eaten pudding and lean back into my pillows. If I *have* lost my skills I'd rather know now instead of after I mess up another mission. I dry my palms against the sheets, snatch at time, and pull it up short. For a split second I think it hasn't worked. Usually freezing causes a slight jolt somewhere deep in my midsection. I've always thought of it as time trying to get away from me. But this transition slides by seamlessly; one instant the world moves, the next it doesn't. Taking a deep breath, I grab hold of the time strands and start to rewind. Shadowy images slide past me with the fluidity of a boat riding a gentle current. I watch my own ghostly arms spoon food from mouth to tray, then wait for Yolly to back into the room, mutter gibberish at me, and remove my meal before I bring the rewind to a halt. Easy. Smooth.

I smile my relief at the still room. Nothing about the rewind feels strange—no difficulty pulling time backward, no struggle to keep the invisible force under control. In fact, I feel extra strong, like I could hold this freeze for hours. I dump the remaining pudding out of my bowl and smear it across my tray. Dipping my fingers in it, I write my name in triumphant brown letters. I can freeze just fine. At least for the short term, everything is going to be OK.

I flop back into my pillows and let time move forward again. It's another seamless transition, without even a hint of dizziness. Melts always go more smoothly when there's less to put back.

The freeze monitor in the clinic's main room beeps.

"Alex?" Yolly's voice drifts in from behind the closed door. "What's going on?"

"Nothing," I call back. "I guess I dozed off."

"I thought you were feeling better?"

Yolly's cell phone meows.

"I'm just tired." I sit up and reach for my pudding. I hear Yolly telling someone that I fell asleep. The monitor goes quiet.

"Was it a bad dream?" she asks.

I don't answer.

"Alex?"

I still don't answer. I can't. What I am seeing is simply not possible because frozen time isn't real. Nothing that happens within it lasts. I close my eyes. Open them again. Chocolate remains smeared across my tray. I look inside the bowl.

All the pudding is gone.

09

"ALEX?" YOLLY'S HEAD POPS AROUND THE EDGE OF my door.

The letters on the tray scream my name like a confession. I turn the bowl over, as if somehow this might make the pudding magically reappear. It doesn't.

"I'm fine," I say.

"I guess calling your recovery amazing was a bit premature." Yolly gathers up the remains of my meal, clucking her tongue at the chocolate mess on my tray.

"Sorry," I mumble.

She wipes up the smeared pudding. "KJ said he wanted to see you as soon as you woke up. Shall I tell him you're ready for visitors?"

I hesitate. I want to see KJ, but I also want to know what happened to my time skills. To do that, I need to freeze again, and the only way I can get away with that is if Yolly thinks I'm asleep.

"I think I need a nap first." I fake a yawn. "Can you ask him to come in an hour?"

Yolly pats my arm and stacks the empty soup bowl into the equally empty pudding bowl. I wait until I hear her close the outer door of the clinic, then force myself to watch the clock tick for five minutes before I reach out. The shafts of noonday sun streaming through the blinds turn dull as everything stops. I climb out of bed. Cold tiles meet my bare feet. I release time.

The sunshine brightens and I remain standing a foot from the bed.

"Oh my God," I whisper. The possibilities flooding my brain make me giddy. *I can affect things that happen in frozen time.*

The freeze monitor in the clinic's office starts beeping. I plunk down on the edge of my bed. If someone calls in a crime, I could get there while it's still in progress. McDennon could have dismantled the bomb while time was still frozen. I could walk into a hostage situation and simply remove the victims. I could disarm someone across the room in a split second. The enormity of the possibilities makes my head spin. My days may be numbered, but, oh, the things I can do in the meantime!

I hop back onto my feet. Amy said Ross will be here this afternoon. I picture his face, the amazement lighting his features when I show him what I can do. I laugh out loud with sheer pleasure, then laugh again when I imagine telling KJ. He was worried about me while I was sick and here I am, not only healthy, but improved.

With a reckless tug, I stop time again. Why wait? The monitor is still beeping. It's not like I can set it off twice. I zip out of the room, not bothering to look for real clothes. The clinic office is empty, the clock on the wall stuck at 12:34. Lunch will just be ending. I race out into the hall. Yolly's stout body blocks the top of the main stairway. Her head is turned over her shoulder—it looks like she's talking to someone coming up the stairs behind her. Afraid I might jostle her if I squeeze past, I skip over to the smaller emergency stairs halfway down the hall. By the time I reach the basement, I'm panting. I don't care. The harder I crash later, the more convincing my tired act will be for Yolly.

The smell of french fries floats in the air outside the cafeteria's open doorway. The Center kids are scattered around the room, some still eating, most clearing their trays or on their feet heading off to their afternoon assignments. I edge my way among them, looking for KJ, before remembering that Yolly said it was Monday. Mondays are the days KJ and I clean up the kitchen. I turn on my heel and trip over a Younger's backpack, sending the purple nylon sack skittering across the floor. I take three more steps before I realize I can't just leave it there—when I melt, the thing's going to look like it teleported. I retrieve the bag and set it back where it came from. Or more or less where it came from. Hopefully no one was actually looking at it at the moment I froze.

The Center kitchen is a large industrial space with rubber mats underfoot and burnished metal everywhere else. KJ is way in the back, pointing a pull-down sprayer at a stack of dirty plates. Steam hovers around him in a vaporous cloud. I check the whole room, even opening the walk-in refrigerator, to make sure the place is empty. Once I'm positive no one can see us, I wrap my hand around his bare wrist and start time.

"Hey, there, buddy."

KJ jumps, splashing us both with hot water.

"Alex! Oh my God, you scared me."

I wipe my face, laughing. After the quiet of the freeze, the clatter from the cafeteria sounds extra loud—rumbling voices, scraping chairs, the faint beep from the monitor.

"Surprised to see me?" I ask.

"Completely." He turns the sprayer off and gathers me into a hug.

"I can't believe you're walking around," he says. "The last time I saw you, you looked awful."

"Gee, thanks."

"You know what I mean."

He steps back, his hands clasped around my elbows.

"Are you really better?"

"Better than better." I'm smiling so widely my cheeks hurt. "Check this out."

With our arms still touching, I freeze time again. Silence returns. KJ's fingers dig into my skin.

"Are you nuts?" he says. "What are you doing?"

His own skills surge between us, further strengthening my hold on time. It feels effortless, like I could hold time for hours, even in my weakened state.

"It's OK." I pry his fingers loose. "Yolly thinks I'm dream-freezing. Look."

I walk all the way across the kitchen, beckoning him to follow me.

"Are you sure you're feeling all right?" KJ trails in my wake. "You seem . . ." He waves a hand, the gesture taking in my pajamas, unwashed hair, and grinning face. I laugh.

"Crazy? No, I promise I'm not crazy." I take his hand. "You ready?"

Real time moves forward. The buzz of noise returns. I wait just long enough for KJ to realize what happened, and then grab the flow up tight again.

KJ's face turns so pale I'm afraid he might faint. He stares down at our clasped hands, then back at the spot by the sink where we were standing when I froze time.

"How did you do that?"

"Isn't it great?" I dance around him, unable to contain the bubbly feeling rippling through my insides. "Things I move in frozen time stay that way. Think how amazing this will be on missions."

KJ keeps staring around the motionless kitchen. He looks like one small tap might knock him over. I make an effort to contain my jubilation.

"It's not just missions," I say, remembering his complaint about my obsession. "We can do lots of things. Fun things."

I start time again, grabbing it back almost immediately, but this time without touching him. Skirting his frozen body, I pick up a squirt bottle of ketchup and write *Alex Rocks!* in huge goopy letters on the countertop closest to him. Then I take his hand and once again release and refreeze time. KJ starts. I point to the scrawled message.

"Tada!"

"Alex—"

His voice holds warning. The bubbles inside me deflate a tiny bit.

"Don't you see how cool this?" I say. "The last time I was in the Youngers' class, I figured out how to freeze time without getting caught. Next time I'm there I'll sneak out and take a dorm key from the security office. We could get out of our rooms at night, maybe even out of the building."

"Alex!" KJ's voice is sharp.

"What?"

"How did this happen?"

KJ sounds strangled, like the idea of my new skill is more than he can swallow. I cross my arms.

"I don't know." The image of Ross digging through my bedside cupboard in the middle of the night flashes into my head. I put it aside.

It's only a theory, and KJ is freaked out enough. He doesn't need to know I agreed to change my meds. "I just woke up and was like this."

"You can't tell anyone." KJ moves away from me. He picks up a rag and starts wiping away my ketchup art.

"I have to tell Ross," I say. "Otherwise I can't use it."

"If anyone knows what you can do, they won't just stop you from using it, they'll stop you from everything."

"What do you mean, everything?" The excited bubbles are definitely gone now, replaced by a prickling sensation that's crawling up the back of my scalp. "Like leash me? All the time?"

"Well, leash you, of course," KJ says, as if this were totally obvious. "They'll send you to the Central Office. They'll want to study you, make you do tests, take blood samples, who knows what else." He erases the last of my message. "They'll test all of us, trying to figure out how this happened. It will be like the old days you read about where spinners were experimented on." KJ tosses the rag into the sink. "The Norms are scared of us already," he says. "Our only saving grace is that nothing we do in a freeze sticks. Think how much they'd fear us if it did."

All the plans building within me since the pudding vanished evaporate in KJ's warning. I imagine a sterile room lined with beds full of spinners, wires sprouting from their heads, machines beeping.

"So you think . . . you think I can't even tell Mr. Ross?"

"*Definitely* don't tell Ross. He might like you, but he's still an agent. If he didn't turn you in he'd lose his job."

The urge to cry is almost overwhelming. All the brilliant plans I'd made for the future disappear in an instant. I am suddenly very aware of how little I've eaten in the past few days. Time, which seemed so easy to hold a minute ago, now tugs on my control.

"But I have to tell him. When we go on a mission . . ."

"Alex." KJ puts a hand on my shoulder. "You can't go on missions like this."

I prop myself against a countertop, fighting the desire to collapse onto the sticky floor. Without time work, my new skills make me nothing but a freak, different even among the outcasts. I'll have to lie to Ross and say I don't want to work with him anymore. I'll have to lie to everyone. The other spinners. Barnard. Yolly.

Yolly!

"Oh, no." Panic pulls me upright.

"What?"

I slide out from under KJ's arm.

"Yolly was coming to check on me when I left." I try to figure out how much real time passed in the few seconds I let it roll forward. I melted and froze three times? Four?

"Go," KJ says, "I'll come up as soon as you melt time."

"No." Thoughts whirl through my head, making it hard to focus. "I'll have to pretend to be asleep. Yolly said she'd come get you in an hour."

KJ opens his mouth, then closes it without speaking. The rebuke hits me anyway. The colossal stupidity of what I've done hangs between us. I ran around like a child showing off a new toy with no thought to the consequences of my actions. Consequences that won't just affect me, but all spinners.

I drag myself back to the stairwell and up the two flights to the clinic. None of the elation that buoyed me on the way down remains to cover my exhaustion. Only the fear of trying to explain to Yolly where I'd gone keeps me moving. If she entered the room and found it empty, what can I say? The main stairs are only a few yards from the clinic door—she'd have seen me if I left. I picture the sickroom, the scattered sheets and minimal furniture. No excuse I can think up seems even faintly plausible.

Opening the door to the hallway feels like shoving a boulder. I stick my head around it. The hallway outside the clinic is empty. So is the main stairwell. Yolly has already entered the clinic's lobby.

My throat tightens. For once I wish the Center raised us with some kind of religion—then at least I'd have someone to pray to. I tiptoe over to the clinic and open the door.

Relief weakens my knees. The door to my room is closed. Yolly hovers halfway to it, head titled to one side as she talks into her cell phone. I don't think I've ever been so happy to see her.

I slide past her, careful not to ruffle any part of her body. I realize I'm shaking, fear and the unexpected reprieve both taking their toll. Maybe I can fall asleep for real before Yolly reaches me. It certainly won't take any effort to pretend I'm exhausted. I open the door and step inside. My heart stops beating.

Next to the bed, attention fixed on the empty sheets, stands Carson Ross.

10

I SINK DOWN ONTO THE COLD TILE FLOOR. PART OF me wants to run back out and ask KJ what to do, but I don't think I can bear to add to his disappointment in me. I try to think of someplace to hide. Side table, sink, storage cabinet. The space under the bed is so exposed Ross would have seen me the instant he walked into the room.

Time whispers inside my head, demanding its release. Regardless of how healthy I feel, two days of bed rest still means less energy. Choice dribbles away. I am going to have to face the consequences of what I've done.

Dragging myself to my feet, I prop my body against the wall near the door, clinging to a vague hope that I might convince Ross I was standing there when he opened it.

With a feeling of imminent doom, I release time.

". . . she all right, Mr. Ross?" Yolly's voice floats in from the main room.

"Mr. Ross." I try to make my whisper sound playful. "Over here." Ross spins around so fast it's as if I've smacked him. I shape my lips into a smile. "Boo."

Ross's mouth falls open. I think he's going to shout, but instead he motions wordlessly, pointing urgently toward the bed.

"Everything's fine, Yolly," he says.

It takes me a second before I understand: Ross is going to cover for me! I dive for my tousled sheets. Ross opens the door a crack, placing his body so he blocks Yolly's view of the room inside. I scramble to lie flat, pulling the blankets up to my throat.

"Just like you thought," Ross says in a hushed voice, "she's sound asleep." I snap my eyes shut. "I thought you said she was acting perky?"

"She was when she first woke up," Yolly says. "But then she fell asleep again as soon as she ate."

The door makes a soft swoosh as Ross opens it all the way. I lie still, breathing as evenly as my hammering heart allows.

"She's still doing really well." Yolly's feet pad close to the bed. "Her fever is gone and she managed to eat her entire lunch." She straightens the covers on my bed. Her hand lingers as she smooths them across my chest. "Poor thing. It's so hard to watch them at the end."

Yolly's voice breaks and I almost open my eyes in surprise. I've never heard any of the staff talk about us dying. For the first time I think about it from her perspective. Yolly spends most of her days here with us and then she has to watch us die off one by one. Pity momentarily lightens my fear. When she moves her hand away, I have to keep myself from reaching out to bring it back.

"It's such a waste," Ross says. I hear the scrape of the visitor's chair as he pulls it over next to the bed. "Mind if I stay a while?"

"You really care for this one, don't you, Mr. Ross?" He must nod, because she adds, "Sure, you can stay. Just don't wake her up."

Ross assures her he won't. Yolly's soft-soled shoes pad from the room. The door closes. I lie still, waiting.

"You can open your eyes now."

I push myself up against my pillows. Ross sits beside the bed, elbows on his knees so he can lean even closer. My fingers twist together under the sheets, twining themselves into a knot so tight my knuckles crack.

"Thanks for not telling Yolly I was out of bed," I say.

"You really feel OK?"

"Pretty good. I'm still tired."

Ross's eyes narrow. "So tell me how you ended up over by the door?"

My heart starts pounding again. KJ's warning plays in my head: *Ross is an agent. If he didn't turn you in he'd lose his job.*

"I heard you coming and got up." I lick my lips. "To show you how healthy I am."

"That's not true. You weren't there when I came in. I checked."

"No, I was there." I shake my head hard enough to knock my pillow onto the floor. I sit up straighter, moving as far from Ross as the bed allows. "Where else could I have been? You just didn't see me."

My voice has risen to a squeak that practically screams I'm lying. I clench my hands together even more tightly.

"Alex." Ross leans back in his chair. My heart pulses in my throat, the beat pounding out my panic: *he knows, he knows, he knows.*

"Remember how we talked about getting you on some different meds?" Ross asks.

My fingers feel like they're about to snap. I know what's coming next. He'll tell me it's too late now for him to help me and that what I can do is dangerous. He'll say how bad he feels about turning me in. He'll talk about duty, mine or his. It doesn't matter. The result will be the same. A chill circles my wrist, as if the leash is already pressing against my flesh.

Ross clears his throat.

"While you were sick, I found a way to get them to you. I wish we'd had time to talk about it first. Dr. Kroger warned me there might be side effects."

He waits. Realization penetrates my brain slowly.

"The new meds." I stare into Ross's sea-blue eyes. They meet mine steadily. "The ones that are supposed to extend my life. They're the reason . . . and you knew . . ."

KJ's warning not to tell anyone plays once more in my head, along with the vision of spinners being experimented on at the Central Office. I shove the images aside. KJ doesn't understand how much Ross has already risked in order to help me. I untwist my fingers and press them flat against the mattress.

"You knew they might make it so the things I moved during a freeze stayed that way after I melted time."

Ross nods. His eyes are bright. "Tell me what happened."

"Not a lot. I wanted to see if I could still freeze, so I tried it. When I melted time the food I'd spilled was still gone. So then I froze and melted a few times to see what would happen. I went out into the hall and . . ." I decide to omit any mention of KJ. Just in case I do get in trouble I don't want him implicated. "I walked around."

"Did you change anything anyone would notice?"

I shake my head. "I got scared that if someone knew what I could do I'd get leashed."

"You're absolutely right." Ross stands up and starts pacing the room with quick strides. "This has to be our secret. You can't let anyone know about your new abilities. None of your friends, none of the staff or doctors. No one." He returns to my bedside, leaning his elbows on the visitor's chair so his face is level with mine. "You understand how important this is? It's not just about getting leashed.

Power like this scares people. If Dr. Barnard finds out what you can do, he'll lock you up. He'll put you back on Aclisote, too, and at the rate you were going, you wouldn't last long."

I nod. After KJ's warning I don't need to be told twice.

"I won't tell anyone," I say, internally amending my statement to *anyone else*. I'm not worried. I know KJ will keep my secret.

Ross seems to sense my slight reservation. He frowns at me.

"You're not the only one with something on the line here. I could go to jail for changing your meds."

I bite my lip. Taking these drugs puts so many people in danger: Ross. The other spinners. I picture KJ's long body laid out on a surgeon's table while doctors cut into his brain. I bite harder, salting my tongue with a thin trickle of blood. Is trying this medicine a selfish choice? Even Ross doesn't know how much more life they might buy me. Is it fair to ask everyone to risk so much for what might turn out to be very little gain?

I wipe my lip with the back of my hand. I'm not being selfish; I'm volunteering for a private research project. If this new medicine can keep me alive, it will help others after me.

"I won't tell anyone," I say again, this time with all the conviction I can muster. "I promise."

"That's my girl." Ross's eyes crinkle at the edges when he smiles. "You rest for a few days. I'm hoping by then you'll be in good enough shape to go out on missions again."

"Are you sure that's safe?" I ask. "I mean, I've thought about it, and I think my new skills can really help our work, but how can I use them without anyone noticing?"

"We'll figure something out," Ross assures me. "If we have to, I'll set it up so we're alone when you freeze."

Memories of our last mission flood my mind. I drop my eyes to my hands. The blood from my lip has left a red smear near my thumb. I rub it.

"Mr. Ross, last time . . . the Torino murder. I couldn't hold it. I'm so, so sorry."

"It's OK," he says. "I got what I needed. In fact, we made an arrest yesterday."

My head jolts upright.

"You arrested Sikes?"

"No, no, someone else. A guy named Karl Wagner."

The cut on my lip stings when I lick it.

"But the rewind . . . I lost hold before anyone came in the room."

Ross gives me a piercing look. "What do you remember about that morning?"

"Not much. The body was there, his blood started moving." I shake my head. "Then everything just kind of ripped away and I passed out."

"That's all?" he asks.

"Yeah. Why? Did you see more?"

"A little. Enough to know who was behind it."

A weight I didn't even realize I was carrying floats away from me.

"And you saw this Karl Wagner? Who is he?"

"He's one of those guys whose name always comes up near Sikes's cases, but never quite in it. I think Sikes uses him as a lookout or an informant. Someone to case his targets before he strikes. I've been trying to nail him on something for years and never found anything that sticks. Now I've finally got him." Ross grins at me. "Here's the best part though. Because of your rewind, I have a lead on Sikes's real identity. When you're better, we can follow it up."

His grin widens. "With your new skills we're going to make a pretty unbeatable team."

Ross's face shines just the way I'd imagined when I first woke up. All the fears brought on by my conversation with KJ fade beneath its warmth.

The chair creaks as Ross straightens.

"I put two weeks' worth of the new medicine in your box." He gestures to the cabinet beside me. "And I'll bring in more as you need it. Before you take a dose, check the label. The doses I swapped in have a typo—your last name is spelled M-A-N-I-N-G, with one *n*. If it's not the right vial, don't take it."

I nod.

"Also," he says. "Make sure Amy is the only one who tests your blood, OK? She's going to help me keep track of your chronotin levels."

Heat floods my cheeks at the mention of Amy. I bend down to pick up my fallen pillow so Ross can't see my face.

"And one last thing," Ross says. "No freezing time, even when you're alone. This is way too important to play with."

"Don't worry, Mr. Ross," I say, returning my pillow to its rightful spot. "I won't let you down."

"Good girl. I knew I could count on you."

The last of my worries evaporates into the air. I settle back into bed, succumbing at last to my exhaustion. I don't have to worry anymore. KJ knows I'm sick. I didn't blow the Torino rewind. And Ross has a lead on Sikes. My future may be short, but at least it's looking bright.

Yolly lets KJ into my room while I'm eating an early dinner: macaroni and cheese, garlic bread, a salad of iceberg lettuce drenched with a bright orange dressing, and a frosted brownie. Between emotional upheaval and two days on an IV, I'm shaky with hunger, so I'm devouring the mediocre menu with monster bites.

"Yolly doesn't suspect anything?" KJ asks as soon as she leaves us.

I gulp down a hunk of lettuce. My meeting with Ross reassured me so much that I forgot about the panicked state I'd left KJ in. I stop shoveling food long enough to tell him that all is well. KJ sinks into the visitor's chair with a relieved sigh.

"That's great." He watches me attack the mac and cheese. "You know, I came to sit with you while you were sick."

"Amy told me," I say. I pop a piece of garlic bread into my mouth, savoring the oily butter as it melts over my tongue. "It must not have been real fun. I was pretty out of it."

"It was awful," KJ says. "For a while I thought you wouldn't make it."

I stop chewing. About a year ago, a baby bird found its way into the courtyard and KJ nursed it back to health. He adored that ball of fluff. Every time KJ came near, the bird would squawk and dance, clacking its little beak to demand its meal of worms or garden spiders, and KJ would laugh and laugh. Then one day a raccoon or a cat or something must have gotten into the courtyard. I was the one that found the pile of feathers. When I told KJ, his face crumpled, like I'd knocked all the air from his body. It's the same expression he's wearing now.

I fiddle with my fork, trying to think of something to say that will erase the melancholy filling the room.

"And here I am." I smile. "Perfectly healthy again."

KJ shakes his head. "Except you're not. Things are different now."

"You mean my time skills?"

"No," he says. "I mean everything."

My smile fades. "It doesn't have to be."

"Things *are* different. We've always avoided talking about the fact that one day we'll both get sick. That we're going to die. We can't pretend anymore."

Silence wraps the sickroom, muting even the faint hum of traffic on the street below. The loudest sound is the ticking of the clock on the wall. KJ places his hand on my sheet-covered leg.

"When I was sitting here with you, a lot of things became clear to me. Remember when you asked me the other day what I would do if I weren't a spinner?"

I nod.

"I figured out my answer," KJ says. "If I were a Norm I'd want to grow up and have a family. I'd want a wife and children and the chance to spend the next sixty years seeing the people I love every day."

I push the last piece of macaroni around my plate. This is why I didn't want KJ to know I was sick. I didn't want him to feel sorry for me. I didn't want to see him looking this sad.

"We're not Norms," I whisper. "Spinners can't have children. We can't have any of those things."

"We can have some of them," KJ says. His hand moves on my leg, stroking my knee with hesitant fingers. "You've always said missions matter to you more than anything else, but now that that's over, we can spend more time together. At least for the few months we have left."

His gently moving hand hypnotizes me. I picture his tanned arms working in the courtyard, the way his nose wrinkles when he laughs, the full lips that define his mouth, and for the first time in years I let myself imagine touching them. My stomach turns over. I shove the images away. KJ is my best friend. Now he thinks I'm dying and he wants . . . what? To comfort me? I tighten my grip on my fork.

"Ross said I may live a lot longer than a few months. He said I can keep working, too, even with my new abilities."

KJ's hand stills. His lips move a few times without making a sound.

"Ross was *here*? And you *told* him?"

"Yes." I trace a pattern in the puddle of orange dressing with my fork. I feel like I'm betraying one of them, but I'm not sure which one. "Ross was in the room when I got back. He saw me reappear."

KJ's breath hisses past his teeth. I plunge on before he can interrupt.

"He's not going to tell anyone."

"Why not?"

"Because he doesn't want me to get in trouble."

KJ's hand is back in his lap. He looks mad now, his brows so low they cast his eyes into shadow.

"If he cares so much, isn't he worried about the fact that your freezing abilities have changed?"

"He . . ." I catch myself. I'd promised Ross I wouldn't tell anyone about the new meds, and the way KJ looks right now I'm not sure I trust him to keep the secret. I struggle to come up with an alternate explanation.

"He said it was nothing to worry about," I lie. "That this is a normal side effect."

KJ's eyes narrow. "A normal side effect? Then how come we've never heard of it? And if it's so normal, why keep quiet?"

I pick at a stray piece of lettuce with my fork. The thin green leaf skitters around in the gloppy dressing, refusing to be impaled.

"It's normal, but really rare. You know how Barnard freaks out about everything. It's better not to mention it."

"Maybe someone should be freaking out," KJ says. "Did Barnard say anything about your chronotin levels?"

"I don't know," I admit. "Ross asked Amy to fake them so I could go out sooner."

The room gets very quiet again. I raise my head from the striped pattern I've drawn on my plate. KJ is staring at me with pure horror.

"Amy is *faking your chronotin results?*"

My eyes fly to the door, afraid someone might have heard him.

"Just for Barnard," I say. "She's telling Ross the real levels. He'll know when it's safe for me to go on another mission."

"Are you insane? Ross isn't a doctor!"

I abandon the lettuce.

"Sikes is out there," I say, "and we have a chance to catch him."

"Sikes." KJ flops back in his chair. "Really? You're dying and all you care about is catching Sikes?"

"Catching Sikes matters. It's important."

I shove a piece of brownie into my mouth before I add what I really mean: Catching Sikes makes *me* important. It makes me matter.

"What if you get sick again?" KJ asks. "What if this weird change is because your chronotin levels are totally out of whack? Barnard won't know to adjust for it."

The brownie dissolves into clods of dirt on my tongue. KJ must sense his advantage, because he leans forward again.

"Forget about Sikes, Alex. Forget about work. This is your *life* we're talking about. You go out there and catch Sikes and what happens? Ross gets his revenge, maybe he even gets his shot at being made Chief, but what will *you* get besides a pat on the head?" KJ's hand reaches out for mine.

"Look at me," he says. "Is that really how you want to spend what little time you have left?"

His hand hovers inches from my own. He's so close to me I can smell the laundry soap in his shirt. My heart starts beating very fast. If I walk away from Ross, I walk away from his new meds and the chance to live a longer life. And what exactly is KJ offering me? When we were a couple all those years ago it didn't work out. And what about Shannon? Even if KJ is lukewarm about her, she certainly wants him. How could I share a room with her after stealing the guy I knew she liked? Questions clutter my brain, making my head hurt worse than any time headache.

"I just want everything to stay the same! I never should have told you any of this."

Frustration puts more anger into my words than I meant. KJ sits back, cradling his rejected hand. His face is as red as if I'd slapped it.

"I was trying to help."

"You're not."

"So you choose catching Sikes over me?"

Over you as a friend or as a boyfriend? The clinic door swings open before I can ask.

"Are you done with your dinner?" Yolly asks, bustling over to pick up my tray.

KJ stands to get out of her way. He moves stiffly, like someone injured. I can tell he's trying to keep his face neutral in front of Yolly, but as he turns away I see the edge of his mouth tremble. A yawning hole opens in my chest. All I wanted was to protect our friendship, and instead I've made things worse. Our conversation plays back in my head. If he hadn't come at me so suddenly, if I'd had time to think . . . Yolly bustles around me, straightening my pillows, fussing with my tray.

"I almost forgot your medicine," she says brightly.

Unlocking the cabinet, she picks up one of the mislabeled dosages and hands it to me. KJ backs away. I gulp down the meds, eager for Yolly to leave so we can continue to talk in private.

"I'll let you rest," KJ says.

The liquid in my mouth prevents me from asking him to wait. I swallow, too quickly, choking as the chemicals slide down my throat. Yolly pats my back. By the time I've stopped coughing, the door has closed and KJ is gone.

11

I SLEEP BADLY THAT NIGHT AND WAKE TO THE SOUND of people talking in the main room of the clinic. Amy's voice, sharp with anxiety, mingles with Julio's. Somebody groans. The squeak of a wheelchair confirms my fear: another spinner is sick. The clinic has two patients now.

Sleepiness vanishes. I lie without moving, straining to make sense of the quick patter of words.

"Did you check his pulse?"

"Get me an IV."

"Watch his head."

His. One of the boys, then. My brain instantly calls up Jack's list of most likely candidates: Jack, Calvin, KJ. I sit bolt upright. Don't let it be KJ. The patient in the hallway moans again. Jack, I bargain. Couldn't it be Jack? At nineteen, he's the oldest spinner. That would be fair. Not that time sickness is ever fair.

The door next to mine shuts, muffling the voices. If it's KJ . . . My mind is incapable of finishing the thought. *Please*, I beg the sterile room, *don't let it be KJ. Please.*

The tiles feel slick under my feet when I slide out of bed. I tiptoe noiselessly from my room and open the door of the one next to mine. Bright overhead light reveals the scene: Julio lifting an inert body onto the bed. Amy setting up an IV bag. I stick my head farther into the room just as Julio steps back to expose the patient. It's Calvin.

My hand grips the doorframe. I must make a noise because Amy whirls around.

"Alex! What are you doing here? Go back to your room."

I can't let go of the door. Calvin's face is damp with sweat, his body so limp that my relief the victim isn't KJ sours. My legs start shaking. I point toward the bed.

"Is he going to be all right?"

Amy presses her lips together.

"Go back to your room," she repeats, though this time she says the words gently. "We'll know more later."

I lie in bed until early morning sunlight squeezes through the blinds to stripe the sheets covering my feet. I trace the pattern with my eyes, listening to the faint noises from next door. Amy comes into my room around 7:00. Her smock looks rumpled, her mouth tight around the edges.

"You're awake," she says.

I sit up. "How is he?"

Amy sighs. "He's stable, for now."

I nod. This is Calvin's third attack. We both know his chances of recovery are slim.

"I'll bring breakfast in a bit," she says. "Right now you need to take your meds."

Amy unlocks the cupboard and pulls out a fresh dose. The letters of my misspelled name stare at me accusingly. Next door, Calvin is dying, and here I am being offered a longer life.

Amy hands me the vial. I want to refuse it, to insist Amy give it to Calvin instead, but I know I can't. Doing that would only get Ross fired, or worse. I accept the bottle and pour the liquid down my throat. I'm a test subject, I remind myself, taking my own chances to support research that might help others later on. Through the walls, I hear Calvin moan.

I crumple the empty vial in my hand.

"Don't worry about breakfast," I tell Amy. "I'm not hungry."

Dr. Barnard releases me from the clinic the next afternoon. I shower and put on a pair of jeans and a long-sleeved shirt I've washed so many times the Nike swoosh across the front has faded to gray. Comfort clothes. The common room is quiet when I make my way downstairs. Someone tuned the TV to a nature show, but the sound is down low and no one seems to be watching it. Aidan, Yuki, and Raul are sitting around a Scrabble board. They all look up when I walk in, offering the barest acknowledgment before returning to their game. It's unclear whose turn it is. Raul idly shuffles the tiles on his tray. Yuki stares around the room with a blank look in her eyes.

When I was a Younger, I remember that the older kids dying seemed sort of distant. All it meant was a different face handing out meds, or a change in the dishwashing schedule. That's not true anymore. Now it isn't the older kids who are dying. It's us. I know that look in Yuki's eyes. Every one of us has it at one time or another. It's the question that haunts us all: *Who's next? Him? Her? Me?*

I skirt the game-playing trio and walk over to where KJ is sitting with Shannon. He's chosen the seat Calvin preferred. The book Calvin was last reading rests in his lap. *The Hidden History of the JFK Assassination.* I wonder how far into it Calvin got. KJ strokes the picture on the front as if it's a small animal.

"Hey," I say. They turn their faces toward me. Both of them have circles under their eyes. KJ's shirt looks like he slept in it. Shannon's usually tidy braid is fuzzy with loose hair.

"How are you doing?" I ask KJ.

He offers me a tight smile. "I should be asking you that."

I shrug. "Barnard let me out, so I must be OK."

KJ doesn't answer. His unspoken disapproval hangs between us. I twist a strand of my shower-wet hair around one finger. Compared to their rumpled state, my clean, soap-scented presence seems somehow disrespectful of Calvin.

"Any news?" I ask.

"His fever is still really high," Shannon says.

She's wearing the nurse's smock I saw her in when she brought me lunch earlier. In the last two days, she's practically taken up residence in the clinic, moving between my room and Calvin's to bring us food, hand out meds, and take temperatures. At least, that's what she was doing for me. Her duties with Calvin may have been more clinical.

KJ sighs. Shannon reaches over to take his hand.

"Dr. Barnard is with him now," she tells him. "He's doing everything that can be done."

The finger wrapping my hair twitches, yanking the strand painfully against my scalp. Barnard is *not* doing everything that could be done. My standing here is proof of it. I shift my weight from one foot to the other, trying to think of a way to help.

"I'm going to head up to my room," I say. "Read for a while."

KJ nods. No one else says anything to me as I leave.

I hurry down the hall, not toward the dorms, but to the main stairs. The floor is wet from a recent mopping and I have to walk carefully so I don't slip. Dr. Barnard's office is off the lobby. I wave at

Charlie behind his glass window before knocking on the door.

"He's out!" Jack yells through the wood, a fact I am perfectly aware of since Shannon said Barnard was in the clinic with Calvin.

"That's all right," I say, loud enough for Charlie to hear. "The message I have is for you."

I open the door, closing it behind me with a snap. Jack is sitting on the floor, surrounded by stacks of medical magazines. He looks to be in the process of sorting them, though at the moment, the process seems to include him lounging against the bookcase flipping through yesterday's sports section.

"What's the message?" he asks me.

"There is none," I say, crossing the room to Barnard's desk. "I need to use the phone."

Jack raises one eyebrow. "I assume you have permission for that?"

"The same permission you have to do that," I say, nodding at the paper in his hand.

"Yeah, but I'm me and you're you. Miss Goody Two Shoes doesn't break the rules." Jack tosses the paper aside. "Who are you calling?"

"My agent."

Jack looks disappointed. I pick up the phone and dial the number listed on the agent contact sheet pinned up beside Barnard's desk. It only rings twice before he answers.

"Carson Ross."

"Mr. Ross. Hi. It's Alex."

"Alex?" He sounds surprised. "Everything OK?"

"Yes." I glance at Jack, who is openly listening to my conversation. I wish I could kick him out, but there's no reason I can think of that won't make Charlie suspicious.

"I was released from the clinic today."

"I heard. I'm so pleased. It even sounds like your chronotin levels are low enough that you can resume time work."

"They are?" I ask, momentarily distracted. Does he mean my real levels or the ones Amy wrote on my chart?

I rub some dust off the phone's base, framing my words with care.

"You know that Calvin's sick now? Well, he's really fond of German food, and I was wondering if maybe you could get him some. Like that stuff you got me the other day."

Silence. Across the room, Jack watches me with a puzzled expression. I squeeze the phone closer to my ear.

"Alex," Ross says, "that stuff I got for you, I only have so much."

Tears burn the edges of my eyes. I turn around so I'm facing the window.

"Couldn't we share it?"

"It won't work. He's too far gone and they're monitoring him way too closely. I'm sorry."

A single tear slides down my cheek. I knew it was a long shot, but the completeness of my failure still stings. I say something I hope sounds understanding. Ross apologizes again and says he'll see me soon. Then he hangs up.

I stand with the phone pressed against my ear, staring out the window. It's raining. One of the gutters in the Center's roof must be clogged because there's a steady drip splattering against the glass.

"Since when does Calvin like German food?" Jack asks.

The gushing water turns the view outside into a blur. All I can see clearly are the bars that keep us locked into our small, short lives. I rub my eyes before turning to replace the phone.

"I just thought it would be nice to do something for him before he, you know."

Jack tips his head to one side.

"And that's what that call was about?"

"Of course," I say, then add, hoping to distract him. "Remember the other day, when you said Dr. Barnard was up to something? What did you mean?"

Jack cracks his knuckles one by one, the pops a counterpoint to the pattering rain.

"Let's just say our Dr. B. likes his reputation as the world's chronotin expert, but resents that his big research projects don't get enough support from this poorly funded public institution."

"So what are you saying? That he pads the budget?"

"Maybe he does." Jack wiggles his eyebrows. "Or maybe *we're* all part of his grand plan to get ahead."

My mind jumps to the confusing Aclisote dosages I'd seen in Calvin's file.

"Are you saying he's experimenting on us?"

The still-wet strands of my hair tickle the back of my neck. The other day at breakfast, Shannon said there wasn't a threshold for the sickness, that everyone had their own level. What if she was wrong? What if there were specific triggers, and Dr. Barnard was manipulating them? Raising and lowering our medication just to see what would happen? I close my eyes, trying to drum up the numbers I'd seen on the others' charts.

Jack bursts out laughing. "You should see your face."

I back up, cheeks flushing. I should have known Jack was just messing with me.

"Forget it," I say. "I've gotta go. Dr. Barnard will be back soon."

"Hey, don't be mad," Jack says, making no effort to stifle his amusement. "I was trying to give you a genuine tip."

"I bet."

I realize everyone deals with fear and grief their own way, but I have no sympathy for Jack's version of it. The door slams behind me as I stomp my way out. Jack's laughter chases me across the lobby and all the way back up the stairs to my room.

Calvin dies later that night. Yolly announces his death while we're at breakfast the next morning, adding a few words about what a great spinner he'd been and how we'll all miss him. Yuki and I are on kitchen duty, so I hear the news from behind the metal counter, where I stand looking out at the other kids scattered around the cafeteria tables. Nobody reacts with surprise. Across the room I see KJ bent low over his plate, absently stirring his scrambled eggs into mush with his fork. I can't see his face, but Jack, sitting beside him, is pale, with all hints of his usual mocking swagger leached from his face.

Yuki starts dragging the tubs of dirty dishes back to the sink. I turn the water on extra hot and we load the dishwasher together in silence. As soon as the kitchen is reasonably clean, I blow off my job with the Youngers and go looking for KJ. Since he doesn't have regular assignments, KJ can be anywhere: in Barnard's office messing with his computer, in the library fixing a wobbly shelf, changing light bulbs in some random hall. It takes twenty minutes before I track him down. He's in the common room, standing directly across from me in front of the shrine Yolly always sets up when someone dies: an eight-by-ten photograph framed in black and surrounded by four tall white candles. The photograph is an old one. Calvin looks about sixteen, unparanoid, with chubby cheeks and longer hair. He's smiling crookedly, as if caught in the middle of telling a joke.

Tears sting my eyes. I hover in the doorway, waiting for the wash of sadness to pass before I go inside.

"Here," a voice says. "That looks better, doesn't it?"

Shannon appears from where she must have been on the far side of the room. She's carrying a handful of flowers from the courtyard stuffed into a glass decorated with beads that spell out Calvin's name. I shrink back into the hall. Shannon places the flowers in front of Calvin's picture, and she and KJ stand side by side, staring at it.

"Thank you," KJ says. His voice sounds husky. Shannon puts her hand on his shoulder and rubs it gently.

"He was peaceful at the end," she says. "I doubt he felt much pain."

The tears in my eyes well over. KJ nods.

"I'm glad you were with him," he says. "I didn't like to think of him up there alone."

Something sharp knifes through my insides. It's not that I envy Shannon's ability to bring KJ solace; it's that it doesn't feel fair. I hung out way more with Calvin when he was alive than Shannon ever did. I should be the one sharing KJ's sorrow.

I wipe the wetness off my cheeks and take a step forward.

"I'll never let any of us go out alone." Shannon's soft voice carries through the space between us. I hesitate, one foot hovering over the threshold, not wanting to interrupt.

"Nothing matters more than all of us spinners supporting each other," she says. "I learned that after Steve died. We're all the family any of us has."

KJ turns to Shannon and wraps his arms around her, his face resting against her bright hair. My foot trembles a little as I set it back on the ground. Shannon strokes KJ's back. She's still talking, but the words have melted into a soothing murmur. KJ's shoulders begin to shake. He says something to her, and she lifts her head. Their lips meet.

The knife in my gut twists. As quietly as possible, I back out of the room. KJ and Shannon remain locked in their embrace. I turn, walking quickly, aimlessly, wanting only to put space between me and the scene I just witnessed. How is it I've managed two voyeuristic encounters in less than a week? The beat of my feet echoes in a brain that seems to have gone blank. It's good they're together, I tell myself, good they can offer each other comfort. Another gut stab denies the generosity of my thoughts. I take the stairs to the second floor at a run.

"Alex!" Yolly calls. "Julie was asking where you were. You're late for class." Her forehead wrinkles as she studies me. "Are you not ready to go back to work?"

"I'm fine," I say. "Sorry. Heading there now."

Tariq is the first name on my list. As soon as the door to the practice room closes behind us, I freeze time without touching him, then lay my head on the table and sob.

The rest of the week drags by in a dark blur. KJ and I exchange stilted conversation when we see each other at mealtimes. At night in our room, Shannon shares breathless confessions about the progress of their romance. When she falls asleep, I lie in my bed, staring up at the dark. In the clinic, when KJ said he wanted to be with someone romantically, I assumed that person was me. I guess I was wrong. I replay our conversation over and over again in my head. Was there a point where things could have gone differently? I want to rewind the whole afternoon, tell him about my new skill less abruptly, and ask him what he meant when he said he wanted to spend more time with me. Except rewinds don't work that way. All you can do is watch an unchanging past, listening to words that no longer make any sense.

It's not until Sunday afternoon that Dr. Barnard gives me the news I've been hoping for all week: I am cleared for time work and Ross is on his way over. We have a mission.

Ross is waiting for me in the lobby. I'm so glad to see him that if Charlie weren't hovering in the guard station, I would have given him a hug. Instead I offer him an eager smile, which he matches with equal enthusiasm. He clicks on my leash, signs out the key, and we head outside.

It's a cool afternoon, the sun hiding under a swath of gray. I hurry down the steps to the squad car parked on the curb.

"What's today's mission?" I ask.

"We have two, actually," Ross says, opening the door for me.

I climb into the car. The interior smells like old burritos, the radio makes unintelligible squawks, and my left leg is crammed under the laptop hanging off the dashboard. I welcome the awkward space like an old friend. Ross gets in on the driver's side and asks me to hold out my arm.

"It's silly to make you wear this thing all the time," he says, unlocking the leash and tossing it over his shoulder into the back seat.

The maddening buzz quiets as soon as the metal band leaves my skin. I touch my wrist. The leash hasn't even been on long enough to leave a pressure mark. Ross laughs at what must be the stunned expression on my face.

"Just don't freeze while we're driving," he says. "The car will stop, but thanks to momentum, you won't."

He starts the engine with a rumble that resonates deep in the center of my chest. A second later the car leaps from the curb, nearly clipping Barnard's sedan, which is parked in the other reserved spot. I watch the Center grow smaller in the side mirror as we drive away. When we turn the corner, it disappears completely. I unroll the window. A breeze blows past me, sending the loose strands of my ponytail dancing against my cheeks.

"Where to first?" I ask.

"Remember that lead I told you about?" Ross says. "I think we're about to prove that one of the suspects Sal visited was Sikes."

"What?"

I twist around so fast the seat belt locks. Before he disappeared, Sal visited three people: a businessman with ties to known drug dealers, a male bartender suspected of money laundering, and an often-arrested female political activist who claimed that wealth should be shared by the masses. Ross had shadowed the investigations that followed, but no shred of evidence was ever found to link any of them with either Sikes's thefts or Sal's death.

I yank the strap crushing my ribs without managing to loosen it.

"I thought they'd all been cleared for Sal's murder ages ago?"

"They were, until your rewind at the butcher shop opened up a new possibility."

Ross makes one of his trademark squealing turns onto the Steel Bridge and heads toward the east side of the city. I dig my fingers into the soft seats, both to keep from lurching sideways and to stop from bouncing around like an excited four-year-old.

"Tell," I demand.

We weave through traffic while Ross fills me in. Torino's death was the first case where he could pin down the timing for a Sikes-related crime to a narrow window. Ross, who still believed one of the three was Sal's murderer, did some poking around to find out where they each were the night Torino died. He figured that even if Karl did the actual killing, there was a good chance Sikes was in contact with him during that time period, if not actually lurking nearby. The drug-dealing businessman had finally been arrested and he'd spent that night in jail. The political activist was hosting an all-night rally in Los Angeles—an event which was live-streamed on the internet.

"And I don't care who you are," Ross says, "it would have been really hard for either of those two to be simultaneously tracking their hired killer. But Matt Thompson, our sketchy bartender, spent most of the night at his bar—in a back office, near an emergency exit, where he worked alone."

"How'd you find that out?"

"An informant. The guy's been keeping an eye on Mr. Thompson for me and he happened to be at the bar that night."

I clap my hands together.

"So that's where we're going."

"Yep. I'm going to need you and your very special skills so we can figure out for sure if we're onto the right guy."

I admire my leashless wrist. This case needs me. Choosing to take the new medicine was worth the costs.

"It's great that Chief is letting you take the lead on this one."

"He isn't," Ross says. "Technically, we only have one mission: the rewind of an armed robbery. We'll head there next."

A vague unease curdles my excitement. I look at Ross. He's focused on the traffic outside, frowning as he swerves around a slow-moving truck.

"What about my tracker?" I ask. "If anybody is watching, they'll know we aren't going to the right place."

"Don't worry. Matt's bar is on the way."

I press my forehead against the window and watch the city flashing past me: used-car lot, taco restaurant, furniture store. People fill the vehicles and sidewalks around us, vulnerable people who would be safer if Sikes were behind bars. And I can help put him there. I straighten up. This work is important. What's wrong with a small lie if it leads to the right results?

Ross pulls the car over on a side street not far from the river. It's a light industrial part of town, full of warehouses and showrooms selling things like marble countertops and plumbing supplies. The building in front of us has blank, windowless walls. On the opposite side of the street, two large semis are backed into loading docks.

"Where's the bar?" I ask.

"A couple blocks away." Ross cranes his neck to peer up and down the street. There's no one in sight.

"I thought we'd freeze here where no one will see us disappear."

I put my hand on his wrist. Ross checks once more that no one can see us, then nods. I reach for the time strands and pull the world to a standstill.

We climb from the car. My stomach is in knots, with anticipation more than worry. My eagerness makes Ross's usual hurried stride feel like a snail's crawl. We wind our way through frozen cars as we cross MLK Boulevard, then up another block and a half. Ross stops. On our left is a four-story brick apartment building. There are two street-level commercial tenants: a secondhand clothing store and a bar called Tom's.

"This is it?" I ask.

Ross nods. I stare up at the façade. The bricks show signs of wear, and the trim on the upper windows cries out for a fresh coat of paint. The bar itself has tinted windows, the interior further obscured by neon twisted into beer logos. The enthusiasm boiling inside me reduces to a low simmer. This building looks way more like some place I might have visited on a vice mission than the luxury digs of a millionaire thief.

"Are you sure? It's so . . . plain."

"What better cover? Plus, a cash business like a bar is a great way to wash stolen money."

Ross jiggles the door handle. It's locked. I lean against the window, cupping my hands around my face to peer inside. A forest of wood meets my searching eyes. The chairs have all been flipped up on the tables, presumably to more easily clean the floors.

"They're closed."

Ross winks at me.

"Let me show you a little unofficial police tool." He digs in his pocket and pulls out something I think is an army knife until he flips the thing open and shows me a pair of thin metal sticks. I step back in surprise.

"You're going to pick the lock?"

"Someone will notice if we break a window."

My laugh sounds hollow. Ross slips on thin gloves, handing a second pair to me, then drops to his knees in front of the door. Automatically, I look to see if anyone is watching. A woman hovers about a block away, arms sunk in her coat pockets, eyes blindly fixed somewhere over my shoulder.

I yank on the end of my ponytail.

"Isn't this illegal? We won't be able to use the evidence if we find any."

"All we're doing today is seeing if my hunch is right. If it is, I'll get a warrant and come back officially." Ross glances up at me. "You're not worried about this are you?"

I shrug.

"Alex, we're talking about Sikes. The guy who murdered Sal in cold blood. He doesn't deserve any rights."

I look down at the pick dangling from Ross's hand. Jack would think this whole situation was hilarious, a thought that almost makes me smile until I replace Jack's face with KJ's. KJ would not think this was a fun game. KJ would most definitely disapprove. Then again,

KJ has never understood the importance of cracking a case. Plus, he's probably, more like definitely, been making out with Shannon every chance he gets, so he's hardly the perfect rule follower anymore either.

"He's the bad guy," I say to Ross. "We're the good guys."

Ross grins and motions me closer. "Why don't you come down here where you can see. This is a trick I think you'll find useful."

I kneel on the hard concrete and watch while Ross sticks a metal rod into the key slot. He moves confidently, all the while describing what he's doing in careful detail: a tension wrench to slightly turn the lock, a pick to feel for the pins, and then some wiggling of the pick until each tumbler raises enough to make the shear line on the pins match up. It doesn't take very long. In less than a minute, we're inside.

Shadows cloak the bar's interior. The air carries the bitter stench of spilled beer and a lingering whiff of deep fry oil. When I step inside, I can feel a slight suck on my shoes from the sticky floor. I guess I was wrong about the chairs.

Ross relocks the door then heads straight for the back, skirting the polished bar to enter a short hallway. To our left is a small kitchen, to the right are three closed doors labeled *Guys*, *Dames*, and *Office*. Another door at the end reads *Emergency Exit*. Ross wiggles the unmoving knob on the office door.

"You want to try out the pick?" Ross says.

"Right now?" Even though time is frozen, I can't help checking over my shoulder. Ever since I thought of him, KJ's frowning face has been hovering in the corner of my brain. *Go away*, I tell his image. *It's just frozen time.* Imaginary KJ looks about as understanding as he did the day I told him Ross was faking my chronotin readings.

"Sure," I say to Ross, who places the pick in my hands, covering my gloved fingers with his own as he moves them through the steps to unlock the door. I'm surprised by how easy it is. A few twists with the metal tools and the door swings open.

Unlike the grimy bar, Matt's office is almost antiseptically clean. The walls are painted a bright white that gleams under a pale shaft streaming from a skylight. The desk is made of blond wood, its surface bare except for a large computer screen, a cup full of matching silver pens, and a neat stack of files in a wire basket. Nearby are a bookcase, a row of wooden filing cabinets, and a large safe.

"If Matt is who we think he is," Ross says, "he's probably using the bar to launder money, so the first thing we need to do is get his passwords so we can look up his accounts. Why don't you start a rewind."

He walks around the desk until he's facing the computer monitor. I run a finger along the outer edge of the doorframe. Despite its neatness, there's something creepy about this room, like we've stepped into one of those tombs that rain curses on excavators.

"Are you sure a rewind will work? What if the change in my freezes affects the rewinds, too?"

"It will be fine, don't worry. Even *you* can't change the past."

I push away thoughts of KJ and curses, and walk toward Ross.

"How far back do I need to go?"

"Just one day. I talked to a waitress who works here. Matt does the books on Saturdays, so he'll be checking account balances then."

Time slides back smoothly once I get the rewind started. I pull quickly at first, whipping us through Sunday morning and into the backward murmurs from Saturday night. Strains of disjointed music drift in from the bar along with unintelligible voices and the clatter of dishes in the kitchen. The clock on the wall shows a little after 9:00 p.m. when the office door opens and a man backs in. I slow the rewind.

"Is that Matt Thompson?" I ask.

Ross nods. Dim, rewound light further brightens the space. The memory of Matt sits down at the desk. I study him hungrily. I realize I've built Sikes up into a dashing figure, a movie version of a worthy adversary. If this man really is him, he's disappointingly normal looking. Midforties, shorter than Ross—maybe a couple inches under six feet—with brown hair clipped over his ears. His face is clean-shaven. He's thin and wears skinny jeans, cowboy boots, and a black T-shirt with a stylized image of an electric guitar printed on the front. The only thing that makes him look rich is a thick gold watch clamped to his left wrist.

Matt settles in to work, intermittently tapping the keyboard and shuffling papers. A couple of times he picks up his phone and engages in a garbled conversation. Ross gestures at me to speed things up. Uncounted minutes slip by as the clock winds back to 7:30, 7:00—

"Stop!" Ross calls. I grab the strands up tight. Ross takes a pen out of the cup on Matt's desk and pulls a mostly blank sheet of paper from the recycle bin.

"OK," he says, "start again, but really slowly."

I move to stand beside him and let the seconds seep past me. Ross's eyes are glued to Matt's fingers as they move over the keyboard. The screen in front of him is pale blue and shows a white sign-in box filled with a string of black dots.

"Four," Ross says, jotting the number down as one of the dots disappears.

"No," I correct him. "It's a dollar sign, look at his pinkie."

"Good catch. OK, so it's: $-U-O-!-V-R-E-p-m-1"

Matt lifts his hands and shakes the computer mouse. The screen goes black. Ross studies the sheet in his hand. A second later, he lifts his head with a smile.

"Impervious," he says.

I accelerate the rewind again. Matt leaves the room for a while, then comes back. I speed up and slow down on Ross's command, occasionally cranking time to a crawl so Ross can copy down more passwords or squint at the faded letters in an email. At 5:30, Matt stands up as another man, this one wearing a black apron folded at his waist, backs into the office. They chat together and Matt kneels down to open the safe, replacing a stack of bills the other guy hands him. Ross makes careful note of the combination when Matt closes the safe's door.

A headache worms its way into my brain, gentler than the throbbing pain that announces the sickness, but still uncomfortable.

"Mr. Ross?" I say. "If we're going to have to do a second rewind after this . . ."

"Is it getting hard?" he asks, capping the pen. "Thanks for warning me. We have enough for now, you can let time go for a bit."

I release the strands, half-expecting the dizzy swing that would return us to Ross's parked car. Instead, we sink into dimness as the rewound light in the office winks out. Ross laughs. He brushes past me and lights up the room for real with a touch of the wall switch.

"Now for the good part," he says. He's radiating so much energy it makes the small room feel even smaller. My own heart rate speeds up in response.

"What can I do?" I ask.

Ross spins slowly, taking in the tidy space.

"Computer, file cabinets, that—" he points to a door I hadn't noticed before, tucked in a corner behind the desk, "—probably has office supplies. How about you start with that beauty," he points at the safe, "and I'll tackle the computer."

Ross hands me his note with the combination and tells me to

look for bank statements, appointment books, or anything that might link Matt to one of the Sikes robberies. I turn the numbers slowly, running through them twice because the first time I forget they're reversed. The door is thick and very heavy. Inside, there are stacks of paper money, tucked into pouches by denomination, with a separate one for coins. I move them aside, setting them out very carefully on the floor in the same pattern so I can return them correctly. Underneath is a pile of folders. I open them one after the other, a process that goes slowly since my gloves make it hard to separate the pages. One holds the deed to the bar, and another seems to be insurance certificates. There's a whole stack of tax returns, which I hand over to Ross. He glances at them, then keeps tapping away on the computer, occasionally printing a page or two on a softly humming printer set on top of the bookcase.

The scream of a siren makes its way into the office. My hands tighten on the folder I'm holding. The siren grows louder. I stare out into the dark hall. I don't realize I'm holding my breath until the noise starts to fade.

"We should go," I tell Ross. "It's two forty-five. We've already been here for fifteen minutes of real time."

"One more sec," Ross says, "I just want to follow this thread."

I'm nearing the end of the files. At the bottom is a final folder, bigger than the others, beige and somewhat wrinkled. The label on the front says *Receipt Copies 2012* in smudgy handwriting. I unclasp the top and tip the contents into my hand. A sheet of canvas slides down, heavy and bright with color. It's not a receipt.

"Mr. Ross?" The canvas trembles in my fingers. "I think I found something."

He must hear the shock in my voice because he's beside me in seconds. I hand it over. It's a painting, unframed, the vase of sunflowers familiar to anyone who knows Vincent Van Gogh. Or Sikes, who was suspected of stealing it from the Portland Art Museum two years ago.

"It's him," I whisper. "Matt Thompson is Sikes."

Ross touches the painting with a reverent finger.

"Sure looks like it."

Every nerve in my body lights up. I feel like I've just drunk ten cups of coffee. My body is electric and my lips can't stop smiling.

"We found Sikes!" I throw my arms in the air, wiggling my whole body in a crazy happy-dance next to the filing cabinet. "*We* did," I shout. "You and me."

Ross laughs.

"We sure did." He salutes me with a high five, slapping my open palm with enough force to make it tingle. His eyes are shining.

"We're unbeatable together, Alex. The perfect partnership."

I laugh, a bark of pure joy that bounces off the plain white walls. Ross takes the envelope from my hand and very carefully slides the painting back inside.

"Why would he keep that?" I ask.

"I don't know," Ross says. "Too well-known to fence? As a souvenir, maybe? This *is* the guy who chose *impervious* as his password."

"Is it enough for you to make an arrest?"

"It certainly makes a strong case for him as a thief," Ross says. "Not necessarily as a murderer. And I'm starting to think there might be a twist there. In the email I was reading it sounds like . . ."

His body stiffens. I don't have to ask why because I've heard it too. Someone just opened the bar's front door.

12

"QUICK," ROSS HISSES, "FREEZE."

I rip the gloves from my hands, reaching for his arm at the same instant I snatch up the time strands. The paper I just picked up flutters to the ground as time slams to a halt.

"Let's go," I say.

Ross turns toward the computer screen.

"Wait," he says. "I want to read the rest of that email chain."

"You can't scroll through email in frozen time. There's no electricity."

"I know that." He crosses to the desk. "But I think the information in it is critical. I only need five more minutes."

I slide my gloves back on. The thin leather sticks against my sweaty palms.

"Whoever is outside will be here in two."

Ross shakes the useless mouse. He's staring at the computer like he's trying to will it into giving up its secrets. I twist my fingers together to push the gloves more firmly over my hands. The new freeze is making my headache worse.

"Alex." Ross looks at me, his expression pleading. "Do you think you could stall him?"

"Stall Sikes?" Jason Torino's limp body flashes before my eyes, followed by the imagined corpse of Sal floating in the green waters of the Willamette. I shudder.

"I . . . I'm not a good liar. What if he suspects something?"

"I wouldn't ask if it weren't important. Just try. If it doesn't work, freeze time and we'll get out of here. I promise."

Everything in my gut tells me to run. Our being here is completely illegal. Ross will lose his job if he gets caught. I'll probably get pulled from time work. Any evidence we found about Sikes will be instantly disallowed. On the other hand . . . I press my fingers together, stretching out the taut muscles. We've come so far. Who knows if we'll get this chance again? As I know all too well, life is short.

"OK," I say, starting to put the safe's contents back in place, "let me just think of a way to distract him."

Ten minutes later I'm outside, sheltered behind a car a few feet from Tom's Bar. I've covered my regulation CIC top with a green Oregon Ducks sweatshirt I borrowed from the secondhand store next to the bar, and I'm holding a clipboard I found on a shelf in the back room. Matt is standing at the bar's entrance. He's holding a cup of coffee in one hand and is leaning into the door, which he's pushed open about six inches. A set of keys dangles from his fingers. I check my surroundings one more time, taking careful note of the windows on both sides of the street. As far as I can tell, no one is watching. I straighten the clipboard and take a deep breath. Time moves forward. The keys in Matt's hand jingle. I stand up.

"Mr. Thompson?"

Matt turns around. Or Sikes does. My brain can't quite hold both thoughts at the same time. This is the man who's eluded capture for a decade. The man who's killed to keep his secret. I shake my head. For right now, I'd rather think of him as plain old Matt.

"Hi." I hope he doesn't notice my hands are trembling. "I'm Jane Maxwell, a student at Grant High School. Could I have a few minutes of your time?"

Matt hesitates. Except for the denseness of his body, he looks exactly like he did in the rewind. Same tidy hair and tight jeans. Today, he's swapped the T-shirt for a leather jacket, beneath which I can see the collar of a plaid button-down. For a dangerous criminal, he's disappointingly bland.

"I'm actually kind of busy," he says, pushing the door open wider.

"Wait!" I scramble over the sidewalk to reach him. "Please? I'll be quick."

Matt frowns. "What's this about?"

"I was hoping you'd agree to a short interview. I'm taking a journalism class and we're writing a piece about revitalizing inner Southeast neighborhoods. As a business owner, your opinions would be really helpful."

The speech rolls off my tongue so fast it's nearly unintelligible. I clutch the clipboard against my chest. Even a normal girl would feel nervous approaching a stranger on the street, wouldn't she?

"Sounds interesting." Matt takes a step inside. "But like I said, I'm busy. Maybe some other day."

My heartbeat ratchets up a notch. There's no way Ross has had time to read more than a few sentences. I consider shouting *I know who you are* but decide that might end badly.

"Another day would work." I push myself forward, catching the door before it can close against me. "Could we schedule a time now? The guy down the street said your bar really adds to the neighborhood's ambiance."

I can tell he's waffling. He's jingling his keys and focusing over my head, probably conjuring a list of possible excuses. I channel Shannon and open my eyes really wide, going for an earnest, innocent look.

"All right," he sighs. "Let me check my calendar."

He moves further inside. For a moment I'm afraid his calendar is in his office, but he only goes as far as the bar, setting down his coffee and taking a cell phone from his pocket.

"I really appreciate this," I say, tripping over the doorstep in my rush to follow him. Matt starts offering times, and I make a pretense of consulting a blank sheet of paper on my clipboard to check my own "schedule." I stretch out our negotiation as long as I dare without annoying him, then sneak a glance at the clock over the bar. How is it possible only two minutes have passed? It's like my skills have morphed from freezing time to just slowing it down.

Matt puts away his phone and picks up his belongings.

"Well, Jane, I guess I'll see you on Wednesday."

He gives me a you-can-go-now look that I pretend not to recognize. Instead I turn my head in an ostentatious study of the room around us.

"This is a really cool bar," I gush.

"Thanks."

He waits for me to leave. I glance at the door and realize I've made a massive tactical error. Panic flutters in my chest. Matt can reach his office in about three seconds. I, however, have to leave the bar, then find somewhere to hide before I can freeze time. By then he will have his office door open and Ross will be exposed. My chest squeezes so hard it hurts. Would he kill Ross on the spot?

I search the bar for anything I can use to lure Matt away from the hall. Besides the stacked chairs there's not much here. A wall of liquor lined up on shelves behind the bar. Two video poker games stuffed in a corner. The unlit neon cluttering the windows. Matt flicks on a light in the back hallway. The flash reflects against something on the wall at the far end of the bar. It's something in a frame, glassed in. I lunge toward it.

"Mr. Thompson?"

"What?"

He's definitely annoyed now. I scurry across the room, trying to think of anything I know about art that I can use to express my fascination with this discovered treasure.

"It's your picture. Can you tell me something about it? It's so . . ."

I reach the wall. The object is not a work of art. It's a framed certificate from the fire marshal. My death grip on the clipboard rams the wood into my palm. I catch a distant humming sound. The engine of a passing car? Or the whir of illicit printing? I turn around. Matt's eyes are narrowed.

"I think it's time for you to leave," he says.

I walk slowly, circling the chairs in the longest route I can manage to reach the door. Matt watches me without moving one step farther from his office. His suspicion worries me less than the fact I don't know how to protect Ross. As soon as I reach the front door Matt will head into his office. Sweat beads my upper lip. Through the neon-crusted windows I can see that the street, so conveniently empty when I entered the bar, now hosts a line of cars, all stopped dead while they wait out the light on the corner. The woman in the car closest to the bar is only a few feet away. She'll see me if I freeze time right outside the bar.

Matt clears his throat. I inch another step toward the door. Sikes wouldn't kill Ross immediately, would he? I can run and hide. Freeze time and come back for him. No one would believe Matt if he said Ross just disappeared. Except Sikes would know Ross was onto him after that. He'd hunt him down, just like he did to Sal . . . My toe drags across the floor, and the nasty beer slime catches the tip of my sneaker. I snatch at a chair to keep from falling when an idea explodes fully formed into my brain. Quick as thought, I lean toward my off-balance foot.

"Oops," I say, and let myself crumple, stopping time the instant I hit the ground.

The concrete floor is hard and dirty and smelly. A wad of long-abandoned gum lies by my cheek, its surface mashed so flat it's barely distinguishable from the dark floor. Moving my body as little as possible, I scout my surroundings. Matt is completely blocked by the tall bar and, from this angle, I can't see the cars at all.

I scramble to my feet and head to the office. My whole body is shaking, both my knees hurt from my fall, and everything about me feels dirty. I want to go back to the Center, hear the click of the many locks, then climb into the shower and scrub myself clean.

Matt takes up half the hallway. I press myself against the wall in order to slide past without touching him. The office door opens under my hand, revealing Ross standing at the copy machine, caught in the act of lifting a small stack of freshly printed sheets. I wrap my hand around his bare wrist, releasing the time strands for the instant it takes to bring him into a new freeze with me.

"We have to go," I say, even before he's registered my presence.

"Alex!" He holds up the papers in his hand and gives me a brilliant smile. "I found it."

I pull on his arm. Even in frozen time, the knowledge that Matt is standing only a few feet away makes me want to throw up.

"Tell me later. Let's *go.*"

Ross waves the sheets at me, making the crisp paper snap loudly in the quiet room.

"I have it, Alex," he says. "I have him."

I tamp down my panic enough to focus on the man standing in front of me. His smile carries enough wattage to light the room. It's not happiness oozing out of him so much as it is triumph. My hand slips from his arm.

"You found more evidence Matt Thompson is Sikes?"

Ross shakes his head. "Sikes isn't the one we're looking for anymore."

The room tilts, everything seems out of focus. I steady myself against the bookcase.

"He's not?"

Ross's blue eyes shine in the frozen room, like chips of ice within the flatness of a painting.

"Matt has a partner. I found the name of the man who killed Sal."

13

"A PARTNER?" I ECHO. "I THOUGHT SIKES WORKED alone."

"So did I." Ross shoves the printed sheets into his pocket. "This changes everything."

He looks at me. He's wearing the expression of someone who just realized they're holding a winning lottery ticket, stunned and only half-believing. He shakes his head.

"Let's get out of here," he says. "We can talk in the car."

Minutes later, Ross and I are zooming toward our "real" mission. I've said my hasty good-byes to Matt and returned the purloined clothing, and Ross has my leash set on the console between us so I can snap it back on as soon as we near our destination. Ross also handed me one of those caffeine-packed energy drinks. It tastes as nasty as the grape-flavored cough medicine Yolly pours down our throats when we get the sniffles, but I chug some anyway.

"So what did you find?" I ask him.

"A whole string of emails between Matt and a guy named Austin Shea. They're not completely explicit, but reading between the lines it's pretty clear what they're plotting. Plus, all their communication lines up with known robberies: dates, locations, everything."

"And the murders?"

"I couldn't scroll back far enough to get to Sal's death, but the one about Torino was pretty clear. The day Jason died, there's an email from Matt to Austin. It's only two words: Franz Meats."

"I thought Karl Wagner killed Torino?"

Ross shrugs. "Hired thug. Our guys didn't want to get their hands dirty."

We turn onto the highway. Ross flicks his flashers on, and the cars in front of us melt out of our way. "It makes sense when you think about it," he says. "One guy with a vision, another who can make it happen."

"Which one is Matt?" I ask.

"Oh, he's Sikes, all right. He's the mastermind. But he couldn't do any of it without Shea."

I unroll the window, leaning my face into the rushing air. Its wildness fills the space left by my receding fear. We did it.

"There's enough evidence in the room to prove Matt is Sikes," I say, "so if you get a search warrant . . ."

"No." Ross shakes his head. "Sikes doesn't matter right now. It's Shea we have to get."

My hair is tangling into a hopeless mess. I pull my face back inside, pushing the wind-whipped strands out of my eyes.

"But I thought . . ."

"Sikes is a thief. Shea is a killer. There may be enough evidence in there to nail Sikes, but not Shea. And he's dangerous. If we arrest Matt before we deal with him, they could both slip through our fingers." Ross swerves around a car dawdling in the fast lane. "You and I are going to have to go out on another mission. Soon. We have to stop Austin Shea."

I smile out the window. Another mission means another day like this one: Ross and I working as partners to solve the biggest case in city history. Will they still let us work together if Ross becomes chief of police? Chief Carson Ross. I roll the name around on my tongue, along with the icky caffeine-fueled dreck. Everything I ever dreamed about suddenly feels within reach. Even Ross's medicine is working, I'm certain of it. I feel perfectly healthy. Strong. We'll catch Sikes and Shea *and* advance science. Dr. Kroger will have to tweak the medicine so everyone doesn't get this side effect, but if it works to extend spinner lives, everything I hid from the Center—and KJ—will be justified. The rushing wind fills my ears with a roaring that sounds like applause.

The car careens to the right as we exit the freeway, and Ross blasts his siren so we can blow through a red light. I toss back the last of the energy drink. Revolting flavor aside, it has made my headache fade enough that I'm not dreading another rewind. I drop the bottle on the floor and snap my leash back on just as Ross pulls in behind two other police cars parked in front of a 7-Eleven.

"Sorry we're late," Ross says, stepping out onto the asphalt. "I thought it would be faster to take surface streets. Big mistake."

Yolly tracks me down the next day in the cafeteria where KJ, Shannon, Yuki, and I are eating lunch, to tell me that Barnard has approved a day pass for me.

"It's for today, and you can take the friend of your choice," she says. "Mr. Ross requested it, because you've worked so hard lately."

I swallow the bite of my sandwich so suddenly it hurts my throat. "A pass? Really?"

Yolly beams at me. Shannon lets out a squeal.

"I'm so jealous. I haven't been out for like three months."

"That's 'cause last time we were half an hour late getting back," Yuki reminds her. I notice she is tactfully not mentioning that they were late because the two of them were talking with some boys in a coffee shop.

"I assume you're taking KJ," Shannon says, "and not your very favorite roommate?"

I look over at KJ. Ever since I got home yesterday, I've been hoping for an opportunity to talk to him. Yesterday's success has made me so happy that I'm eager to heal the rift between us. This pass is the perfect chance.

"What do you think?" I ask KJ.

He's focused on his fruit salad, trying to impale a lone grape lost in a sea of melon chunks, and for a split second I'm afraid he's going to refuse, but instead he raises his head and says, "Sure."

A huge grin erupts over my face. The edges of KJ's mouth twitch upwards.

"All right," Yolly says. "I'll let Charlie know. You'll be excused at twelve thirty and have exactly two hours."

"You don't care that she's going out with your boyfriend?" Yuki asks Shannon, after Yolly shuffles off. Her voice is light, teasing, but I feel the color rise in my cheeks. Shannon tosses her head.

"Worry about those two?" She laughs. "They're like brother and sister."

KJ drops his eyes and goes back to picking at his salad with great concentration.

Shannon leans her head on his shoulder. "Will you bring me back a present?"

"Guess it depends where Alex wants to go," he mumbles around a mouthful of fruit.

Yuki spends the rest of our half-hour lunch telling us all the best stores at the downtown mall. I half-listen. KJ and I usually spend our time just walking around. I love feeling like one anonymous person among thousands cramming the streets. Yuki rolls her eyes when I tell her this. Shannon claims the pass is wasted on me, though she seems consoled when I promise to help KJ find her a gift.

At 12:15, people start trickling out of the cafeteria, heading to their afternoon activities. Five minutes later, KJ and I are the only ones left. I wipe my hands with a paper napkin, cleaning both sides of each finger with studious attention. I can't remember ever being in the cafeteria practically alone, or if I have, I never noticed how cavernous it is. KJ stabs his fork repeatedly into a stray piece of melon. I watch him, trying to think of something appropriately casual—or maybe witty?—to say. Nothing comes to mind. Over our heads, the wall clock ticks softly as the second hand makes its way around the dial.

KJ clears his throat. "We should go," he says.

"Yeah," I say, standing so quickly my thigh collides with the edge of the table. We busy ourselves scraping our plates into the compost before heading for the stairs. KJ takes them two at a time, leaving me to scramble to keep up.

Charlie fills in the sign-out book and attaches our leashes. I find the routine comforting. I'm still panting a little, both because of our brisk stair climb and because my chest feels like it's wrapped in a straitjacket. Maybe I should have taken Shannon after all. It would make the day a lot more relaxing.

Outside, it's a typical Portland fall afternoon, wet without actually raining. The skies are gray, and the air smells like damp concrete. A protester stands on the steps holding a placard that reads *My times are in Your hand (Psalms 31:15).* When he sees the Center door open, he lowers his sign like a shield. Charlie runs interference by telling the guy to beat it before KJ and I walk past. We turn the corner, jackets covering our leashed wrists, and blend into the rest of the Monday afternoon crowd.

Silence builds between us, as tangible as the moisture seeping into our clothes. My expectations for our afternoon, so high when Yolly offered the passes, sink to match the dreary weather. I've ruined our friendship. KJ will never forgive me for all the lies I told him plus being so mean that day in the clinic. He only said he'd come with me because he would never be rude to a dying girl in front of her friends. He'd rather be back at the Center with Shannon.

I'm so sunk in my own head I don't even notice KJ has stopped in front of me until I hit my forehead against his chest.

"I have to tell you this," he says.

I step back and face him. His lips are pursed, eyes darting everywhere except at me. I slip my hands in my pockets, tightening my fingers into fists. This is it. The point where he tells me he never wants to hang out with me again.

"I'm sorry about the other day," KJ says. "You were right—it's your choice what you do with your life. If you want to track down Sikes, that's OK. I just want us to be friends again."

The gray afternoon grows brighter. KJ is finally meeting my eyes. His are dark, as familiar to me as my own, but the expression filling them is brand new. There's pain there, and regret. For an instant, I imagine reaching out, placing my bare fingers against his neck, the two of us escaping into a freeze, that time that doesn't really exist.

KJ holds out his hand. "Friends?" he asks.

I brush hair off my damp forehead, forcing the fantasy back down where it belongs, deep in the land of lost opportunities and impossible dreams.

"Friends," I agree, taking his hand.

KJ tightens his fingers, then playfully twists my arm until he's pulled it behind my back.

"Then, as your friend, I demand that we go to Powell's Bookstore."

The unexpected move makes me laugh, which is probably why he's doing it. I squirm from his grasp and force myself to match his casual tone.

"OK, OK, you win," I say, as we start down the sidewalk again. "But why Powell's?"

"I think we need to do some research."

"Most people go to libraries to do research."

"Powell's is closer. And they have more books."

My sneaker catches on a crack in the pavement. I know KJ well enough to guess what he's after: he wants to look up information about time sickness and my new "rare" condition. My heart starts pumping much faster than our walk deserves.

KJ frowns at me. "Come on, Alex, don't you want to know?"

"I do. I'm just . . ." I adjust the leash through my jacket's sleeve. "Scared. It's like Jack said, if you knew someone could tell you when you're going to die, would you want to know?"

KJ shakes his head.

"It's not like that at all. This is a disease. The more we know, the better we can fight it. Like, if we only did short freezes, would we live longer than if we held long ones? Or maybe we should be freezing all the time, that the sickness hits when we're not using our skills and all that time energy gets bottled up inside somehow."

His speech is so classic KJ—the logical thinker searching for a strategy to make the situation better—that I have to smile.

"You'd think Dr. Barnard would already know that stuff."

"He might not care. I mean, yeah, he monitors our chronotin levels to keep us alive, but what difference does it make to him if we die a couple months early?"

I wrap a strand of my hair around my finger. KJ is asking good questions, but my current state of health is complicated by the medication Ross is giving me—the one I promised I wouldn't talk about. I cast a sidelong look at KJ. The sight of him loping along beside me fills me with a happiness that's almost as potent as catching Sikes. I don't want to lose him again. He was so upset that I'm letting Ross hide my blood tests, he might give up on me completely if I tell him about the meds.

I push the secret aside, and instead share with KJ what I can. In a rush, I pour out everything I learned from my investigation into the clinic files: Calvin's strange chronotin readings, the varying "normal" ranges each of us seems to have, even the hints Jack shared that Dr. Barnard might be using us for his own research. By the time we reach Powell's, KJ's forehead is laced with frown lines. I, however, am feeling lighter than I have in days.

Powell's, Portland's famous three-story, full-city-block bookstore, welcomes us into its bright warmth. The usual eclectic mix of people wanders the aisles, eyes slightly glazed as they scan the overstuffed twelve-foot shelves. The air carries the musk of ink and old paper mixed with the scent of coffee drifting from the in-store café.

KJ marches off through the color-coded rooms, past the green of new arrivals and up the stairs into purple, home to the medical books. I follow him as he moves down an aisle to stop squarely in front of the section with books about spinners. I scan the row from left to right. The books in the health section aren't as popular as fiction, and at the moment there's no one here. I still lower my voice.

"What are we looking for?"

"Chronotin levels," KJ says, handing me a particularly dense looking medical textbook. "What's normal, what isn't, and any mention of rare mutations."

I flip over the volume in my hands. It's a hardback, dark blue, with the title printed in gold. *Translational Research Methods for Chronotin Usage: A Focus on Early Phase Clinical Studies.* KJ slides another book from the shelf. It's thinner than mine, though with an equally mind-numbing title: *Chronotin Levels in Adolescence.* We both sit on the floor and start reading.

Time crawls by, the minutes, and my frustration, piling up with the books stacked around us. We share everything we can find, but between our lack of scientific training and the density of the texts, we're not getting much. At 1:45, I toss *Aclisote: A Treatise on Chronotin Suppression* onto the floor and roll my shoulders.

"Anything new?" KJ asks.

I shake my head. "Just more of the same. Higher chronotin levels—which they're saying is anything that averages over 170—equates with earlier death rates, as well as erratic behavior and more intense bouts of time sickness."

"This one says the opposite." KJ holds up the book in his hands. "These guys did a study that showed a correlation between time sickness and deeply suppressed levels of chronotin."

"What's a suppressed level?" I ask.

"Under 150."

I kick at one of the abandoned medical texts, sending the heavy tome skittering across the floor.

"Calvin's levels were both too high *and* too low," I say. "So which one triggered his illness? Did Barnard mean for Calvin's chronotin levels to drop so dramatically when he raised his Aclisote? Or did he set it up on purpose as some kind of test?"

"Maybe, once you get sick, the way you react to Aclisote isn't predictable. I read in a science journal once about—"

"Shhh," I say, holding up my hand. There's a muffled announcement winding down from an overhead speaker.

. . . please come to the customer service desk in the gold room. You have a message.

"What?" KJ asks.

"I think they said my name."

KJ tips his head, but the intercom has stopped squawking.

"Couldn't be," he says. "No one knows we're here."

I touch the back of my neck, brushing my fingers across the tiny bump that marks the tracker.

"The Sick does," I say. "Something important must have come up."

I'm on my feet, books tumbling from my lap. The only reason I can think that the Center would call me is that Ross needs me on a mission. *The* mission.

"I'll just go check," I say. KJ starts to protest but I scurry away before he manages a question. The peace between us still feels tenuous; I don't want to mess it up by mentioning missions unless I have to.

The customer service desk is at the end of a wall of books. The man sitting at it has greasy hair and an intricate dragon tattoo that snakes up his arm and under the sleeve of his black T-shirt.

"Hi." I pull on my ponytail. "I'm Alexandra Manning. Did you page me?"

The man peers up at me from under his bangs, eyes wary.

"Are you a spinner?" he asks.

I jump. "What?"

"The guy said he was calling from the CIC." Tattoo Man's mouth twists. "They don't let spinners just run around freely do they?"

I'm tempted to tell him spinners wander the city all the time but my irritation is dampened by fear he'll make a scene. I wrap my hand around the leash on my left wrist. The rain jacket covering it feels like flimsy coverage.

"No," I say. "I . . . work there. Volunteer. It's a school project."

The man leans forward. "Really? Isn't it creepy?"

"Not really." I don't smile. "What's the message?"

He rummages through some papers scattered on his desk and hands me a hot-pink sticky note with a phone number scrawled on it. I don't recognize it, which isn't surprising. I don't know anyone's phone number.

"Did the caller say who he was?" I ask.

Tattoo Man shrugs. "He just said it was important." He nods at a phone set on the edge of the counter. "You can use that if you need to."

I dial quickly.

"Crime Investigation Center," a voice answers. I nearly drop the phone.

"Jack?"

"Hey, Alex. You got my message."

"What's going on?" I turn my body away from Tattoo Man and lower my voice. "Does Ross need me?"

"Ross? No, Barnard does. His computer crashed and he wants KJ back at the Sick ASAP."

"We have to leave now? But we have leave for another forty-five minutes."

"KJ has to go back now. You have to run an errand for Dr. B."

"By myself?" I glance over my shoulder. Tattoo Man is tapping something into a laptop on the desk but by the slow way his fingers are moving I'm pretty sure he's mostly listening to my conversation. I stretch the phone as far as I can and wrap my hand around the mouthpiece.

"We're not allowed," I whisper.

"You are when the good doctor tells you to. He sends me out on errands by myself all the time."

"He does?" I say, forgetting to keep my voice down.

Tattoo Man gives up his pretense. He props his chin in his hands, head swiveled in my direction. I scowl at him.

"Hey," Jack says, "I don't make the rules, I just follow them."

"No, you don't," I snap into the receiver. Jack laughs.

"True," he says. "But you do, and if you come back without doing his errand, Dr. B will be pissed."

Tattoo Man's eyes narrow. I try and think what my side of the conversation sounds like—have I said anything that would make him suspect I'm a spinner?

"What does he want me to do?" I ask Jack.

"A guy named James Sidell called to say he has a plaque ready for tonight's agent meeting. It's for Ross for that bomb scare thing you guys rewound the other day. Dr. B didn't know anyone had ordered it and he doesn't have time to pick it up, so he wants you to go get it."

My hand tightens around the phone. This whole story is so strange it makes me wonder if something else is going on. Did Ross arrange for me to have a pass as a cover so we could go out on another secret mission together? He could have called in the plaque order himself so we'd have a place to meet.

"Hello?" Jack's voice jolts me back to my surroundings. "You still there?"

"Yeah, sorry." I grab a pen from the counter. "Where do I go?"

I scribble the address on the bottom of the sticky note and slip it in my pocket. I've just hung up when KJ emerges from a nearby aisle.

"So you really did have a message?" he asks.

Tattoo Man looks expectant. I drag KJ away from the counter before repeating my conversation with Jack, without adding my suspicion that it's all a cover. It will be better if KJ goes back without knowing anything. KJ's eyebrows climb his forehead as I talk, rising until they disappear under his floppy bangs.

"Barnard wants us to separate?" he asks.

"Jack says Barnard sends him out alone all the time."

"Are you sure he's not just messing with you?"

"I don't know." I replay the phone call in my head. I can't really remember the subtleties of Jack's tone. I'd been so distracted, first by Tattoo Man and then by my brain wave, that I'd mostly been thinking about how quickly I could hang up.

"He sounded serious," I decide. "I mean, serious for Jack."

KJ looks skeptical.

"Something about this feels off," he says. "Maybe I should go with you."

I shake my head. I can hardly bring KJ along if it turns out to be a mission—not when I promised Ross I wouldn't tell anyone about my new skills.

"I'll be fine," I say. "Besides, Jack said Barnard's freaking out about his computer. Go do your magic and maybe he'll reward you with another pass. We'll need it if we want to do more research."

KJ argues with me all the way through the store. I finally get rid of him by reminding him he has to buy Shannon a present. We part ways in the orange room—me heading out to the street, KJ scanning the store for something he can bring back. I feel bad about not telling him everything, but the glimmer of guilt is buried under my excitement at the possibility of getting closer to Sikes.

The weather has deteriorated from damp to drizzly. Even though my walk is only a few blocks, by the time I find the right address my jeans are so wet they stick to my legs. My destination turns out to be a squat one-story building, marooned on a corner between a self-pay parking lot and a warehouse offering doggy day care. Dust-colored stucco coats the outside walls. To my surprise, it really is a trophy shop. The sign over the door reads *Just Rewards*, and decals plastered on the large windows advertise sports trophies and garish plaques. Behind them, blinds cover all but the top few inches of glass.

Muffled barks from the neighboring business mingle with the hum of passing cars. I twist the doorknob and push the door open. Stuffy air, dim as the blinded windows promised, greets me when I step inside. Display tables fill the main part of the room, showcasing the store's wares: athletic figures waving baseball bats, round medallions like wannabe Olympic medals, and framed monstrosities with room for full paragraphs of accolades. I suspect business isn't going well. All the merchandise needs a good dusting.

"Hello?" I call.

A woman flipping through a magazine at the front counter raises her head with a nervous start.

"Can I help you?" she asks.

"I'm looking for . . ." I check the note, "Mr. Sidell."

The woman's face pales. She's middle-aged, with no makeup and graying hair hanging loose just past her shoulders. Her skin has the papery texture of a heavy smoker, and even in the half light I can see circles beneath her eyes.

"You're Alexandra Manning?"

"Yeah." I take a step closer, doubt gnawing at the edges of my excitement. "Is Mr. Ross here?"

"Who?"

The woman is watching me like I'm one of the dogs from next door and she's trying to decide if I'll bite. I crumple the note in my pocket. I guess I was wrong. Barnard really did send me on an errand.

"You have a plaque for me," I say.

The woman lets loose a phlegmy cough before dragging herself to her feet.

"Back here," she says, pushing open a door behind her. "Mr. Sidell is waiting for you."

The space behind the door is even darker than the poorly lit showroom. I squint into it, a trickle of unease replacing my earlier eagerness. This situation is starting to feel really weird. I wish I had let KJ come with me—then I'd be walking in there with a six-foot ally instead of just this tired-looking spinner-hater.

I shrug off my regrets and follow the woman into a workshop lined with tables and benches. One table is heaped with a stack of unfinished plaques; another holds a pile of soccer trophies, spilling out of a tipped-over cardboard box. The overhead lights buzz loudly in the deserted room.

The woman gestures toward a door at the back corner.

"He's in his office."

She doesn't offer to walk with me and cringes when I pass her. I stomp my way across the jumbled space, hoping against hope that Mr. Sidell isn't as narrow-minded as his staff. I can't believe Barnard cut short my fleeting hours of freedom with an errand as unpleasant as this one.

I reach the office and knock so hard the door rattles in its frame.

"Come in."

The room is small, made even smaller by a large wooden desk, its surface crowded with stacks of paper and random trophies, most of them broken. Two men are crammed in with the furniture: one sitting behind the desk and the other in a chair directly to my left. The guy next to me is wearing a black tracksuit and has very short hair. I can't see his face because he's bent over an expensive looking cell phone, jabbing at the screen with a thick thumb. The man at the desk is balding, overweight, and wears a wrinkled button-down shirt. He looks as downtrodden as the woman in the front room, with unwashed hair and sagging jowls.

"Mr. Sidell?" I ask the man at the desk.

He nods. "You're Alexandra."

My uneasiness grows from a trickle to a steady flow. What difference does it make what my name is? I'm just the gopher Dr. Barnard sent to pick up a plaque.

I wipe my hand on my pant leg, a useless effort given they're equally wet.

"You have a plaque for me?" I say.

Mr. Sidell's eyes move from the wet strings of my hair to the small puddle I'm dripping onto his floor. His face wears a curious expression, a mix between eagerness and anxiety that seems wildly inappropriate for our transaction. My skin prickles.

"I have a few questions for you." Mr. Sidell points to a chair.

I rub my arms. The office is unheated and manages to feel both stuffy and cold. My wet jacket does nothing to add any warmth.

"I don't really have time," I say. "I have to get back."

Footsteps sound behind me. I spin around in time to see a big guy ducking his head as he enters the room. He's young and clean-shaven, wearing a tight shirt that shows off the many hours he must spend working out. He reeks of cologne. Gym Guy gives me a quick appraisal, then shuts the door and leans against it. My heart flutters up to my throat and starts beating very fast. In the moment he raised his arm to close the door, I got a clear view of a gun holstered under one of Gym Guy's well-muscled arms.

I turn to Mr. Sidell.

"If the plaque isn't ready, I could come back later."

Even as I say the words, I realize how idiotic I sound. It's pretty clear by now that whoever tricked Barnard into sending me here was motivated by something that had nothing to do with plaques.

Gym Guy's arrival seems to have bolstered Sidell's confidence. He straightens in his chair. "You work with Carson Ross."

It's a statement, not a question. My uneasiness is now completely drowned under a tidal wave of anxiety. My brain whips through a thousand scenarios where this question might make sense, none of them reassuring. Gym Guy's presence looms behind me.

Sidell links his fingers and places them on the desk. "I'd like you to tell me about a job you two did together."

"A mission I went on with Mr. Ross?" I cross my arms. I'm hoping this makes me look confident, though my real intention is to keep my body from shaking. "Why are you asking?"

"Because the police arrested the wrong man."

My fingers clench. I run my mind back over the missions Ross and I have been on in the last few months. There must have been dozens, half of which ended in someone's arrest. I lick my lips.

"I don't have anything to do with the arrest side of things. All I do is rewind the event. If you have a question about an arrest you need to talk to the cops."

Sidell leans his forearms on the desk. Drops of sweat are collecting in the creases of his skin above his collar. I try not to stare at them.

"I have talked to the cops," he says. "And Officer Cannon here agrees that what was written up in Carson Ross's report has some errors."

Sidell gestures to the man sitting beside me. I'd almost forgotten there was a third person in the room. I turn my head with a sense of foreboding. The man has lifted his head and even then at first I don't recognize him. Then the word "officer" clicks into place and I realize he's the cop with the red hair and squashed nose I saw at the butcher shop. The breath catches in my throat. This means the arrest that Sidell is talking about is the arrest of Karl Wagner. The man who works with Sikes.

Heat climbs up my cheeks. The stink of Gym Guy's cologne seems to be getting stronger. I'm intensely aware of how crowded this room is, and how very much smaller I am than any of the men inside it. If I screamed would anyone hear me? I picture the sparsely filled parking lot and the loud yelps from the howling dogs, and hope gutters out. No one is coming to rescue me.

Sidell is watching me intently.

"According to Officer Cannon, you said some interesting things when you came out of the freeze. Something about not being able to hold time, about being sorry." He leaned closer. "In fact, you told Agent Ross you messed up."

A bead of sweat slides along my rib cage. The only windows in the room are set high up above Sidell's desk. Both are small, like those in a basement. They're also barred and opaque with grime. I lick my lips again. My tongue feels dry.

"I don't have to tell you anything."

"Look." Sidell sounds strained. "I'm just trying to find out the truth here."

"Why?" The cold from the unheated room seeps into my bones. I wrap my arms more tightly across my chest. "What does Jason Torino's murder have to do with you?"

Sidell's shoulders droop. The eyes that meet mine turn pleading.

"Karl Wagner is my son."

I open my mouth and find no words. I've never met a relative of someone we've arrested. I only see the crimes, grisly acts committed by isolated humans. They are criminals, not someone's family, not someone who might be loved.

"He's my son," Sidell repeats. "And you and Ross framed him."

"We didn't," I croak. "Mr. Ross saw him enter the room."

"He can't have." Sidell leans forward. "Karl was home with me all that night. Carson Ross lied. You have to help me. You're the only one who can."

Memory floods my brain: Jason's body flickering on the ground, blood seeping back into the wound, the jolt as the unraveling slipped. What if Sidell is telling the truth? I never saw anyone and Ross could have caught only the briefest glimpse of the killer. What if he ID'd the wrong guy? I shake my head, denying Sidell's words as much as my ability to help.

"I can't." I make an effort to keep my voice steady. "I don't remember. I got sick that night. You have to ask Mr. Ross."

"Agent Ross is not the type to say he made a mistake on a high-profile case."

Sidell's hands are lying on the table. They are old-man hands, the skin mottled, the knuckles thick. I wonder how many times those fingers touched his son's hair. How many tears they wiped away. How many skinned knees they bandaged. Then I remember Jason and the gaping wound flapping in his neck.

"It has to be *you*," Sidell is saying. "You have to tell the police that you never saw Karl in the rewind. Please, I'm begging you. Tell them Ross isn't credible. Tell them he lied."

I tear my gaze away from the pleading fingers. This man is a father. These could all be lies to protect his son. I don't know him. I do know Ross. Ross would never frame an innocent man.

"I can't," I say again. "I'm sorry."

Sidell lowers his head. To my horror, I see tears leaking into the lines around his eyes.

"Jim," says Officer Cannon, getting up from his chair and putting an arm around Sidell. "It's OK, buddy. Calm down. We got a backup plan, remember?" He cocks his head toward the door. "We tried your way. Now we've got Buck here for Plan B."

14

GYM GUY SHIFTS AGAINST THE DOOR. EVEN THE WAY he moves sounds muscle-bound. Another bead of sweat slides along my ribs, its path as cold as the rain matting my hair.

Officer Cannon comes around to perch on the edge of the desk.

"I think you can tell that my friend here is pretty upset. Your type doesn't have families. I warned him you might not understand how a father would feel in this situation."

He smiles at me, a thin-lipped grimace offering no more warmth than the unheated room.

"We'll try this the nice way one more time. Tell us everything you remember about that night."

I can no longer stop my body from shaking. Sidell may be doing this because he's Karl's father, but I'm convinced these other men were hired by Sikes, a man who has his own reasons for keeping Karl off the witness stand. The fact that one of them is a cop doesn't surprise me. Ross has always speculated that Sikes has inside help.

"I already told you," I say, doing my best to keep my voice level. "I don't remember much. I got sick."

"But you saw the murderer?"

I swallow. "I passed out."

"So how could Ross have seen him?"

A flare of anger overshadows the fear rattling my body. These men are nothing but thugs—the kind of people it is my job to put in jail. I won't let them use me to discredit the only man who has ever stood up for me. I square my shoulders.

"I said *I* passed out, not Mr. Ross."

Cannon's eyes narrow and I grab on to the tiny hesitation. Surely these men are bluffing. No one here is actually going to hurt me.

I take a step back. Gym Guy—Buck's—hand lands on my shoulder like a sack of lead. The weight bows my knees.

"This will all go much easier for you," Cannon says, "if you tell us the truth."

Buck's hand tightens hard enough to make me aware of how little padding protects my clavicle. I twist out from under his meaty paw.

"You're wasting your time," I say. "Even if I contradicted Mr. Ross no one would believe me. If you haven't noticed, spinners aren't very popular with most people."

Cannon's cold smile widens. "Some people are not as fond of Mr. Ross as you seem to be. They would be happy to champion anyone who discredited him. You have nothing to be afraid of. Mr. Ross can't hurt you if you're under our protection."

"Mr. Ross would never hurt me," I say. "It's your boss who's the killer."

A bubble of silence expands into the room. Sidell shoots a nervous look at Cannon, who has lost his false cheer. I push my advantage, giddy in the knowledge that my guess was right.

"He thinks he's safe, doesn't he?" I taunt. "Why don't you tell him that Ross and I are on to him. I expect it will only be a matter of days before Sikes gets arrested. Maybe if you turn on him before then, you can get a plea deal."

Sidell's eyes go wide.

Buck's hand crashes back onto my shoulder. For the first time, he speaks, his voice low and gravelly:

"I told you questioning her was a stupid idea. All she's good for is as a warning to tell Ross to back off."

The flicker of bravado that has carried me through the last few minutes snuffs out. I claw at Buck's fingers, trying to pry them off of me. He shifts his grip almost casually, wrapping his free arm across my chest to pin me against him. The gun bites into my shoulder blade. I kick at his shins. He's holding me so close the blow lacks force.

Officer Cannon lifts his palms in a well-I-tried gesture.

"I guess she's all yours, then," he says to Buck. "Make sure you leave her body somewhere Ross will find it. Eventually."

The room spins. Dimly, I hear Sidell protesting, something about someone knowing I'm at his shop.

"Well, he's hardly likely to tell anyone that, is he?" Cannon snaps.

I hear the door swing open and Buck starts pulling me away.

"No!" I scream. "Let me go. Help!"

The shock of Cannon's hand across my cheek stops my words. I close my mouth and taste blood. Sidell drops his face into his hands.

"Please," I beg him. "Don't let them do this. I told you what I know. How can hurting me help your son?"

Sidell's shoulders start shaking, but any sympathy I had for him is gone. Buck drags me from the room. My wet shoes scrabble uselessly against the concrete floor. I reach out for time, and the leash yanks the power away from me with a jolt that hurts almost as much as Cannon's slap. I scream again. Buck shakes me so hard my ear slams against my own shoulder.

"Shut up," he growls.

He hauls me out into the workroom. I'm breathing in jagged gasps, unable to fill my lungs. Cannon and Sidell edge past us, heading toward an exit in the back of the room. The woman who let me in is nowhere in sight.

Buck pulls a tarp from a shelf with one hand and drops it on the ground. I thrash, kicking at every piece of him I can reach. My legs feel weak, their thrusts without impact. The air shimmers with the electric sparks of my terror. I find skin and sink my nails into it. Buck swears and adjusts his grip. His fingers grab the leash, smashing the hard edges against my bone. I moan. Buck rips my sleeve back, exposing the band. The metal gleams in the overhead light, its CIC logo a dark etching in its center.

"What's this?" he demands.

Tears clog my throat. Buck is going to kill me. He's going to wrap me up in this tarp and dump me somewhere so far away no one will find me until it is way too late.

"I said, what's that?" Buck repeats, shaking me to make his point.

"A leash," I sob.

My vision blurs, blending the blue plastic into the dusty floor. Is this the last thing I'll ever see? I try to call up images of the people I care about: KJ, Ross, even Yolly, but all I can picture is Buck's gun.

Buck slaps me. "What's it do?"

I blink. The world snaps back into focus: Buck doesn't know what a leash is.

"It's how they track us," I say.

Buck's eyes narrow. "I thought you had implants?"

"Those only monitor our freezes." I sniffle. "That's why we wear these when we leave the Center."

Buck's gaze moves from my arm to my face, searching for truth. Tears wet my cheeks. Snot leaks from my nose.

"They won't find you this time." Buck's grip tightens again around my arm. He yanks me toward the workbench, searching one-handed through drawers of tools until his fingers close on a pair of metal cutters. The unsparing light gleams against the sharp blade.

New fears pile on top of the mountain already threatening to overwhelm me. I don't have to pretend that I think this is a really bad idea. Buck slams my arm on the workbench, holding it steady while he forces the metal cutter under the leash. I scream. The jaws of the cutter close around the band. It doesn't break. Buck swears again. He twists the blade to try another angle, and when he does, the sharp tip gouges my wrist. Pain sears my skin like a brand. My screams dissolve into sobs. Crimson wells up from the gash, splattering onto the bench and floor. Buck works the cutter, each press of his hand making the slice in my arm vomit up another gush of blood. It feels like he's stabbing me over and over and over. Dots careen across my vision. I clutch at the workbench with my free hand. The leash's band bends upwards.

Release comes suddenly. Buck's arm flies up from the abrupt lack of resistance, nearly stabbing himself in the mouth. He snatches up the battered leash and tosses it onto the workbench.

"It's into the river with you," he mutters to the twisted remains.

Clarity slices through the fog in my head as the leash's buzz recedes. For a moment we both stand there, panting.

"Come on." Buck, still holding my arm, drags me toward the tarp. I force myself to ignore the ache in my wrist and just breathe. Once. Twice. Buck shoves me to the ground and reaches for his gun. I wait only until I am absolutely sure Buck isn't touching me before reaching out and freezing time.

Silence—perfect, absolute silence—descends. I'm shaking so violently I can't stand up so I scoot myself away. Buck remains bent over the tarp, one hand frozen over the clasp that will release the gun. Even from here I can smell the mix of mold and paint thinner emanating from the tarp.

I use the wall to pull myself onto to my feet. When I melt time it will seem to Buck as if I've vanished into thin air. I picture his shout of surprise, the others coming back, their confusion and anger. Their first call will be to Sikes, which means that within minutes of real time Sikes will know what I've done, and know the kind of power I control. What will someone like Sikes do next? Will he tell someone? Or will he try even harder to get rid of me?

Fear gives me the strength to keep moving. I have to get back to the Center. The Center, with its locked doors and twenty-four-hour security is the one place that can keep out Sikes. I wipe my nose on the back of my hand. My whole body feels tender: my jaw aching from Cannon's slap, my muscles strained from the struggle to free myself, and my arm . . . I look down. The gash across my wrist is about an inch long and deep enough that it probably needs stitches. Fresh blood trickles steadily along my arm, leaving red drops on the concrete floor.

I strip off my jacket and rip off the torn arm to make an improvised bandage before staggering for the exit. Rain hangs in the air outside. I dash through it, dodging the scattering of frozen people. I'm holding on to time so tightly it feels like I'm gripping strands of steel. The image of Buck and his gun keeps popping into my head, and every time it does, I wobble and nearly crash into unmoving pedestrians. The third time this happens I move onto the street. Stalled cars are less likely to be affected by a bump than stationary people.

The stone walls of the Center rise into view a block before I reach them. I run faster. My foot is on the first step before I realize I can't just melt time and appear at the Sick's front door. Too many potential witnesses crowd the streets, not to mention the Center's video surveillance. I scan my surroundings, settling on a dumpster-filled alley a half block away. I search the narrow space to make sure it isn't already occupied, then crouch down, out of sight, and let time go.

Returning sound blasts my ears: squealing brakes, a rattling bicycle, chattering voices. After gripping the time strands so tightly for so long, the release makes me woozy and I have to grab the dumpster to keep from falling over.

A woman gasps when I step out onto the sidewalk. The window behind her reflects something out of a zombie movie. Strips of mangled windbreaker hang from my arm. My hair sticks to my face and neck in sopping strands. Blood stripes my left hand and leaves splatters on my shirt.

I turn away and race toward the safety of the Sick. I'm terrified Buck will somehow appear before I can reach the Center. People step back when they see my blood-smeared clothes.

"Are you all right?" a man asks.

I ignore him, leaping up the Center's wide steps to ring the front bell. The door camera's red eye blinks over my head. Eternal seconds pass before an electronic buzz tells me someone has punched the code to open the door.

Charlie's mouth goes slack when I stumble inside.

"What happened to you?" he asks.

The freeze monitor is beeping. I push the door shut behind me. When I hear the click of the lock resetting itself, I sag against the wood.

"They tried to kill me," I pant. "Call Mr. Ross. I need to . . ."

"Alex!" Yolly's voice echoes across the tiled foyer. "What's going on? KJ got back ten minutes ago, babbling about Dr. Barnard's computer being broken." She stops when she sees me. "Oh my God."

"It was a trap." Relief at being back in the Center returns the shivers that started in the workshop. "The guy who called Dr. Barnard about a plaque. It was a set-up—they didn't have anything for us to pick up. The men there took me to a back room and they . . ."

A lump rises up in the back of my throat. I swallow. Just picturing Buck turns me into a quivering mess. Yolly comes over and wraps an arm around me. I turn my head and bury my face in her shoulder.

"Slow down," Yolly says, patting my back. "What plaque are you talking about?"

"Jack gave me the message," I say. "When he called Powell's."

Yolly tilts my head up so she can see my face. There's a frown creasing the space between her brows.

"The one KJ said you got?"

"Yes!" The relentless beep of the freeze monitor is making my head hurt. I can't figure out why Yolly is looking so confused. I try explaining more clearly.

"Jack called and said Dr. Barnard needed KJ to fix his computer and that I was supposed to go pick up some plaque."

"Alex." Yolly places her palm against my forehead. "Dr. Barnard doesn't send spinners off on errands by themselves."

"I know. But Jack said . . ."

Jack's face dances before me. Was KJ right? Was this Jack's idea of a joke? I cradle my swaddled arm against my chest. No, the message was real, the people at the store were expecting me. I suddenly remember Jack telling me that he worked with people who were more important than Ross. He couldn't mean Sikes. Could he?

"Jack," I say, just as Jack himself descends the staircase.

"Dr. Barnard wants to know who set off the monitor." He catches sight of me and halts, one foot hovering above the last step. "What happened to you?"

Rage like I've never felt fills my face with heat. I clench my fists.

"The men at the trophy shop," I say. "The place you sent me."

Jack's gaze flicks to Yolly.

"I didn't . . . ," he says. "I never sent you anywhere."

His denial hits me like a slap. I lunge toward him, wanting to scratch the composure off his lying face. Yolly grabs my arm to restrain me. When her hand closes on my bound wrist, I scream.

"What is it?" Yolly looks down at my arm. My homemade bandage has unraveled, exposing my bare wrist. Yolly's head jerks toward the guard station, where my name must be scrolling across the monitor's small screen.

"Where's your leash?" she demands.

"I told you." Tears of pain well up in my eyes. "The guy tried to kill me. He cut the leash off so you couldn't trace me."

"Leashes don't have a trace." Yolly turns back to me. Her face has gone soft, the frown replaced by an expression of deep sadness. With one hand she reaches out and smooths a strand of wet hair off my cheek.

"Alex, if you're not feeling well, you need to tell someone. You can't just run off in the city and—what is it?"

Tears are pouring freely down my cheeks and I'm pretty sure from the wooziness threatening my ability to stand up that I'm turning something way past pale.

"My arm," I moan.

Yolly unwraps the remains of my jacket. The final layer sticks to my skin and I whimper when she rips it free. Yolly draws a sharp breath. Dried blood smears the skin on my forearm, framing the raw mouth of the incision. My wooziness takes a turn for the worse.

"Oh, honey," Yolly says. "Charlie, call Amy. Tell her I'm bringing Alex in and she'll need a room. And turn off that wretched monitor."

She slips an arm around my shoulders, hooking her hand under my armpit.

"Come on. Can you walk?"

Jack hurries forward to take my other arm.

"Alex, I'm so sorry," he murmurs into my ear, so only I can hear. "Dr. B. told me to keep the errand secret. I'd never have passed the message if I thought you'd get hurt."

If I felt even slightly less shaky I would punch him.

"Leave me alone," I hiss.

Jack drops my arm as Yolly helps me to the elevator. He stands there as the door closes, body hunched over as if the blow I wanted to deliver had actually landed in his gut. The elevator creaks upward. Fear, pain, anger, and confusion battle for dominance inside me. I lean against Yolly's warm bulk, trying to think. My advantage, as always, is time. It's been only minutes since the men attacked me. Plenty of time to track them down in a rewind.

"Damn sickness . . . ," Yolly mutters, "stupid . . . should have known . . . so unpredictable."

Sickness? Yolly thinks I'm sick? I want to protest, but I'm so tired the effort doesn't seem worth it. The door opens, and I let her half-carry me down the hall to the clinic.

Amy meets us just inside the door. "What's going on?" she asks.

Yolly holds up my arm. "She'll need stitches."

Amy shakes her head. "Put her in the exam room. I'll go make up a shot of lidocaine."

Dry paper crackles as Yolly helps me up onto the exam room's padded bench.

"Lie down," she says.

I collapse onto the thin foam. My head hurts, the inevitable ache claiming its due as the adrenaline leaves my system. Yolly dampens a cotton swab and starts wiping the dried blood from my arm.

"Everyone has a hard time after a bout of sickness," Yolly says. "It's nothing to be ashamed of. You can always come talk to me if you're feeling depressed."

I nod. I don't get why she keeps talking about the sickness, but I'm glad she isn't threatening to get me in trouble for freezing time.

"You have to call Ross," I say.

Yolly sighs. "Alex."

Amy walks in with a tray loaded with the supplies she needs to stitch me up. She sets it down and pulls on a pair of rubber gloves. I keep my gaze firmly fixed on Yolly so I don't have to watch.

"I can lead him back to the trophy shop." The smell of iodine fills the small room. I try not to flinch while Amy cleans my wound. "I'll rewind it for him, and he can identify the men who attacked me."

"Not now, Alex," Yolly says.

"My arm's not that bad. I can still go on a mission."

Yolly shakes her head. I swallow my frustration.

"Then send someone else," I say. "KJ will go."

The outer door to the clinic slams open and a voice roars from the waiting room.

"Where is she?"

Amy winces. I'm glad she hasn't started stitching yet.

Yolly squeezes behind Amy to get out of the exam room. "Dr. Barnard?"

"Is Alex here?" He's still yelling. I'm surprised he sounds so upset. He's certainly unemotional about us dying.

"Yes," I hear Yolly say. "I'm afraid she slashed her wrist. Amy will keep her here for a while, until we're sure she's not going to hurt herself again."

Hurt myself? A sharp jab tells me Amy has injected the numbing agent. Is that what they think? That I cut my arm *myself*?

"Stop wiggling," Amy says.

Dr. Barnard bursts into the exam room. The straggly hairs around his bald head stand out like an attacking dog's ruff.

"What happened?"

"Jack called me with a message," I explain, for what feels like the twentieth time. "He said someone called you about a . . ."

Barnard makes an impatient noise and in that instant his distraught state takes on a whole different meaning. The blood drains from my face. My cheeks prickle. What if Jack was telling the truth? What if the message he gave me really did come from Barnard?

"They beat me up," I say. I choose my words carefully. Did Barnard send me to the trophy store on what he thought was a legitimate errand? Or did he know that Sikes's men would be waiting for me?

The safe feeling that has comforted me since I heard the front door lock evaporates. My eyes flick around the tiny room. Amy holds my arm in a firm grip. Barnard's body blocks the door. Even without a leash there is no way out.

Yolly's head bobs behind Barnard's. She speaks softly, but I can still hear every word.

"The sickness must be causing hallucinations," she murmurs. "Alex claims she got paged at the bookstore, but KJ didn't hear anything, and he wasn't there when she talked on the phone. When did you last adjust her dosage?"

Dr. Barnard isn't listening. He moves so close to me that Amy has to stop stitching.

"How did you get away?" he asks me.

My mouth goes dry. "They said they were going to kill me. He cut my leash off. I . . . I . . ."

"What. Did. You. Do."

A new terror stalls my tongue. I'm sure Dr. Barnard knows I can change things in frozen time. Did Buck call him? Or . . . my mind wheels through possibilities. The tracker. That's how they knew I was at Powell's. Barnard could have watched the monitor, following my progress all the way to the trophy store. The tracker would have winked out when I froze time and reappeared a half block from the Center. My mouth opens without making any sounds. Barnard stands so close to me I can smell the bitter scent of old coffee on his breath.

"I ran away," I manage. The words come out in a whisper.

Barnard's lips press together so tightly they disappear.

"Amy," he snaps. "Go get a syringe. I need to test this girl's blood right now."

15

I WATCH, HELPLESS, AS AMY SCURRIES OVER TO A supply cabinet. Yolly is staring at Barnard, confusion stamped across her features. None of us say anything. The tiny exam room is so crowded with bodies it feels like there isn't enough air for us all. When Amy turns around, her face is pale. I remember Ross telling her they could never trace her faked test results and wonder if that's true. Amy must be wondering the same thing. Her hands shake so much she can't rip open the package holding the needle.

Barnard extracts the syringe himself. He swabs my arm above the half-stitched gash and plunges the needle into the vein at my elbow. Blood, dark and rich, fills the tube of the syringe with my secret. My mouth goes dry. Once the test is complete, whatever Ross is giving me will be exposed. Barnard will grill everyone to find out how I got it, and the way Amy looks now I can't imagine her standing up to Barnard for longer than it takes her to draw breath. Ross will be ruined. And I . . .

Barnard slips the needle from my skin and presses a cotton ball over the prick in one smooth motion.

"Yolanda."

Yolly starts.

"Take her arm," he says, "and don't let go of her. I don't want her freezing time alone."

"Freezing time? What difference . . . ?"

"Just do it."

Yolly wraps one hand around the bare skin of my unhurt arm.

Barnard points to Amy. "I'm sending Charlie up with a leash. I want her leashed, in a room, with the door locked. She's to stay there until I say she can be released. Is that clear?"

The two women nod dumbly. Barnard walks away, carrying with him the bloody evidence that will guarantee my imprisonment for the rest of my short life.

Amy's face has gone dead white. She keeps shooting glances at Yolly while stitching up my arm. I know they want to talk but won't as long as I'm there. I don't mind. Their silence gives me space to think. Shannon has described the blood tests to me before. She says you have to pour the sample into a vial and add a few drops of a separating solution. Then you have to swirl the mixture for at least five minutes to engage the chemicals and let it sit for five more. After that you smear some on a slide and run it through the chronotin analyzer, a buzzing little metal box that looks like a miniature copy machine.

Ten minutes. I check the clock. 2:46. Say it takes Dr. Barnard thirty seconds to get to the lab room and maybe ten seconds more to mix up the solution. Ten minutes for the chemical reaction and he'll be putting the sample in the analyzer no later than 2:57. That gives me until 2:56 to figure out a way to stop him.

Amy's fingers move methodically through her task. Prick, pull, snip. My skin slides together into a neat seam. I try not to fidget. 2:49. Yolly's hand squeezes my other arm. Not only will I have to get away from her, I'll have to cover up the fact that I've frozen time. The impossibility of my task makes my head hurt worse than the stitches. 2:52.

"That should do it." Amy pulls off her gloves and rubs a hand over her forehead, which is damp with sweat. Yolly touches her shoulder.

"You feeling OK?" she asks. "You look kind of pale."

Amy mumbles something about Barnard yelling at her and starts picking up the bits of bloody cotton and thread. I look at the clock again. A plan is forming in my head, but unless these two start moving faster I'm going to run out of time.

"I'll do that," Yolly says to Amy, "you go get the room ready."

Amy trails off toward the sickroom.

"You don't have to hold my arm," I tell Yolly as soon as Amy leaves. She casts me an uncomfortable look.

"Dr. Barnard was very explicit," she says. One-handed, she dumps the leavings Amy collected into the trash. Her movements are awkward and painfully slow. The clock counts down another minute. My knee starts jiggling. I could try to wrench my arm from Yolly's grasp. Is it worth it? She's pretty strong, and if it doesn't work my aggressiveness will make her distrust me.

Yolly tosses the last of the garbage and lets out a long sigh. "Let's go set you up in a room."

I slide off the exam bed. Yolly keeps a firm grip on my arm as we leave. 2:54. The main clinic door opens. Charlie is here with the leash. This is it. Game time.

"Will you let Amy take me in the room by herself?"

It takes all I have not to scream the words. Yolly hesitates.

"Please," I say. "It's just that last time I was sick I was here with you, Yolly, and going back in together will make it feel like it's happening all over again. Like the worst days of my life are being endlessly rewound."

I'm babbling. Even to myself the excuse makes no sense, but Yolly's face crumples. She blinks hard and strokes my arm with her free hand.

"Of course, dear. I understand."

She calls for Amy. Charlie walks toward us, looking nervous. I lower my head, doing my best to look meek and harmless. Amy's hand replaces Yolly's. She takes the leash from Charlie and reaches for my unhurt wrist, but I've already started walking, pulling her with me as I step into the cheerless sickroom. The door closes behind us. No one locks it.

"Let go of me," I say, keeping my voice barely over a murmur. Amy shakes her head and reaches for my wrist again. I raise it over my head.

"If you don't, Barnard is going to find out you faked my blood tests."

Amy gasps. "What do you mean?"

There's a clock over her head. 2:55. One more minute.

"Let go of my arm," I say, "for five seconds, and I'll cover for you."

Her grip loosens, but not enough. "How?" she asks.

I shake my head. The clock is ticking relentlessly forward.

"It doesn't matter, but it has to be now." I pull against her hand. Her fingers tighten.

"I can't."

"You can." I stare into her eyes, forcing my will into her. I could freeze time and take her with me, but then what? She has no reason to keep my secret. I play my last card.

"It's what Mr. Ross would want you to do if he were here."

Amy's mouth quivers. "Carson?"

"Close your eyes, let go of me, and count to five. Right now."

Amy's eyelids flutter. Her fingers loosen. I pull my arm free and yank time to a halt.

The world stops. Amy stands before me, eyes closed, looking scared. I memorize my position, checking the set of my feet, the angle of my head, and move away—carefully—so I don't bump her. The sickroom door opens at my touch. I pull it wide, inching around Yolly and Charlie who are standing just outside. When I gain the waiting room, I check the clock again. 2:56.

Adrenaline makes me run when I don't need to. I charge back to the empty exam room and grab up the materials I need—a clean syringe, a rubber tie, and a handful of cotton balls—then race to where Dr. Barnard stands in his narrow lab. The green light of the chronotin analyzer sends out a weak beam. My heart squeezes painfully until I see that Barnard is still holding the tube with my blood. His other hand is stretched toward the counter, fingers inches from an eyedropper. I've made it with seconds to spare.

The fragments of my plan flutter around my brain like bits of paper caught in a windstorm. I grab at the scattered pieces, forcing them together as I race through the Center's silent halls. Already, I can feel time pulling at me; my injuries aren't going to allow me much time to hold on. I find KJ in the third place I try. He's in a storage room, putting away a box of computer supplies. Snatching up his frozen hands, I melt and refreeze time as fast as I can manage the commands.

"Alex!" KJ's body jerks. "You can't just appear like . . ."

His eyes blink. The box he's holding slides from his fingers, landing on the floor with an unfortunate cracking sound. He puts a hand on my shoulder.

"What happened to you?" he asks.

I tell my story quickly, trying to gloss over the worst parts. KJ looks sick when I finish.

"Alex, I . . ." He moves as if to pull me into a hug and I step back automatically. KJ shoves his hands into his jeans pockets.

"How badly did they hurt you?"

"Nothing permanent." I hold up my arm to show the small bandage Amy taped over the wound. "This is the worst of it."

KJ shakes his head, clearly still trying to fit my story into his brain. "And now you think Dr. Barnard has ties with Sikes?"

"Yes. I don't know. Maybe. But I'm sure he suspects what I can do."

"Then why did you freeze again? This is only going to make things worse."

I study the floor. I'm not looking forward to this part. "I didn't tell you the full story before. There's a reason Ross is faking my blood tests. He's giving me an experimental medicine. It's supposed to let me live longer, and this new skill is a side effect. If Barnard runs a test, he'll figure it out."

"You let Ross give you drugs?" KJ speaks with ominous calm.

I nod.

"Then letting Barnard run the test is the best thing for you," KJ says. "He'll take you off Ross's drug and put you back to normal."

My head snaps up. KJ wears a look of grim determination. A beat of panic rises in the back in my throat.

"This new medicine might be the only reason I'm alive right now," I say. "Plus, if some other drug shows up in my system, Barnard will run a bunch of tests. He'll make me freeze time and figure out I can change things. You said it yourself. They'll send me to the Central Office. I can't just appear places. It's too much. They won't let anyone have this kind of power."

We stare at each other for a long time. I know KJ so well I can see the struggle beneath his skin: desire to get me back on Aclisote, fear of the consequences if my secret is discovered, anger that I lied to him. Finally he lets out a long sigh.

"You'll help me?" I ask.

"On one condition."

"What?"

"You get your blood tested."

"KJ, I told you, I can't. If they test my blood, they'll . . ."

He shakes his head. "Shannon can run the test."

Shannon. Of all the people he could have chosen to involve, Shannon is probably at the bottom of my list. I bite my lip, trying to think of another option. The image of Dr. Barnard holding the vial of my tainted blood leaves me with little choice.

"OK," I say. "She can test it. But don't tell her that my skills have changed."

KJ uncrosses his arms. "What do you need?"

Relief hits me so hard my eyes spark with tears. KJ is back on my side. I allow myself to believe my plan might work.

"Your blood." I hold up the stuff I took from the clinic. "I need your blood."

"To swap out your sample?"

I nod.

"It's a temporary fix," KJ warns. "He can draw more."

"It buys me time." I grimace. "It always comes down to time, doesn't it?"

KJ gives a wry smile. He's already rolling up his sleeve.

Drawing blood turns out to be harder than the clinic staff makes it look. Even after I've tied off KJ's arm to make the blood vessels pop up, the actual injection takes a while. Skin is tough. By the time I'm done, KJ's face has turned slightly green.

"You might want to practice that if you're going to make a habit of it."

"Sorry," I mutter.

I cap the filled syringe while KJ unties his arm.

"We have another problem." I dab his arm with a cotton ball, then stick it and the rubber tie into my pocket. "I need to block the grid somehow so Barnard doesn't know I stopped time. You know, like they do when we're on missions."

"It's too late for that. You've already triggered the system. The alarm will go off in a few seconds." KJ scratches his chin. "I suppose we could unplug the server." He must notice my blank look because he adds: "If we unplug the server that the monitor runs on, the whole system will reset, which should clear your freeze from its memory. It happens sometimes when the power goes out. You'll have to melt time long enough for the monitor to recognize the power was cut and then freeze again as soon as we plug it back in."

"Is there any way to disable my tracker permanently so that I'm not on the system?"

"Not unless we cut it out of your neck."

I touch the barely discernable bump just below my hairline.

"They'd probably notice that, wouldn't they."

The server lives in an electrical closet that's locked with a key card. KJ and I run through the options, settling on one that will use the least fragments of real time. We retrieve the key card from Charlie's guard station, then hurry to the closet, blessedly located in a little used side hall. I take KJ's hand.

"Remember," he says, "you have to be fast or the monitor will register your freeze."

With the image of Barnard's vial floating in the forefront of my brain, I drop hold of time. KJ swipes the card. We snatch the door open, and I refreeze. It's not easy, even with the supportive energy I get from the link with KJ. Time fights me, a powerful force straining for freedom. I clench my teeth and drag it under my control.

The closet is dark, lit by only a few small lights on the monitor's control panel. KJ crawls around on the floor, patting wires and cords as he traces the right one to the power outlet. One hard tug and it's unplugged. I prop the door open and move closer so I can put my hand against the back of his neck.

"Ready?" I ask.

KJ nods. Time runs forward. The lights on the server wink out. KJ thrusts the plug back into the wall.

Freeze time.

The two of us sink back on our heels. For a while we just sit there. My hand lingers on the back of his neck. It seems hard to believe it was only a few hours ago I imagined doing this so we could freeze together, picturing those moments as some kind of illicit romance. This stark reality is both less and more than I imagined—less in that there isn't an inch of romance in this cramped closet, and more because sitting here makes me realize that my bond with KJ is much deeper than a few stolen kisses. He might not be my boyfriend, but he's still my rock. I know he will always be there for me.

My headache gives an insistent throb.

"We'd better get moving," I say. I lift my hand, missing his warmth as soon as I've stopped touching his skin.

We return the key card to the guard station. Charlie is sitting where we left him, completely engrossed in his cell phone. When we reach the lab, we find that Dr. Barnard hasn't moved much either, only shifted the eyedropper from the counter to rest on the lip of the vial. I pour KJ's blood into a fresh tube and add a few drops of the separating solution. I swirl it slowly, checking the original vial to try and match the blood wash up the sides of the glass.

"We should be timing this," KJ says.

I automatically check the clock. 2:56. That isn't going to work.

"Count," I say.

KJ starts counting in a steady cadence. I swirl the vial until he reaches three hundred. Five minutes, halfway there. Very carefully, I slide the vial with my blood out of Barnard's inert fingers and replace it with the tube of KJ's. KJ takes the vial with my blood and caps it with a stopper.

"Can you get back in five minutes?" I ask. KJ nods. Without pausing his count, he pulls the medical trash from my pocket and wraps it around the tube of my blood.

"I'll get rid of this," he says between numbers, then takes off down the hall at a run.

I pick up his count and head back to the clinic, easing past Yolly to return to the sickroom. I'm so tired it's hard to keep the numbers straight. Amy is right where I left her, eyes squeezed shut. I fit my arm back into the open curve of her fingers, making sure not to touch them, and realign my feet and body as close to my former posture as I can remember. At six hundred I release time, tensed for the scream of the monitor. Amy opens her eyes.

"You're still here," she says.

The monitor remains quiet. I let out a shaky breath.

"Of course I am."

"I thought you were . . . " Amy's mouth hangs open, suspended just like her sentence.

"Thought I was what? Going to run away?" I shrug. "How could

I? I just wanted a few seconds to think before you put the leash on. It makes my head so fuzzy."

Amy closes her mouth. Her hand wraps around my arm again. She lifts the leash, hesitates.

"So will you cover for me?" she whispers.

I rub my temple. "You don't have to worry."

Amy gives herself a little shake, either dismissing her fears or reclaiming her role as the responsible person in the room. She snaps the leash on my wrist and leads me to the bed.

"You'd better lie down," she says. "You lost quite a bit of blood. Those stitches might hurt once the lidocaine wears off."

I climb into bed without protest and stare up at the ceiling. The stress of the past hour, combined with the strain of holding time so long, has left me so tired I can barely move. Amy heads for the door. I hear it shut and then the snap as the lock clicks. My head aches, the pain worsened by the buzzing of the leash's interference. So many things could still go wrong: the beep of the reawakened monitor exposing my freeze, KJ not making it back to the storage room and appearing out of nowhere in some random hall, Barnard figuring out he's been tricked.

The murmur of Yolly and Amy's voices drifts through the locked door—soft, worried sounds unintelligible from where I lie. Across from me, high on the wall, a clock with a thin red second hand ticks relentlessly. Time moves forward, out of my control. I close my eyes and wait.

Barnard turns up in my room a half hour later. He's calmer now, though apparently still too worked up to sit. Instead, he paces around my room, spinning the watch on his wrist as he walks.

"Tell me again what happened today."

I tell my story the way I had before: Jack calling me with a message, the woman sending me to the back room, the men threatening me. I add that they wanted me to testify against the evidence of my rewind. I don't mention Ross or Sikes. Instead, I keep the focus on Sidell's role as Karl Wagner's father.

When I finish, Barnard stops pacing and rests his hands on the metal bedrail at the foot of my bed. His eyes are bright behind his glasses.

"And tell me again how you got away?"

I meet Barnard's gaze with all the innocence I can muster. The half hour has given me time to think up a faintly possible cover story.

"I managed to grab up one of the trophies, and I hit the big guy with it and ran. The other two had left, and I figured Buck wouldn't chase me once I hit the street."

Barnard studies my thin frame. If he's actually met Buck, he must know I'm lying. I hurry to change the topic.

"Mr. Ross will want to know what happened. Have you called him?"

Barnard releases the bedrail and walks to the window. "You have to admit your story is pretty farfetched, Alexandra."

I swallow. "It's the truth."

Barnard lifts a slat and peers out the window into the depthless gray of lowering clouds. I wonder what he's thinking. He's had time to run my blood test at least twice. Does the fact that I'm not being dragged to the Central Office mean my secret is safe? Or is he even now plotting how to turn me over to Sikes?

"Yolanda thinks your wounds are self-inflicted," Barnard says. "That the sickness is making you hallucinate."

I pick at the bandage covering my wrist. Does Barnard really believe I'm sick, or is he using Yolly's fears as a convenient cover story? If Barnard really does have ties with Sikes, it won't take long before he hears about my disappearance in front of Buck. And if he doesn't, there's still Sikes himself. My probing fingers catch the edge of one of my stitches, sending a dart of pain along my arm. I don't see Sikes as a man who takes defeat easily. If he wants to stop Ross from pursuing his investigation, one unexplained escape isn't going to slow him down. He'll either come back for me and do it right, or change his tactic and go straight for Ross instead.

I smooth the bandage against my arm, wishing the motion could just as easily smooth away the fear clamping my chest. If I want protection from Sikes, then he needs to go to jail, and right now I'm the only one who can make sure that happens.

"How long until I'm cleared for time work?" I ask.

"Time work?" Barnard drops the slat and turns back toward my bed. "Oh, you won't be doing any more time work. Not if you're so unstable you'd consider suicide."

I bolt upright. Barnard moves across the room.

"We'll just keep an eye on you here for a while. Maybe run a few more tests."

"No!"

Barnard pulls out his keys. I scramble to get out of bed.

"You can't do that." My hands fumble with the sheets, which tangle around my legs. "I can still go on missions. Ask Mr. Ross."

"Carson Ross is not a medical expert," Barnard says, not even bothering to turn around.

The lock clicks. I manage to tear the sheets away, half-falling out of bed.

"Wait!" I say. "You don't understand."

Before the door even opens all the way, Barnard slips through it and yanks it shut.

"I'm not sick!" I wrench the handle just as the lock falls back into place.

"Come on." I bang against the unresponsive wood. "I didn't try to hurt myself. I feel fine. You saw my chronotin levels."

Footsteps retreat on the other side of the door. I press my ear against the crack and catch the thump as the outer door to the clinic closes.

Tears swell the back of my nose. Sikes is out there, a dark menace with the power to destroy everything I care about. I crumple to the floor and let the tears fall. All my planning, all my lies and desperate tricks, have landed me exactly where I didn't want to be: leashed and alone in a locked room.

16

TIME GROWS UNRULY. I LOOK UP AT THE CLOCK AND see only five minutes have crawled past, and then the next instant an entire hour is gone. I pace the room, tracing Barnard's steps around the bed to search the street for signs of Sikes's men, then looping back to try the door, which is locked. Always locked. I finger the rough keyhole. The unmoving knob doesn't offer me any protection. Not if Barnard is the only thing standing between me and Sikes.

The clock reads 5:30 when I finally hear voices in the clinic lobby. My body tenses until I recognize them. Yolly. And KJ. I'm standing a foot from the door when it swings open.

"KJ!" I hurl myself at him. KJ returns the hug, his arms tight against my back.

"He's insistent, your friend," Yolly says, pretending to frown at us. "He can only stay for five minutes. Dr. Barnard didn't explicitly say no visitors, but I'm not sure he'd approve."

"Thanks, Yolly," I say, blinking back tears. "I really appreciate it."

Yolly dabs at the corner of her eye, trying to make it look like she's fishing out an eyelash.

"I'll go rustle up some dinner for you," she says as she backs out of the room.

I press my face into KJ's chest, taking in the earthy scent that is so uniquely his. The solidity of him calms me, and I wish I could stand here forever.

"I'm so glad you're here," I say. "I have to get a message to Ross. I need . . ."

KJ makes an odd gulping sound. I realize he hasn't moved since he entered the room. I loosen my hold on him and take my first good look at his face. His jaw is taut, eyes wide, like he's trying really hard not to cry. The comfort I'd felt in his arms evaporates.

"What happened?" I ask.

"Shannon tested your blood."

I move away from him.

"What? How?"

"That sample Barnard took. We snuck it down to the lab an hour ago. Alex, your chronotin, it's high."

He's holding his hands at his sides, fingers clenched into fists.

"How high?" My voice squeaks. "Like over 175?"

"Higher." He swallows. "It's 317."

"317?" I back away from him, stopping only when I hit the hard edge of the bed. "That's impossible. Nobody tests anywhere near that high."

"We ran it twice."

My knees give way. I collapse against the bed.

"How?" I say, though I'm not even sure what I'm asking. *How is that possible? How can I still be alive?* KJ comes over and sits next to me.

"You have to get back on Aclisote. Now. It's a miracle you haven't had another attack."

"Will Shannon tell Barnard?" I ask.

"I told her I had to talk to you first. But she's worried about you, too."

I shake my head. "This can't be right. Ever since I started Ross's medicine I've felt completely healthy. Normal. Better than normal."

"It's all in your head, Alex." KJ puts his arm around my shoulders. "You wanted to believe the medicine was working, so it did. And even if you do feel OK, Jack says how you feel is no way to predict an attack. He said he felt fine the day before his."

I stiffen. "You talked to Jack?"

"Yes, I . . ."

I shake his arm off my shoulder, wrenching my body away so it no longer touches his.

"He's the one that sent me to the trophy store."

KJ flinches.

"I know. He told me . . ." KJ rubs his forehead. "I'm not explaining this right. Let me start at the beginning.

"After you melted time, I went to find Jack. I wanted to hit him like you'd been hit, but he wouldn't fight me. He just stood there and swore that he thought the errand was legit."

"And you believe him?"

"I do." KJ twists on the bed so he's facing me. "He looked completely un-Jack-like—no showing off, just scared. He told me he's pretty sure Sikes pays Barnard to do favors for him and that Barnard covers up Sikes's crimes. Nothing huge, just stuff like stalling an investigation or making sure only weak spinners get sent to do rewinds on Sikes cases. Sometimes Barnard sends Jack out on his own to deliver messages to this mailbox over at some rent-a-box place. He'll sneak him out through the parking garage so there's no record of him leaving. That's why Jack never gets in trouble when he breaks rules. The two of them have an understanding."

"An understanding that it's OK to work for murderers."

"A really rich murderer."

Jack's mocking hints flash through my brain. *Dr. B. likes his reputation as the world's chronotin expert . . . his big research projects don't get enough support.* Barnard isn't experimenting on us, he's doing illegal favors to underwrite his research. I rub at a bloodstain on my shirt. No one has bothered to bring me clean clothes.

"So it's true, then. Dr. Barnard was willing to let Sikes kill me."

KJ puts his hand on my knee, squeezing until I look up at him.

"We don't know what Barnard knew," he says. "Maybe he thought they were just going to rough you up. But whatever he's doing is not as important as what's going on with you."

KJ's eyes bore into mine. Fear lurks in those dark depths, fear for me, for himself. I can feel my body tensing in response.

"Sikes may or may not hurt you," he says. "Sky-high chronotin will. Let's deal with the immediate threat first. Get back on Aclisote. Bring your chronotin levels back down to normal."

Normal. I'm on my feet, pacing again. What is normal? The leash buzzes in my brain. Am I more in danger from Barnard or Sikes? The new drugs or the old? From someone else hurting me or my own body losing its fight with time?

I reach the door and by habit test the knob. It doesn't budge.

"How would I even do it?" I ask KJ. "The medicine is all premeasured and stocked in the cabinet."

"Amy. Tell her the truth and ask her to swap it out. This way you'll free her, too. She could lose her job over this."

Another person I'm putting at risk. I cross the room again, lifting the blinds to stare out at the darkening street. Do the bars protecting the glass keep out threats or just keep me trapped?

"If I stop taking Ross's medicine, we won't be able to catch Sikes."

"If Ross knows who Sikes is," KJ says, "he'll figure out a way to arrest him."

"Not soon enough."

KJ's face appears over my shoulder, reflected in the window. "Forget Sikes," he says. "Think about yourself."

The last time he said those words to me, he'd put himself in the equation. *Look at me*, he'd said. *Is that really how you want to spend what little time you have left?* If I could go back in time, I'd answer differently, but that kind of rewind isn't possible, even with my new skills. Time is not a soft, flexible thing. It's a harsh master that marches relentlessly forward. I've made decisions I can't take back, found out things I can't forget. I shake my head.

"Thinking about myself is what created this mess. Now I have to do what I can to make things better."

KJ is standing so close to me I can feel heat radiating from his chest. I would only have to lean back a few inches to rest against him. I keep my spine stiff.

"I have to do this, KJ. Just one more mission, and then I promise I'll give it up."

KJ's reflection shakes its head. The image is hazy, as insubstantial as a rewind. "Alex . . ."

"Please, KJ. Ask Jack to call Ross and tell him what happened. He can use Barnard's phone."

The outer door to the clinic opens. KJ and I spring apart. I paste on a smile to match his expression of forced cheer.

"Dinner's here," Yolly announces as she enters my room. KJ walks over to help her with the tray. I go to the bed and busy myself raising the arm of the bedside table.

"You'd better leave now, KJ," Yolly says. "Alex needs her rest. I'm sure she'll be back with the rest of you soon."

KJ moves slowly, lingering at the door to gaze back at me. *Please*, I mouth, and, very slowly, he nods his head.

Yolly fusses with my tray: setting out a glass of water, unwrapping the plastic cutlery. I notice she hasn't included a knife. When it's ready, I climb dutifully back into bed. In two minutes they are both gone.

I pick up my fork. It's chicken tonight. Yolly gave me drumsticks to make up for my knifeless state, along with a blob of mashed potatoes and a scattered pile of peas. I spear a bite of dinner and put it in into my mouth, forcing myself to chew and swallow. Whatever is coming, I'm going to need my strength.

At 7:30, I am lying in bed feeling as refreshed as a sponge bath, clean pajamas, and a restless nap can make me. I'm staring at a book I'm not reading when I hear the clinic door open again. Footsteps patter across the linoleum at a clip that slow-moving Yolly could never match. I jump out of bed, book tight in my hand, ready to hurl the meager weapon at whoever is rattling the doorknob.

"Alex?" Ross pokes his head into the room. My clenched hand loosens.

"How's my best partner doing?" he asks.

His smile lights up the room. I scramble back onto the bed.

"You came! Did Jack call you?"

Ross nods. The visitor's chair scrapes across the floor as he pulls it close.

"He didn't say much, though. Just that someone attacked you and that Barnard locked you in the clinic."

All the fears and questions that have been bubbling in my brain come pouring out. I tell him everything—the trophy shop, Barnard's attempt to test my blood, Jack's claims that he works with Sikes, the crazy-high chronotin reading. Ross sits on the edge of the chair. He looks stricken when I describe how I refused to turn on him at the trophy shop and winces when I describe Buck. When I tell him about the blood test KJ ran that revealed my chronotin levels, he drops his face in his hands.

"Alex, I am so sorry."

A flush of guilt prickles my skin. I'd been so eager to unburden myself I didn't consider how all this would sound to him. Ross put everything on the line to get me the new drugs, and I just blurted out that they were killing me.

I reach for the pitcher Yolly left by my bed and pour out a glass of water so I don't have to look at the drooping curve of his shoulders.

"It's not your fault," I say. "I knew what I was getting into."

"You're wrong." Ross's voice is tight with emotion. "All of this is my fault. Those monsters attacked you because they thought they could use you to get at me." He raises his head. "But I can fix this. I promise I will make you safe."

"I know you will." I sip some water. "As soon as we can get enough evidence to arrest Sikes and Shea—"

"No." Ross slams a fist onto the chair's arm. "That won't be enough. There's still Dr. Barnard. If he knows what you can do, he's never going to let you out of this room. There's only one way to make this right. You have to leave the Center."

The glass in my hand slips, splattering water down the front of my sweatshirt.

"What?"

Ross takes the cup from me and sets it on the table. He leans forward, eyes burning into mine so intensely it's hard for me to look at him.

"It was stupid to give you a new medication without tracking your chronotin more closely. I should have taken you away from Barnard right away so you could get proper medical care. Dr. Kroger says he's eager to have you as an official patient. We'll find a way to tweak the dosage, or get you back on Aclisote if that's the best decision. Either way, we can get you the treatment you need to stay alive."

The walls, so recently a prison, suddenly feel expansive—their bare white no longer a screaming emptiness but a blank canvas waiting to be filled in.

"How could we do it?" I ask.

The edges of Ross's eyes crinkle as he smiles. "They think you're suicidal, right? I'll get you out of here, then we'll cut out your tracker and throw it in the river. It won't be the first drowning where the body never turns up. Meanwhile, I'll find you an apartment, someplace far out of town. You lay low for a bit, buy new clothes, maybe change your hair. I'll get you some ID. You could go to school, live a normal life for as long as you have left."

The future Ross's words paint is more than I can take in. I pull my legs up, hugging them against my chest. The hard point where my arm squeezes my shinbone feels like the only real thing in this room.

"I'm still a teenager," I say. "No one would rent me an apartment."

"I'll rent it," Ross says. "I'll tell them you're my niece."

I squeeze my eyes shut, then open them again. Ross is still there, sitting a foot away from me, the gentle smile still crinkling the corners of his eyes.

"You'd do that for me?"

"Of course I would. I owe it to you after all this. We could even still work together. If you want to."

If I want to? Technicolor images explode in my head: the two of us running around the city like secret superhero vigilantes, laughing over a meal at a restaurant, Sikes jailed, Ross being made chief of police while I applaud from the shadows, a hat artfully tipped to shield my identity.

A blot mars the perfection of my dreams. It's KJ's face, his mouth open in horror as Barnard tells him that I'm gone. That I committed suicide. I dab at the wet spot on my shirt. KJ will get time sick himself before too long. How can I accept a way out when he's still doomed to die? When all of them are?

"What about the others?" I say. "We have to help them, too."

Ross clasps his hands together. "We will. We are. By testing these new meds, you may be finding a way to help every spinner in the world live longer."

I twist a strand of hair around my finger so tightly I can feel it cutting off my circulation.

"Can I at least tell KJ what's going on?"

"Not yet. He has to be as shocked as everyone else when you leave, or else Barnard won't believe it. We can't have anyone out there looking for you. Once you're settled, we'll find a way to let KJ know you're OK."

A tear slides down my cheek. I turn my head toward the windows, not wanting Ross to see me wipe it away. The blinds are drawn again, but I can see the darkness between their narrow slats. Who hides out there in the sheltering night? What plots are being laid while I wait here in this locked room? I hug my legs more tightly. Ross is right. Leaving KJ may be hard, but staying here is not an option.

I turn back to him and release my knees. "When can we go?"

Ross dips his head once, a mute approval of my decision.

"Tomorrow," he says. "I need to get a place lined up where you can stay, and I don't want you to disappear on a day when they know I was in the building. We can't have anyone suspect we're in this together."

I nod. I'm actually kind of relieved. As much as I understand this is my best option, I'm not quite ready to walk out the door of the only place I know to call home.

"There's one thing we have to do first." Ross sounds serious. I wipe my nose on the edge of the sheet and do my best to look prepared. "We have to deal with Austin Shea. You won't be safe out there if he's free, and it's better if we do this while you are known to be locked in the Center. You up for a mission tonight?"

"Right now?"

Ross shakes his head. "Officially I'm here because there's an agents' meeting." He glances at his watch. "Which I'm already late for. We can leave when it's over."

I point at the door, using the arm encircled by the leash. "How do I get out?"

"With this." Ross digs in his pocket and pulls out a lockpick. "One of your very own. Think you can learn to unlock that door in the next three hours?"

I nod. Ross takes my arm and works his magic on the leash. Clarity fills my head as the awful buzzing drops away.

"I'll leave the building at exactly ten thirty," Ross says. "You get out of your room just before then and hide somewhere where you can see the front door. At the point when I am outside, but the door hasn't shut yet, freeze time."

"I'll trip the monitors."

"It will be after lights out, the monitors will be off. Even if someone does notice, by the time they come to check on you, you'll be back here, sound asleep, and firmly leashed."

I nod again. Ross presses the pick into my hand. The edge is sharp, the metal warm from Ross's touch. I close my hand around it. This is my future: comfort and pain and the promise of escape.

17

IT TAKES AN HOUR BEFORE I CAN CONSISTENTLY manage to pick the door lock. The following two hours last forever. Every time I check the clock it seems like the hands have moved backward. Twice I go into a panic, thinking that I've somehow frozen time by accident. At 9:30, Yolly comes to check on me, carrying clean clothes for the morning. I lie in bed with the leash unlatched around my arm. She's gone by 9:40. At 10:20, I dress and kneel down one last time to unlock the door. At 10:25, I open it and creep downstairs.

The Center's halls are deserted. I float ghostlike through the passages until I reach the main staircase. Ross stands in the lobby, under a clock reading 10:28. He seems in no hurry to leave, entertaining Charlie with a long-winded story that makes them both laugh. I hide behind a pillar and chew my thumbnail. Finally, Ross saunters toward the exit. Charlie presses the code that unlocks the front door, and Ross steps out into the night. The instant the darkness swallows him, I freeze time.

Released from my impatient crouch, I hurry down the stairs.

Charlie's hand hovers motionless over the keypad, the remains of a smile curving the edges of his lips. I run past him and out the half-closed front door.

Cool air greets me. It's a clear night, though it must be windy because the trees are all leaning to one side, leaves hovering around them like large brown snowflakes. Ross stands just outside the door, one hand on the outer knob, his head turned toward the shadowy corners of the front entrance, presumably searching for me. He wears jeans, the nice kind that don't show up in donation boxes. He's zipped a leather jacket over them and added a scarf and gloves to balance the cold. Over one shoulder he carries a messenger bag.

I slip behind the door, out of reach of the security camera's electronic eye, and touch the bare skin on his wrist. Time barely pulses forward before I pull it to a stop again.

"Alex." Ross smiles at me. "It's amazing. Even when I'm expecting it."

For a moment I let myself relax into the pleasure of his presence, then I straighten my shoulders and tuck a stray hair behind my ear.

"Where are we going?" I ask.

Ross bends down to wedge a wad of paper under the door. He releases the handle slowly, making sure the heavy wood doesn't shift positions before letting go completely.

"We're heading up into the west hills." He straightens. "We'll have to bike there, think you can manage it?"

"I've never ridden a bike."

"I figured," Ross says. "I stashed a tandem one around the corner. We'll ride together."

I grin. "You think of everything."

Ross tilts his head, considering me.

"You actually don't need to come. It's kind of a long way and if the bike ride will tire you too much, you can always wait here holding time until I get back."

My smile fades. Under the shadows of the Center's awning, it's hard to make out his expression.

"I thought we were a team," I say, unable to hide the hurt in my voice.

"Of course we are." Ross puts a hand on my shoulder. "It's just that it might be a long night and I know you're tired. We'll be in big trouble if you lose control of time while we're out there."

"I'm fine," I say. "I've had plenty of time to rest since this afternoon. I won't let you down."

Ross gives my shoulder a quick squeeze before letting go. I follow him down the concrete steps. I've rarely been outside the Center at night. The streetlights shine with a mustard glow that makes everything kind of mono-colored. Fallen leaves crunch under my feet. I scurry to catch up with Ross so I can walk by his side.

Balancing on the bike turns out to be easy with Ross steadying it from up front. Within a few blocks I feel reasonably stable. Wind whips my hair and cuts through my clothes as we ride. The only jacket in my room was a thin CIC raincoat, and it doesn't provide much protection, but since we very quickly start pedaling uphill, I'm warm enough to break a sweat by the time Ross pulls over to stop.

I lean on the handlebar, panting. We're in a residential area a few miles west of downtown. Unlike most of the city grid, the streets here curve in lazy bends. There are no sidewalks, but there are lots of basketball hoops and plastic swings dangling from tree limbs.

"Hop off," Ross says.

I climb from the bike, which he wheels over to lean against a tree.

Away from the city lights, the moon shines clear silver, illuminating the house before us. It sits on a weed-free lawn, edged with beds of carefully selected plants. There's a neat brick path leading from the driveway to a lighted front porch, and on one side, a huge oak tree towers like a sentinel. It's the kind of house I used to dream of when I was little. A perfect house. A home. I picture Ross and me living in a place like this after I leave the Center. He'd come in and I'd be doing homework behind one of those curtained windows, my chores done, eager to tell him about my day.

"You ready?" Ross asks.

His voice is clipped. I'm reminded that we're on a mission—*the* mission—the one that will finally stop Sikes. I pull myself from my reverie as we head to the side of the house.

Ross opens the locked door with a few efficient twists of his pick. We step into a utility room with a cherry-red washer-dryer on the right. The smell of laundry detergent hangs in the air. High on one wall, the lights of a burglar alarm shine uselessly.

"Let's split up," Ross says. "We can work faster that way. Do you want to search upstairs or down?"

"What are we looking for?"

"The same stuff we did before—anything that ties Shea to either the robberies or Matt Thompson."

The dryer to our right is full of clothes. Ross bends to peer through the clear panel on its front door. The bright metal feels warm when I touch it; someone must have run the load very recently.

"I'll search downstairs," I say. If someone is home I don't really want to stumble across them tucked in their beds. It's creepy enough to dig through someone's house without having their frozen bodies bear witness.

Ross nods before striding out of the room. I listen to the thump of his shoes until they fade away. There's a small part of me that kind of wishes I'd taken his suggestion and stayed behind. The search of Matt's office felt invasive, but this midnight trip makes me feel like I'm in a horror movie. The burglar alarm's unblinking light glares at me through the darkness, and the closed cupboards hint at grisly secrets, their knobs poised to start turning on their own.

I give myself a mental shake. There's nothing to be afraid of in a freeze. Ross only suggested we separate so I don't have to hold time as long. I move out of the utility room into an open kitchen. Stainless steel appliances gleam in the moonlight. A dirty bowl lies on the marble countertop near the sink. I look for somewhere to search. Ross forgot to give me gloves this time, so I cover my hands with my sleeves, just in case. There's a formal dining room off the kitchen, but all it has is a cupboard with plates and wine glasses. The living room has pillows, lots of books, and an abstract painting on the wall that looks like a hundred eyes all watching me. I scurry past it into a family room, which has a huge TV and is very, very dark.

Something creaks. I jump, stifling the scream strangling my throat. Which is ridiculous. Ross must be walking around up there. He probably found a study, really the most likely place to find any kind of evidence. No one is going to hide notes for their next burglary under the TV remote. There's not even a mysterious trunk or anything I could unlock with my pick. I should go help Ross instead of wasting time down here. I pad over soft carpeting and climb the stairs to the upper floor with more eagerness than the task deserves.

"Mr. Ross?" I call, but so softly my words melt into the surrounding silence. I turn on the spot, trying to choose among the line of closed doors, when a slight rustling sound tells me where to go. I hurry forward and push the door open.

Moonlight spills through an open curtain, illuminating a bed resting in a carved wood frame. A man lies there, eyes closed, his mouth hanging slightly open. There's an empty glass on his bedside table, next to a photo of a smiling woman holding a small child.

Ross is standing beside the bed. I am about to announce myself, when something about his stance stops me. He's staring at the man, his face blazing with a triumph that looks more hungry than celebratory. It's somehow intensely personal, and I hesitate, torn between offering help and withdrawing to give him privacy. Before I can decide, Ross moves. He slings the messenger bag over his head and pulls something from it, then turns back toward Shea. My heart stutters.

Ross is holding a knife.

18 ◀◀

IT FEELS LIKE SOMETHING HARD JUST SLAMMED INTO my chest. I can't breathe. I try to call Ross's name and all that comes out is a choked burble. The knife glints in the moonlight. It's a long blade, the top edge serrated with jagged cuts.

Ross raises his hand. Surely he's going to set the blade on the bedside table. A warning. A threat. Ross's hand swoops down and slashes across the man's neck. I scream.

Ross whirls around.

"Alex! You're supposed to be downstairs."

My breath comes so fast it makes me dizzy. A small drip of blood leaks from the gash in the man's neck, the first hint of the flood that time will eventually release. Ross moves toward me, the knife loose in his hand. I back away.

"What did you do?" I whisper.

"I had to." Ross's voice is gentle, soothing. He approaches me like I'm a wild animal that might bolt. I take another step and hit a wall.

"You could never be safe as long as he was alive," Ross says. "Neither of us could."

I can't tear my eyes away from the frozen figure on the bed. He's a big man. There will be a lot of blood.

"You killed him."

"That's Austin Shea. He killed lots of people. He killed Sal. He deserves to die."

"We were going to arrest him." I flatten myself against the wall. "We were looking for evidence."

Ross shakes his head. "I never said we would arrest him. I said we'd take care of him. Austin Shea . . . he's not like a normal criminal, he's too well protected. Until last week no one even knew he existed. We would never be able to send him to jail."

"But . . . you killed him." The bald fact seems insurmountable. That and the idea that Ross stands before me brandishing a knife. I rub my eyes. I want to wipe away the images in front of me, but as soon as I close my lids I see Ross's hand plunging toward its victim, his face lit with that terrible triumph. I look up.

"You used me. You've been using me all along. Mr. Sidell was right, wasn't he? Karl Wagner never showed up in that rewind."

"I told you. Karl Wagner was a bad man. He deserves to be in jail."

"Not for a crime he didn't commit!"

Ross frowns. "I thought we had a partnership. That you understood. Sometimes the truth doesn't make things right. Remember Mrs. Montgomery? You were OK telling a lie for her. We only managed to ID Sikes by doing things that were technically illegal and because I flushed him out with a rumor that Jason Torino was blabbing his secrets. Are you saying we shouldn't have done those things?"

"Yes. No." The dizziness isn't getting any better. I press my hands against the wall, the single point of solidity in a world turned upside-down. "This is different. Sneaking around in frozen time. He never had a chance. It's not fair."

"You think the bad guys play fair? This is justice, Alex. This is making the world a better place. It's what we both wanted."

"This isn't *better*." I point toward the bed. "I never wanted *this*."

Ross and I stare at each other. He's still frowning. A headache pulses in my temple, the first twinge of time resisting my control. The pain sets off a string of associations: the sickness, Aclisote, whispers in the dark. I touch my brow.

"You've been planning this for weeks," I say. "Longer. It's why you changed my meds. You knew what would happen."

Ross adjusts his grip on the knife. A drop of blood drips from the blade in his hand, and for a confused instant I'm convinced that it's mine.

"I saved your life by taking you off Aclisote," he says.

"Saved my life?" I push myself away from the wall. "Your drugs sent my chronotin levels sky-high. I'll probably die *sooner* thanks to you."

A flicker crosses Ross's face, a small spasm as if I'd said something amusing. "Drugs? What drugs?"

"The ones you've been giving me!" I'm yelling now, the words tearing from me like chunks of my own flesh.

Ross sighs. "I was waiting to tell you this until after you got away from the Center. High chronotin is normal for spinners. It's suppressing it with Aclisote that makes you sick."

Comprehension bursts over me with the force of a bomb. I slide down to the floor, crumpling onto the thick carpet. Drugs didn't change my skills. It's me. Me, unfettered by any medicine. No wonder freezes feel easier now, the melts more smooth. Spinners are supposed to have high chronotin levels. We're supposed to be able to change things in frozen time. And Aclisote . . . I look up at Ross.

"Dr. Barnard is killing us?" From my position he looks very tall, like an adult does to a very small child. "You knew this, and you never did anything?"

Ross's eyes slide away from mine. "What was I supposed to do? Take on some crusade to save the spinners? Nothing would have changed. It's not like people in power don't know. They'd have lots of ways to prove me wrong. At least I saved *you*."

"But . . ." I touch the aching spot on my temple, forcing my thoughts into order. "You didn't save me because you cared about me, you saved me so I could do *this* for you." I wave my hand around the darkened room.

"*We* did this," Ross says. "Just like we always said we would. This is our dream, remember? Stop Sikes and get justice for Sal."

I struggle back onto my feet.

"*You* did this," I say, "not me. And I'm going to tell everyone the truth. I'm going to tell Chief Graham that you're a murderer."

Ross's mouth draws into a tight line.

"Do you know what I've risked for you? I put my job in jeopardy. My reputation."

"I didn't ask for any of it."

"No, but you were certainly quick to accept it, weren't you?"

Ross steps closer. I shrink back, from him, from his words. I'm abruptly aware that this man is dangerous, and that I have just made him very, very angry. Ross's hand snakes out, his fingers digging into the soft skin of my upper arm.

"You will tell no one." The sentence sounds like it's chipped from ice. Ross's hand rakes the length of my arm, his fingers dragging along the bone. He presses the handle of the knife into my right palm, forcing my fist to close around it. The wood is smooth, the blade below it wet with blood.

"I was never here." He's standing so close I can smell the bitter tang of his sweat. The scent makes me gag. Ross yanks me toward the bedroom's door.

"You," he says, wrapping my free hand around the knob, "are everywhere." He shoves me deeper into the room, ripping the knife away as I fall back.

"If you do anything to betray me—*anything*—I'll say you've been acting strangely, tell the police to fingerprint you. It will be a familiar tale of another spinner gone mad with time sickness and attacking random strangers."

Ross stands before me, his body blocking the door with its incriminating knob. Little imperfections I never noticed reveal themselves: a stray hair sprouting from one nostril, a wrinkle twisting a bitter line through his upper lip.

"Someone will find him," I say. "The police will come. They'll rewind the whole thing . . ."

"No one will find him for days. His wife and son are out of town until Thursday."

The words I'd said to him earlier this evening ring in my head. *You think of everything.* My stomach twists.

"Even if they do rewind the scene," Ross adds, "what do you think they'll see? This is frozen time. It didn't happen. They'll see his throat slit, but they won't see who did it. There are a few people who might figure out *how* it happened but all that would prove is that a spinner was involved."

Dots fleck my vision. I am trapped in a maze with no exits.

Everywhere I turn, Ross throws up a wall. I look down at my hands. A smear of blood from the knife smudges my palm. In the half light, the blood appears black.

"What happens now?" I ask.

Ross sighs again, a heavy release of air that shivers his entire body.

"Oh, Alex," he says. "You and I are not supposed to fight. We're a team. Partners." His shoulders slump. "What happens next is completely your choice. Take some time and think things over. If you choose to stick with our original plan, you can live a long life. I'll spring you tomorrow, just like I promised, and set you up in a place of your own. We can solve more crimes, do some good with your skills. Or you can refuse and stay at the Center. Given the trouble you've caused, I'd guess Barnard will increase your Aclisote right away. If you're lucky you'll live a week."

My headache pulses. I want to scream at him, hit him, scratch the sympathetic expression off his face. Even more than that, I want to cry. Not because I know he has me trapped. Not because a man is dead because of me. I want to cry because I've lost the person I admired most.

Ross crosses the room and picks up the messenger bag. Pulling out a plastic sack, he carefully wraps the murder weapon and places it inside. When he walks out I follow him. What choice do I have? If I melt time, my tracker will place me at the scene of the crime. I could run, but I don't know how to ride the double bike by myself. Plus, we're so far from downtown I'm not sure I can find my way back before I lose control. If I can't, Ross will get there before me and then all he has to do to secure his alibi is wait until I inevitably let time go.

We ride back without speaking. It's mostly downhill, so this time the wind is chilling. I clench the handlebars, not bothering to pedal.

Ross stops along the way to drop his gloves into a sewer. I catch a faint splash as they hit water, two small bits of leather swallowed up in an underground river of trash.

By the time we reach the Center, I'm shivering with cold and shock. Ross stashes the bike, using a cloth to wipe away our prints. I drag my feet up the Center's front steps. The door stands half open, just like we left it. Charlie's hand hovers over the controls at the front desk, lips smiling over Ross's jokes. Nothing has changed, yet everything is different.

"Tomorrow afternoon," Ross says, "if you decide to come with me, freeze time just before six o'clock and leave your room. It's the shift change, so hide out by the entrance until one of the staff leaves and slip out after them. I'll be waiting for you in an unmarked car at the corner of Northwest Second and Davis."

I nod my head without really listening. Ross ducks into his spot behind the front door when I cross the threshold. My footsteps echo through the hallways, reverberations no one will ever hear. Without conscious thought, I head to the only consolation I know.

KJ's door opens with a twist of my pick. He's asleep, knees half bent, face turned toward the wall. I climb over his inert form and coil myself into the curve of his body.

At this instant Austin Shea is alive. Frozen, but alive. He is still a husband. A father.

I close my eyes and inhale the night's dark air. It fills my body, slowing the shudders. When I am nothing but an empty shadow, I let time go.

A breeze finishes its journey through the window. The thrum of the highway resumes. KJ's sleeping form twitches.

And in that perfect house, far away across the city, Austin Shea's stilled heart begins to pump. I picture the blood pouring through his slashed veins, red soaking his sheets, his body arching in a final spasm. I wonder if he feels pain. Tears burn against my eyelids. I keep them back. I do not deserve the relief of crying.

Carson Ross may have slit Austin Shea's throat, but I am the one responsible for his death.

19

KJ WAKES WITH A START. HE STARTS PUSHING ME AWAY, then stops and puts a tentative hand on my shoulder.

"Alex?" His voice is muffled with sleep.

My body is shaking again. I curl into a ball, pulling my knees close against my chest.

"What's wrong?" he whispers. I can't answer. KJ's hand brushes my arm. "You're cold."

He tugs his blankets out from under me and drapes them over both of us. I duck my head, burying myself inside his shelter. It smells musky and intimate—safe. KJ wraps his arms around me and holds me close.

We lie like that for a long time, my back against his chest, his legs curled against mine. I try to focus all my attention on the warmth radiating from his body. It doesn't work. Images of Ross and Shea keep crashing into my head, ripping away any pockets of peace. Eventually, the blanket tent fills with my recycled breath and turns claustrophobic. I raise my head into the night.

KJ strokes the hair back from my forehead. His hand moves gently, as if I might break if he presses too hard. I stare at the wall in front of me. Pencil scratches mark the surface, some faded, some fresh.

KJ freezes time so we can talk without anyone hearing us.

"What happened?" he asks.

I tell him everything: how Ross and I found Sikes and learned about the existence of Shea, about Ross's plans to move me out of the Center tomorrow, and about tonight's mission and the perfect house high up in the hills. KJ's hand never stops stroking my hair. I touch my fingers against the wall. He's written my name there, *Alex*, over and over in his neat writing. I rub at the pencil marks, trying to erase the letters.

I tell him about the gash along Shea's neck.

KJ's hand pauses.

"He's dead?" he asks.

I nod. "I killed him."

"No, Alex." KJ's arm tightens around me. "It wasn't you, it was Ross. This isn't your fault."

I shrug. "There's more. Aclisote is not a miracle drug that keeps us alive, it's a poison that makes us sick. Spinners are supposed to have high chronotin levels, we're supposed to be able to change things in frozen time. Ross figured it out. He's been giving me a placebo all this time so he can use my skills."

KJ rolls over and stares at the ceiling.

"Are you saying that the Sick," he says, "Dr. Barnard . . . ?"

"They're killing us off. It's like you said, no one can let us have this much power. It's too dangerous."

Even for frozen time, the room feels very quiet. I stare at the wall. It's a long time before KJ speaks.

"So all those old stories are true," he says, "the ones about spinners appearing places and about them being adults." The bed creaks as he shifts his weight. "Do you think they all know? Amy, the teachers, Yolly?"

"I don't know," I say. "Probably not."

KJ turns toward me again. "We'll have to leave," he says to the back of my head.

We. I blink at the wall. The letters are smudged but I can still read them.

"Do you mean the two of us?" I ask. "Or all the spinners?"

"There's over twenty of us. That's too many to take at once. We'll have to figure out a place to hide first, and then come back for them." He pauses. "I mean, if you want us to go together."

I turn around. KJ's face lies inches from mine. Familiar and unfamiliar. The person I know best in all the world and the only one I know who will never let me down. I've been so afraid of things changing between us, I nearly destroyed our friendship. And now everything has changed anyway.

"I'm a mess," I say. "Everything I do turns into a disaster."

KJ touches my cheek. "You're not a mess. You're the bravest person I know."

"I'm not."

"You don't have to do all this alone. I'll be with you. Whatever happens next, we'll face it together."

I let the world shrink until there is nothing in it but the two of us. The sweetness in KJ's face eases my fears, the light in his brown eyes finally warms the chill in my chest. He leans toward me, and when we kiss, his lips block out the past and fill up the future. I taste his tongue. It's warm and rich, like new grass growing in the spring. Like life and the chance to live it.

We cling together for a long time. With each caress, the burdens I carry grow a little bit more bearable.

KJ strokes the curve of my nose. I trace the line of his cheekbone, letting my fingers drift over the roughness of his cheeks. KJ sighs.

"Do you know how long I've wanted to do this?" he whispers.

I touch his lips. KJ slides his teeth over my finger, nibbling with exquisite gentleness. My world grows a little wider, steadied by the comfort of his presence.

"What about Shannon?" I ask.

KJ lets go of my finger.

"Yeah, that." He studies my chin. "I was stupid. I was mad at you and she was so . . ." He shakes his head. "I'll tell her it's over in the morning."

A flare of guilt dims my pleasure and, as if the ugly emotion opened a door, other worries crowd in. I wriggle out of KJ's embrace and sit up.

"How are we going to survive out there?" I ask. "We have nowhere to live. We don't have IDs or money."

KJ moves to sit beside me. "If we stay here, we won't survive at all," he says.

His hand slides around to the back of my neck, fingers skimming the tiny bump that lives beneath my skin.

"We'll have to cut our trackers out," he says.

I nod. The idea doesn't sound so scary anymore.

"What about everyone else?" I ask. "If we can't take them, at least we should tell them. They can stop taking Aclisote."

"That only works until the next blood test. Besides, it's better if Barnard doesn't suspect that we know Aclisote is bad."

Out of nowhere, Calvin's face pops into my head—the cheerful, unparanoid Calvin, who used to rag on KJ about his fascination with computers, the one who loved history books and once told me that he wished he had time to learn to play the guitar. I gnaw on one of my thumbnails. The agonized moans I'd heard through the clinic walls come back to me. My jaw tightens. So many deaths, so much suffering, and all because the Norms don't trust us with the skills we were born with.

I bite down on my thumb hard enough to pierce the skin.

"At least *you* have to stop taking Aclisote," I tell KJ.

"I have a blood test first thing tomorrow morning. I won't take any after that."

"Ross's plan was for me to leave at the shift change tomorrow night." I spit a shred of thumbnail onto the floor. "He was going to cut out my tracker and throw it in the river so it looked like I killed myself. It's not a bad idea, we can use it ourselves."

"I'll come up to my room at six o'clock and wait for you here." KJ takes my hand in his. "Make sure you grab a scalpel before you leave the clinic."

The world scalpel makes my neck tingle. I have a momentary burst of panic that we should leave now, right this minute, except I know we can't. The doors are all locked, we have no idea where to go, and with all that's happened today, I'm not sure how long I could hold a new freeze. I lean my head on KJ's shoulder.

"I'm sorry," he says.

"For what?"

"Sorry that Ross isn't who you thought he was. I know how much he meant to you."

"Yeah, well." I look down at our clasped hands, at my bitten thumb sheltered in his palm. "Trusting him wasn't my biggest mistake."

"No?" KJ's voice is soft. "What was?"

In answer, I sink my fingers into his hair and bring his face to mine. KJ pulls me close, both of us sliding back down on the bed. Time passes. I don't think about Ross, or Shea, or Shannon.

"I should get back," I say, eventually. "You can't hold this freeze all night."

"You're right," KJ mumbles into my neck.

Despite our best intentions, it's another half hour before I make my way to the empty bed waiting for me in the clinic.

I wake before dawn, my mind already buzzing with all the worries that KJ's caresses temporarily hid. Rain patters against the clinic's windows. I watch the dull light slowly change the room from dark to pale gray. Where will we sleep tonight? What will we eat?

My stomach rumbles. Objectively, it's been hours and hours since my last meal, but given that my insides feel like they're drowning in bile, I don't have much desire to eat. I yank the covers off and resume the pacing I started the day before, looping uselessly from locked door to barred window. The leash, reattached to my wrist, makes my head fuzzy. How many people will the Center send after us? What will Ross do when he figures out I've abandoned him?

The questions circle around in my head, as pointless as my pacing. By 8:00 I feel like I've walked ten miles. My muscles are tight and I've chewed all ten fingernails down to stubs. When I hear noises in the outer clinic room, I race to my door and stand there, bouncing on the tips of my toes. Maybe I can convince Yolly to give me some kind of sedative. Then I could sleep a few hours, kill half the day so I can fast forward to the part where we can leave.

Multiple voices fill the space outside the door. I put my hand on the knob, waiting for it to turn.

"Over here," someone says.

"Watch the feet."

The commotion is ominously familiar. My hand clenches on the metal knob. There's a squeaking sound, the shuffle of padding shoes. The blood drains from my face.

"Yolly?" I bang on the door.

The people outside pass by me and head to the room beside mine. They're moving fast, talking about IV drips and fresh sheets. A ball forms in my stomach, heavy as lead.

"Who's out there?" I yell. "Amy? What's going on?"

A door shuts. The voices grow muffled.

"Hello?" I beg. No one answers. I run to the other side of the room and press my ear against the wall that separates the two rooms. It doesn't help. All I can hear are murmurs and the vague rustle of people moving.

I rest my cheek against cool plaster. I can't let anyone else die. Not now. Not when I know the truth. I shut my eyes and call up the faces of my fellow spinners the last time I was in the common room. Did Shannon look drained? Had Jack mentioned a particularly bad headache? I roll my head against the wall, knowing predictions are useless, that symptoms mean nothing. The sickness doesn't give warnings.

The door to my room opens. I spring toward it, then stop abruptly when I see who it is.

"Shannon!"

I edge away from her. Shannon's eyes are ringed with red, her hair fuzzy where it has slipped from her braid.

"What are you doing here?" I ask.

"Yolly sent me to tell you. She knew you'd want to hear right away."

Shannon reaches her arms toward me. I put a hand up to stop her. I don't want comfort, I want facts.

"Who is it?"

Shannon makes a choking sound.

"Dr. Barnard says it happened really fast," she says. "He said he collapsed during his blood test."

Goose bumps erupt along my skin. My hands feel like they're encased in ice.

"Who collapsed?"

"Oh, Alex." Shannon's eyes fill with tears. "It's KJ."

20

"NO," I SAY, THE WORD MORE DENIAL THAN DOUBT. Shannon reaches to hug me again, and again I step away.

"Is it bad?" I ask.

Her lip trembles. She nods.

I clench my hands so tightly that my fingers ache. I should have woken KJ as soon as I got back and refrozen time while the front door was still open. We could have left right then, run away, gone anywhere as long as it was somewhere that Barnard couldn't poison him. I picture KJ in the hospital bed, imagine the IV dripping Aclisote into his veins.

"Is he . . . ," I start. The only clear idea in my head is that I have to get KJ out of the Center. "Do you think he can walk?"

"Walk?" Fresh tears well up and trickle down Shannon's cheeks. "He can't even sit up. I just came from his room. He looks . . ." She pauses, clearly struggling to find a word terrible enough to describe how KJ looks, "like someone drained all the life from his body. He's pale and quiet and so, so still."

My body feels like someone reached inside and ripped out all my guts. I'm hollow, almost too weak to stand.

"I have to go to him." I stumble toward the door.

"You can't." Shannon spreads her arms to block my way. "You're not supposed to leave your room. Yolly said she'll come see you as soon as she can. And Alex—don't be mad at me—but after I saw KJ, I told Yolly about your chronotin levels."

Horror freezes my feeble efforts to get past her. "You *told* Yolly?"

"I couldn't let you get sick, too! Don't worry," she adds, placing her hand on mine, "it will be OK. Dr. Barnard says he'll change your Aclisote dosage right away."

"Dr. Barnard." I repeat the words like an automaton. Shannon gives my hand a gentle stroke.

"Yes. Dr. Barnard will make sure you're all right."

The walls of the room seem to be closing in around me. It doesn't matter how sick KJ is. I have to get us both out of here right now.

I duck around Shannon and shove open the door, ignoring her *oh* of surprise. My heart thuds like it wants to leap from my chest and get to KJ first. It's two steps to reach the second sickroom. I nearly yank the door from its hinges in my rush to rip it open.

KJ lies on his back with the sheets pulled up to his chin. I'm at his side with no memory of crossing the room.

"KJ?"

Dried spit forms an uneven line on his lips. The hair I'd run my hands through just a few hours ago flops on the pillow. An IV drips fluid into his arm from a plastic bag mounted over his bed. My vision blurs. How much Aclisote has Barnard given him to make him this sick, this fast?

Footsteps patter behind me.

"I'm so sorry." Despite the short distance, Shannon is panting. "I tried to stop her."

I raise my head, my panic lifting enough to register the other occupants of the room. Yolly stands on the far side of the bed, her face tight with anxiety. The night guard, Julio, is in one corner folding up a portable wheelchair. On my side of the bed, inches from me, stands Dr. Barnard.

"That's all right." Barnard slides neatly behind Shannon and closes the door. "We were just coming to get her."

Yolly clasps her hands against her chest.

"We heard about your chronotin levels," she says. "We're so worried about you."

My cheeks prickle as all the blood rushes from my face. How could I have been so stupid as to rush in here without a plan? Now I'm wedged in a corner between the bed and the wall, wearing a leash, surrounded by people who think I'm sick. I put a hand on KJ's shoulder. Even though the sheets, I can tell he's burning with fever.

"There's nothing wrong with me," I say.

Yolly sighs. "I can take a blood sample now, if you'd like," she tells Barnard.

"No." Barnard settles himself against the door. My grip on KJ tightens.

"If they're as high as Shannon reports," Barnard says, "I have to take Alexandra to the Central Office."

My insides turn liquid. "What?"

"You may not realize it, but you're a very sick girl." Barnard pushes his glasses higher on his nose. No one else in the room moves. Yolly is blinking a lot, the way little kids do when they're trying not to cry.

"I feel fine," I say.

Barnard shakes his head. "We can't keep you here in this condition. You might hurt yourself again."

The metal rails around KJ's bed are digging into my spine. I focus on the pain to keep from screaming. Yolly and Shannon are both looking at me with a mixture of pity and fear. Barnard's eyes are cold.

"You know that's not true," I tell him.

Barnard's eyes narrow and any doubt I might have had disappears. He knows exactly what I'm capable of doing. In desperation, I reach out for time. The leash blocks me like a locked door. I turn to Yolly.

"Can't we wait until KJ wakes up? I'll go back to my room. You can keep me leashed. I just . . ." My voice cracks. "I just want to make sure he's OK."

Yolly gives an audible sniff. "Surely you can put it off one day," she says to Barnard.

"No," he snaps. "It's too dangerous."

"Dangerous for who?" My voice is rising.

Yolly lowers her chin. Shannon slips around the bed to stand beside her, blond head resting against Yolly's dark one. Julio starts pretending the wheelchair needs his focused attention.

Barnard moves in my direction and a burst of sheer hatred blasts through me. This is the man who decides our fates, and his decision for me is clear: Barnard has no intention of letting me live past tonight. At the Central Office, no one will ask any awkward questions.

I wait until he's almost reached me, then dive for the door. Barnard moves just as quickly. When my hand closes on the knob, he slams me against it.

"Let me go!" I shout. His secrets are my only remaining weapons. I hurl them at him, each small burst of knowledge a thrust I hope will find a home.

"You're killing me. You're killing all of us!"

Barnard pushes me into the door so hard my face smashes into the wood, cutting off my words. I squirm beneath the pressure. One flailing arm catches his jacket, and I dig my fingers into the rough cotton, ripping, tearing.

"Give me something to restrain her," Barnard barks.

"Don't hurt her," Yolly moans. "It's not her fault. She's sick."

I hear someone rummaging in a cupboard. Barnard is leaning his shoulder into my ribs so hard I can only breathe in shallow gasps.

"Here," Julio says from behind me.

Barnard gives a grunt of acknowledgment. The two work together to pull my arms behind my back, tying them together with some kind of thin rope. Only when I am secured does Barnard lift his weight from me. I fall forward, inhaling gulps of air. My nose feels like it's listing sideways.

Barnard keeps a tight grip on my arm. "I'll drive her out there now."

I try to pull away. Barnard grips me harder. *Think*, I scream at myself.

"Yolanda," Barnard says, "keep an eye on KJ. When Amy gets in, tell her to test his blood twice a day. If his chronotin levels go above 125, raise his dosage."

"125?!" I shriek. Barnard, his ear inches from my mouth, recoils.

"Please." I bend my knees, pulling down on the monster holding me, trying to keep him from taking me away. "You'll kill him."

Shannon puts a hand over her mouth. Tears are pouring down her cheeks. "Don't worry," she tells me. "I'll take care of him."

Barnard yanks me to my feet, his fingers pinching the thin skin of my upper arm.

"You don't know what you're talking about," he mutters through clenched teeth.

"Liar!" I writhe under his grip.

"Aclisote is dangerous," I shout at Yolly and Shannon. "We *should* have high chronotin levels."

Barnard opens the door. Julio takes my other arm, and together they start to drag me outside. I twist frantically, gripping the doorframe in my bound hands.

"Please," I beg Yolly, "listen to me. We're not meant to have chronotin readings that low. Suppressing it that much will kill him."

"That's enough!" Barnard pulls so hard I think my arms might pop from the sockets. "Don't listen to her, Yolanda. You can see what the chronotin is doing to her. She's getting irrational."

"No!" I'm sobbing now, fighting Barnard's grip like a person possessed.

"Alex." Yolly reaches toward me even though she is too far away to touch me. I fight harder. If only I can make her understand, Yolly will help me. Yolly will—

"Do you want me to give her a sedative, doctor?"

Hope leaks out of me and I sag in my captors' arms. The lies about spinner madness have been around for too long. They're so ingrained that no one will believe me. Barnard adjusts his grip.

"No," he says. "I can manage."

Barnard and Julio propel me through the door. I stop struggling. Fighting them is useless, and I might as well save my strength. We are halfway down the hall when I hear the pad of Yolly's soft-soled shoes running after us.

"Wait," she said. "Let her have this. It's raining out there."

Barnard waits while Yolly wraps a raincoat around my shoulders. The cheap nylon flutters like a cape over my bound hands. I keep my head lowered. The small kindness offers no relief from my despair.

Barnard's car is parked on the street. Charlie buzzes us out the front door, and he and Julio watch the two of us leave. News of my transfer will be all over the Center within the hour.

Outside, the soft rain has turned into torrents. Barnard splashes down the Center's steps, dragging me with him. Water drenches my hair almost immediately, drops seeping down the neck of my clothes and soaking the mesh of my sneakers. The rush of cold focuses my thoughts on a single point: the leash. I have to find a way to overcome the leash.

Barnard clicks his key fob to unlock a beige sedan. He opens the door and maneuvers me into the front passenger seat. My clasped hands make sitting awkward. I perch on the edge, back arched, mind concentrating on the flow of time. It taunts me from the other side of the leash's block, a river of freedom completely out of my reach. Barnard leans over me, trying to wrap a seat belt around my body. The wet jacket slips from my shoulders and tangles in the belt's buckle.

"Damn it," Barnard mumbles. He slams the door and walks around to the driver's side. Rain pounds the car's metal roof. I try reaching for the door handle, but my bound hands make the stretch too awkward.

Barnard slides into the seat beside me.

"Here." He shoves the jacket into my lap and clicks the buckle into place. The soggy nylon feels slimy against my skin. My fingers are growing numb from lack of circulation.

Barnard considers me. "Lean forward."

I shrink away from him. What now? Will he inject me with Aclisote right here?

"Come on." Barnard pushes my shoulder so hard my cheek collides with the glove box. Barnard pulls my bound hands toward himself.

"Can't have you jumping out at the first stoplight."

My cheek stings. I rest it against the smooth plastic while he unwraps the cords around my wrists. The returning blood stings my fingers. Barnard reties the cord around my left arm, just below my stitches, fastening the other end to the base of the seat belt. I pull on the cord. My motion is limited to about a four-inch distance, and the cord is strong enough that there is little hope of breaking free.

"There," Barnard says. "Now you're not going anywhere."

He turns from me and starts the car. It's a newer model, the kind whose engine hums so quietly I can barely hear it beneath the drumming of the rain. The car slides out into the street, and I rest my head against the seat. Water from the abandoned raincoat oozes onto my lap. I pick up the pile of wet nylon, intending to toss it on the floor, but when I do, something heavy scrapes my leg. A pulse beats in my throat. I glance at Barnard. He's concentrating on making a left turn. As casually as possible I wad the raincoat up in my lap, burying both my hands in its folds as if I'm cold.

We wind our way toward the freeway. The going is slow; every light turns red at our approach. I wriggle one hand through the jacket's folds until I find the weighted pocket. With stealthy slowness, my fingers inch their way until they reach the small lump. A grim smile thins my lips. The raincoat Yolly brought me is the same one I wore last night. The one where I left Ross's lockpick.

I slide my prize out and finger the thin bits of metal. The nylon sheltering my hands rustles. Barnard looks down. I hold still, watching the regular pass of the windshield wipers. We drive for a while in silence. When I move again, the rustling sounds loud in the enclosed space. I need a distraction.

"Any one of us could do it without the Aclisote, couldn't we?" I transfer the pick to my left hand, which is awkward, but necessary, since the leash is on my right arm to avoid the stitches.

"Do what?" Barnard asks with false naiveté.

"Change things in frozen time."

His hands clench the steering wheel. "That's not possible."

"If it's not possible, then why am I leashed?"

"To keep you safe," Barnard says. "With your chronotin so high, freezing might make you sick. Clearly, it's already causing hallucinations."

I take out the tension wrench and run it against the flat face of the leash. Without looking, it's hard to tell exactly where the lock is.

"Freezing doesn't make spinners sick," I say, "and I am *not* hallucinating. You've been giving me Aclisote my whole life to prevent this very thing from happening."

The windshield wipers smear rain across the windshield. Barnard frowns out into the blurry world. The wrench slots into the keyhole.

"You would do the same," Barnard says, "if you were in my position."

My fingers twitch, nearly jerking the wrench free. His admission surprises me less than his tone. He sounds defensive. Barnard gives me a sidelong glance.

"Think about it," he says, "the world can't have a bunch of spinners running around changing things whenever they want."

"Why not?" I ask, trying to sound like I'm really curious so he'll keep talking. Beneath the raincoat, I twist the wrench to the right like Ross taught me: just hard enough to tighten the pins without pushing them so far the mechanism locks up. I bend my right hand down to hold it in place and reach for the pick. The awkward motion makes my palm cramp.

"It's a matter of balance." Barnard seems to have warmed to his topic. I wonder how often he gets to talk so openly. There can't be too many people who know. "For a society, free-roaming spinners would cause total chaos. You could be anywhere, doing anything, and the rest of us would never know. We'd never feel safe."

"So you have to kill us?"

Barnard has the grace to flinch. "It's for the good of society."

"Why not just do it when we're tested, then?" I jam the pick too sharply and feel the soft give of a pin falling. I slide it out and try again.

"Why let us grow up at all?" I ask.

"Killing babies is monstrous."

"And killing teenagers isn't?"

"You might not die. I'm overseeing a very exciting study right now at the Central Office. It's showing a lot of promise . . ."

A study. If the idea wasn't so horrifying it would be funny in a macabre way.

"How many people have you personally murdered?"

"Most of you would have died anyway." Barnard turns the car onto the freeway with Ross-like aggressiveness. "Aclisote isn't all bad. When it was first discovered everyone saw it as a blessing. No one is sure if the strain is mental or physical, but before Aclisote, hardly any spinners survived their childhood. Time really does kill."

Barnard gives a little chuckle. I feed the pick back into the lock, making tiny wiggling motions to try and set the invisible pins. Something clicks. I shift the wrench a hair farther to the right and feel around for the next one.

"I know it sounds harsh from your perspective," Barnard continues, "but all in all it's not a bad compromise. You're guaranteed life for at least fifteen years. You're taken care of, kept sane, you do good work—it's more than a lot of people get."

His words make me so angry I have to stop messing with the lock.

"So all you Norms," I say, "sit around being self-righteous while we're drugged and locked up?"

"Oh no," Barnard protests, "most people have no idea. That's the gift we give them. They get to enjoy their happy, safe, peaceful lives, unsettled by neither excess crime nor out-of-control spinners. Only Center directors and a handful of politicians know the truth. *We're* the ones who bear the burden. The ones who know. It's hardest on us."

The car hums along in the center lane. I check the speedometer. Sixty-eight miles per hour. I concentrate on the lock, making tiny motions with the pick. Another pin falls into place. Another. The leash falls open. The faint buzz in my brain fades. I swallow. I know this is a desperate plan, a terrible plan, dependent on so many variables it's more likely to fail than to succeed. It's a plan that might kill me. It's the only chance I have.

I lift my unleashed arm out from under the raincoat.

"Alexandra?" Barnard has noticed my silence. He turns his head and sees me reaching for him. The car swerves as he jerks away from me.

"What are you doing?" he asks.

It's now or never. I wrap my fingers around his wrist. I say the command out loud. I want him to know.

"Freeze time."

Barnard's eyes widen as the world stops. All of it. The falling rain, the speeding traffic, Barnard's fancy car. All of it except us, our bodies, still moving sixty-eight miles per hour as we fly toward the immobile dashboard.

The airbags do not deploy. The seat belts do not lock. Barnard's body careens forward, the steering wheel plunging into the soft curve above his belt. An instant later my head hits the glove box with enough force to stun me. Pain explodes through my brain, physical impact combining with the whiplash jolt of time ripping away from me. The car leaps ahead. I hear myself scream as we swerve wildly across the highway. Barnard wrenches the steering wheel. The car skids sideways. Brakes screech.

A cement divider rears up, filling the windshield with a wall of solid concrete.

21

A SIREN WAILS. RED LIGHTS BURN THE BACKS OF MY eyelids. Words, urgent and meaningless, attack my ears. The smell of burnt rubber and wet pavement soaks the air. When I take a breath, stabbing pain shoots through my side.

Someone pulls up my eyelid and I wince under a bright light. My mouth tastes like metal. I close my eyes again.

"Responsive." A brisk voice. Female. "Nothing obvious broken. They'll need to suture the forehead." She places something soft against my head, holding it in place with a few bands of medical tape.

"Can we move her?" A younger voice, male, with a slight southern twang.

"Yeah, bring a gurney."

"What about him?"

"Unconscious. Send Riker over."

Someone places a brace around my neck. Strong hands reach under my shoulders to lift me from the car. They stop when they realize my left arm is attached to the seat belt.

"What's that?" Southern Boy asks.

I feel a pull as he yanks on the cord.

"There's a Crime Investigation Center jacket on the floor," the woman says. Her voice carries the rolling consonants of a native Spanish speaker. "She must be a spinner. I didn't know they tied them down."

"What do we do?" Southern Boy sounds nervous.

I force my eyes open. A face bends over mine. A woman, about thirty, with tan skin and thick hair pulled back in a ponytail.

"You awake?" Her hands move professionally over my body. "What hurts?"

Everything, I think. I hold up my bound wrist.

"This."

She takes hold of my forearm. My wrist is raw and the bandage covering my stitches has come off. The rope must have ripped it from my arm when we crashed.

The woman calls to someone over her shoulder. A quick snip and I'm free. I try to climb out of the car. It's awkward moving in the enclosed space, made smaller still by the floppy airbags the real-time crash released.

"Not yet." The woman pushes me back, her hands gentle but firm. She wears a blue uniform with *Portland EMT* woven on her chest. Beneath that, a nametag reads *Teresa Gonzales*.

"We'll take you on the gurney," she says. "OK? You might have internal injuries."

"I have to go," I say.

"Not yet, *chica*, you're still in shock." She slides one arm under my back.

"You gonna help me here?" she calls over her shoulder.

A man in a matching blue uniform moves forward with a tentative step. Southern Boy. He isn't as young as I'd thought, maybe late-twenties. Dirty blond hair cut short and skin as raw as if he shaved over pimples with a rusty blade. He hesitates a minute, then grabs hold of my legs. As soon as he deposits me on the gurney he steps away.

I turn my head as best I can in the neck brace. Barnard's car is totaled. Glass from the shattered windshield sparkles through the drizzling rain. It looks like a gem heist gone bad, diamonds an inch thick on the car's seats, and more spilling across the pavement. The front hood bends upward. Steam billows from under the crumpled metal. A line of traffic has already piled up behind us. On the far side of the car, two more EMTs lean over Barnard, who seems to be out cold. A flicker of hope flutters inside me. My ridiculous plan has worked. I am out of the car, alive and unleashed.

Teresa pulls a blanket over me and pushes the gurney toward the waiting ambulance. "What's your name, *chica*?"

"A . . . Amanda. Jones. Amanda Jones." I touch my side. It feels bruised. I take a few more breaths. There's definitely something not right. "What's wrong with me?" I ask.

"You're going to be fine, Amanda," Teresa says. The gurney rolls into the ambulance with hardly a jolt. Southern Boy is already inside, grabbing straps to secure me. Teresa takes a seat by my head.

"Who should we call?" she asks.

"Call?" The adrenaline coursing through my body spikes. If the Center staff meet me at the hospital, all of this will be for nothing. I should freeze time now, get out. I struggle to push away Southern Boy's hands. The ambulance's engine roars as the van rolls out. Too late. I sag back onto the gurney.

"Nobody," I say. "There's nobody to call."

"You're a spinner, right?" Teresa touches the bruised marks on my wrist. She has very smooth skin and the soft eyes of a doe.

"I know you're all orphans, but whatever Center you work for cares about you, too."

The patent falseness of her statement makes me want to scream. I swallow hard, trying to keep the anger from my face.

"I live at the San Francisco Crime Investigation Center," I say. They've probably already called in Barnard's license plates, but maybe I can buy myself a little time with misdirection. "We're up here to help on a case."

Teresa nods to Southern Boy, who picks up a walkie-talkie and passes on my information. I keep watching Teresa. I have to remind myself that she doesn't know spinners are poisoned, that not everyone is part of the conspiracy. The thought only helps a little.

Teresa leans forward and reaches for a needle. Taking my arm, she pats at my inner elbow. I yank it away.

"What's that for?" I demand.

"Just a saline drip. The doctors like to have it going before you get in so they can easily administer whatever medicine you need."

"No." I cradle my arm, holding it away from her. Teresa holds up her hands in an I-surrender gesture. I curl my arms closer to my chest. "Where are we going?"

"The closest hospital is City General," she says. "We should be there in five minutes."

I nod. City General is good—only a couple miles from the Center. I stare at the ceiling, trying to do a mental survey of my injuries. I tense and relax the muscles in my arms and legs. Besides my sore side, all there seems to be is the bandage fastened around my forehead.

Teresa said something about sutures. It's probably from the first crash, the one *without* the airbags. I lie still, trying to be grateful the pain isn't worse.

Our ride is brief. The ambulance doors bang open almost before the van stops. Southern Boy hops down, and he and Teresa maneuver my gurney out in seconds. A doctor waits outside. Teresa starts spouting words like *contusions*, *shock*, and *BP*, followed by more acronyms I can't follow. I switch my attention to the figures hurrying in the background. I see Julio almost at once. My lie about San Francisco fooled no one; they must have called the Sick as soon as someone reported the crash.

Julio is making his way toward the ambulance at a rapid clip. In his hand he holds a leash.

"Doctor!" he shouts. The man leaning over me hesitates, half-turning at the call. Julio jogs closer.

I don't have a choice. There is no waiting for an opportune moment, no careful covering of my tracks. I reach out and stop time.

The freeze mutes the crowd. I undo the straps holding me on the gurney and sit up. Very gingerly, I take the brace from around my neck and twist my head back and forth. Stiff, but not terrible. Walking doesn't go as well. My knees wobble, my head spins, and I'm dizzy to the point of nausea. I balance myself against the gurney. All I want is to curl up in a ball and go to sleep, but I know that isn't an option. If I sleep, time will start again, and they will catch me. And every second of real time that passes means another drop of Aclisote into KJ's veins.

Thinking of KJ propels me forward. I fix an image of him firmly in my mind—a happy one of the two of us talking in the courtyard—and head away from the chaotic hospital entrance, out toward the street. I walk three blocks before I find someone on a bicycle, and then strain to drag the guy onto the sidewalk. I feel bad about stealing his bike. One minute, the poor guy will be riding down the street, and the next he'll be sitting on the ground, bikeless. It can't be helped. I don't have the time or the strength to walk.

The ride to the Center feels endless. One trip on the back of a tandem bike isn't enough training. I fall over eight times before I master a semblance of balance and still walk the bike down hills because I don't trust the brakes. Raindrops hang in the air, plastering themselves against me. Only panic keeps me going. If I take too long, I'll lose control of time.

I'm shivering by the time I reach the Center. The tall stone building blurs through the haze of rain, like the setting of a dream. Or a nightmare. I drop the bike and drag myself up to the front door. Locked, of course. I melt time and ring the bell.

"Alex?" Charlie's voice crackles through the intercom. "What are you doing out there?"

I turn my face up to the camera that monitors the front door.

"Dr. Barnard was driving me to the Central Office," I say, too tired to make up a lie. I lean against the door. "We got in an accident. Let me in."

The door buzzes and I half-fall inside when it opens. Charlie is already out of his chair, a phone pressed against his ear. I freeze time before he gets any closer and then take off my shoe and use it to prop open the door.

Urgency bites at my heels as I stagger toward the clinic. *KJ*, I keep repeating in my head. *I have to save KJ*. The door opens under my touch. The room is empty, except for KJ who lies in the same prone position I left him in. He looks worse than I remember. Sweat dampens his forehead. His mouth has gone slack. I place my hand against the skin of his exposed arm, the one linked to the snaking tube of an IV.

Melt time. Freeze time.

KJ doesn't move. I rip off the tape holding the IV in place and press down on the insertion point the way I've seen Amy do before pulling out the needle. No response. I look for the reassurance of his pulse. It's faint, the soft flutter of a wounded moth.

"KJ." I shake him. Nothing. I slap his cheek, lightly, and then harder.

"Come on, KJ, wake up. We have to go." Not even a moan. I shove my arms under his torso, trying to drag his six-foot frame upright with arms no stronger than blades of grass. Something wet slides out from under the bandage around my head. I don't have to touch it to know I'm bleeding.

Tears of frustration spill onto my cheeks. I climb up onto KJ's bed and wrap myself around him. Exhaustion pulls at me like a second layer of gravity. I know I can't hold time much longer. Failure taunts me from every corner. I've tried so hard, risked so much, just to end up here, helpless and alone in a frozen world. Time pulls at me, straining my control.

A keening whine leaks from my between my lips, punctuated by gasping sobs. Tears and blood drip onto KJ's white sheets. I lay my head on his chest.

"I need you, KJ. I can't do this by myself."

The words make me cry harder. Last night KJ promised me that he would be there to help me. Except he isn't. He's dying and I'm too weak to save him. I twine myself more closely around his limp body. The abandoned IV line dangles a foot from my face, the snaking tube inviting me to stab it into my own arm, drink in the poison, and let the two of us die together, our fake suicide made real. I am so very, very tired.

A soft beat pulses in my ear. It's weak, but it's also the loudest thing there is in the silent freeze. I stop crying. The beat has an echo. KJ's heart and my own, both captured by my ear pressing against his chest. Hope lives in that beat. Life lives there, too. However hard they're trying, the Center hasn't killed us yet.

I lie still. It's as if the sound is talking to me, sending me a message of hope and strength. I listen until I understand what it is I have to do.

Dragging myself from KJ's bed is the hardest thing I've ever done. I release time for a second and let KJ go. I'll need all my energy to get through the next half hour, and keeping KJ unfrozen will only drain my meager stores. I set off through the familiar hallways, searching for the two people I'm going to need.

I find Jack first.

He's not my favorite person, but he is strong, and, as he himself pointed out, he's spent more time than most of us in the outside world. He's also likely to believe me without too much explanation and, given his age, doesn't have much to lose.

Jack is in the gym, curled in the tight crouch of a half-finished sit-up. Aidan floats just above the ground on the treadmill to his right. I kneel at Jack's side and touch his arm. Melt time. Freeze time.

"What the . . . ?"

Jack is on his feet so fast I rock back on my heels.

"Hey, Jack."

"Where did you come from?" He squints at me. "And what happened to you?"

I glance at my reflection in the mirror over his shoulder. Blood drips from the bandage around my head and clusters in dried flakes along my eyebrow. There's an abrasion from the seat belt on my neck and collarbone.

"It doesn't matter," I say. "I don't have a lot of time, so listen carefully. The Sick doesn't give us Aclisote to stabilize us, they do it to suppress our power. If we were left alone we'd be able to change things in frozen time. And it's not time that makes us sick. It's the Aclisote. Dr. Barnard is killing us."

Jack backs away from me. "Is this a joke?"

"You just saw me appear out of nowhere."

He considers me a moment. "How do you know all this?" he asks.

"Trust me, Jack." I try to keep the impatience out of my voice. "We have to leave the Sick. I can get us out, but I need your help."

Jack's eyes narrow. "What do you want me to do?"

"Help me with KJ. I can't carry him by myself."

"And if I go with you, you'll show me how to change stuff in frozen time?"

A twinge of unease makes me hesitate. I push it aside.

"It's not a question of teaching. As soon as the Aclisote is out of your system, you'll be able to do it, too."

Jack nods slowly. "And if I don't help you . . ."

"Then I'll melt time and find someone else." Fatigue makes me sharp. "I can't hold time much longer, and we still need to find Shannon."

"Shannon? Why her?"

"She's got the skills to take care of KJ. Plus, we need someone to cut out our trackers."

Jack touches the back of his neck. "You're serious."

"You coming?"

"Shannon's in the common room."

Shannon is harder to convince than Jack. She doesn't believe me when I say Barnard is killing us and she nearly faints when I drag her out of the common room during frozen time to prove to her that changes stick. Finally, Jack steps in and tells her this is the only way to save KJ's life. He says he knows a place outside that can heal KJ, that we need her help to take him there, and that we can all come back when it's over. I don't like bringing Shannon along under so many lies, but I don't have the energy to argue about it.

Back in the clinic, Shannon unwraps a sterile scalpel and sets to work slicing out the trackers. It hurts less than I expected. Maybe all my nerves are so shocked they don't have anything left to respond with. Shannon takes out KJ's tracker while he's still frozen. I take all four of them and flush them down the toilet. Let Barnard track that.

Jack unfolds the wheelchair Julio left in the corner while Shannon rummages in a cupboard to fill a bag with medical supplies. We all work together to lift KJ's slack body into the chair. Getting down the stairs is harder. My shoeless foot slips on the slick tiles and Jack keeps letting the front end of the chair bounce against the steps. KJ flops around dangerously and I'm grateful to Shannon when she demands that Jack be more careful.

Charlie is standing almost exactly where I left him in the lobby. He's staring up toward the stairs with his mouth half open, probably wondering where I went. I put on my shoe and push open the Center's door. Time pulls at my mind, the whisper now grown into a full roar. Shannon eases KJ's wheelchair down the accessible ramp. I take the stairs, holding the banister like a crutch.

Jack bounds ahead, whooping as he hurtles down to the sidewalk. He stands there a moment, feet planted, hands on hips. I see him raise one hand to touch the bandage Shannon stuck on the back of his neck. The wet banister slips under my hand. Jack is unmonitored. I've set him free, and now he's going to abandon us. Shannon and KJ reach the street. Time licks at my temples.

Jack spins on his heel.

"Come on," he says. "I thought we were in a hurry."

The smile I give him is watery.

"I'm going to need some help," I say, making my way to the bottom of the stairs. "I'm starting to lose my grip on time."

Jack reaches out and clasps my hand. His time skills surge to meet mine, bolstering my control of the invisible force. I hold his fingers tightly.

"Do you have a plan?" Jack asks as Shannon joins us. I slip my other hand over hers where it rests on the back of the wheelchair. More energy mingles with my fading strength. I shake the hair from my eyes.

"Is it true you can drive a car?" I ask Jack.

He grins. "Well enough."

"Then let's go get one. If we can find someone who is just about to get in or out of their car, we can take their keys and . . ."

"I have a better idea," Jack says. "There's one of those parking garages over on Fourth Ave. The ones where you leave your keys with the attendant. We can take one of those."

"We're going to steal a car?" Shannon asks, horrified.

"Not steal," Jack says. "Borrow. It's the only way to transport KJ where we need to go."

I study the two faces flanking me. Shannon has her lips pursed, as if she's about to swallow something nasty that she knows is good for her. Jack beams like it's Christmas morning. I squeeze both their hands.

"You should know," I tell them, "I don't have a plan after this."

Jack shrugs. "We'll figure it out."

We start walking. It's awkward to stay connected like this—three people on foot and KJ in the wheelchair, bumping down a city street littered with unmoving obstacles. Awkward—yet oddly comforting. It's true what I'd said to the others. I don't know what to do next. I know that, even without trackers, the Center will try to find us. We are four kids, alone and unequipped to survive on our own. It will take days for me to heal completely, longer for KJ, and I don't know how long it will take for the others to be able to freeze time like I can. Until then, we'll all be vulnerable.

But right now, I don't care. Right now, holding on to these two people who have given up everything to come with me, what I feel is hope. At least now we have a chance. And as Ross once told me, a chance is all you ever get. After that, life is what you make of it.

I put one foot in front of the other and concentrate on holding the freeze. It won't be for much longer. When time starts again, our lives as fugitives will begin. Shannon and Jack's hands wrap me with warmth. The pulse of their power urges me forward.

This is the life I choose—the life *we* choose. A life with a future. Somehow, together, we'll find a way to survive.

Acknowledgments

Whenever I think about acknowledgements, I imagine the Oscars with their interminable speeches about people I've never heard of. The beauty of literary acknowledgements is that I can say whatever I want without fear of boring my audience, since nobody is required to read them. (The downside being, of course, that I don't get to wear one of those fancy dresses.)

There are many people I want to thank, primarily those who read all or parts of this novel along the way and encouraged me to keep going. Many of these chapters were critiqued by my fellow students and the wonderful faculty members at the Attic Institute, Portland's premier haven for writers. My entire book group dedicated one month's selection to this novel—the first time I'd allowed anyone outside my family to read the manuscript in its entirety—which means cheers to Laurie Stabenow, Randi Wexler, Suzanne Lacampagne, Deb Walker, and especially Ella Howard, honorary member, who provided not only detailed line edits but invaluable teen insights. Jasmine Pittenger shared much advice and many cups of tea. Sonja Thomas offered detailed beta feedback, as did Diana and Sylvia Tesh. Without their careful critiques and, even more, their enthusiastic support, this novel would not be what it is today.

This book would not exist at all if it weren't for the two years I spent as an MFA student at Stonecoast. Being part of that community gave me the confidence to call myself a writer and the skills I needed to actually create an entire novel. Thanks to my four fabulous mentors: David Anthony Durham, Michael Kimball, Elizabeth Searle, and James Patrick Kelly, as well as every single person who attended a residency between January 2009 and January 2011. It was all of you, together, that made the place so very special, and if I could, I would still go back twice a year to spend time with you all.

Writing can be a solitary endeavor, so I also want to thank all my local writing friends who share with me the joys and frustrations of creating fiction. Vannessa McClelland, Mark McCarron-Fraser, Sonja Thomas, Joe Morreale, and Paul McKlendin have edited more of my words than I can count. David Biespiel, Merridawn Duckler, and G. Xavier Robillard were part of my Hawthorne Fellows family, along with Emily Gillespie, Ryan Meranger, and Rich Perin. Thanks to all of you for understanding the fascination in talking about plot holes and narrative tension and characters who just won't cooperate with the story.

My agent, Alison McDonald, rescued this book from her slush pile, for which I will be eternally grateful. She and her staff provided excellent editing suggestions, and Ali made me more happy than I can express when she found *Rewind* a publishing home. Mary Colgan and all the people at Boyds Mills Press have been a dream to work with, and I am delighted with the final version we've created.

Finally, thanks to my husband, Dan O'Doherty, without whom I would be missing everything in my life that I love the most.

Greenville Public Library-Adult
YA ODOHERTY
Rewind